Two for Interference

A SECRET IDENTITY OPPOSITES ATTRACT ROMANCE

LASAIRIONA MCMASTER

DRAMA LLAMA PUBLISHING

Dedication

For anyone who has ever struggled to look at their own reflection.

CHAPTER 1

Cleo

Cleo's best friend, Molly, snorted over her shoulder. Cleo clutched the phone against her chest, cheeks on fire.

"Too late, I saw it. But I know for sure that message wasn't meant for you." Molly snapped the bra strap on her shoulder. "You're wearing your regular Tuesday bra. And even if by some miracle you *were* possessed by a demon long enough to let your hair down for a hook-up, there's no way you'd be careless enough to leave your bra behind. You'd break out in hives at the idea of being seen with your girls hanging free. Not to mention, you were here watching Pitch Perfect with Ben and Jerry last night."

"I don't have a regular Tuesday bra." Cleo reached for the spaghetti strap of her tank, as though it would somehow cover the bra strap in question. Why she was embarrassed by it was anyone's guess.

"Wanna go open your underwear drawer and do a head-count? Ten bucks says I'd know whether whoever that is on your phone actually has one of yours or not. In under five seconds."

Cleo groaned and hung her head. She and Molly had been besties since the first day of Cleo's freshman year over a year ago. They'd met in the library, throwing dirty looks and shushing the same obnoxious group of jocks. Despite Molly being a year older, a beautiful friendship had been born over a mutual respect for the rules, a shared love of the smell of musty old books, and grilled cheese.

Cleo placed her phone screen-down on the desk. "It's a wrong number. I'm just going to ignore it. I have to finish this assignment for tomorrow anyway."

"Uh huh. It's not even the third week of term and you're already charging ahead. You *can* have a little fun sometimes, you know? That's kinda the whole point of college."

"The whole point of college is to graduate with honors and get a good job. Now, shush. I got shit to do." Cleo shifted her glasses up her nose and slid the end of her pen between her teeth. Her phone chimed again and her fingers twitched, itching to flip it over. Was there another instalment to be had of the mysterious #BraGate she'd found herself in the middle of? Maybe if she stared at it long enough, it would turn over by itself.

"Maybe he's got her panties, too."

"What makes you think it's a he?"

"Oh sweet, summer child. Let's go with 'intuition'. Go on. I can tell you're bursting to see if that's him again. I'm giving you permission to take a look."

Cleo picked up the phone.

Unknown number: I'd drop it off but I dunno where you live. Are you in the dorms? I know these things are expensive as shit or I wouldn't have messaged, I know last night was a one-time deal.

Unknown number: Why do women pay so
much money for such a flimsy piece of
fabric?

Cleo wrinkled her nose. She'd never been a one-night-stand kinda girl. In truth, she'd never really been a dating-of-any-kind sort of girl. Her parents had kept a tight rein on her social life throughout high school. Her two previous boyfriends had never understood her academic drive.

Molly elbowed her. "One-time deal? Huh. You're a changed woman, Cleo Martinez. I had no idea you'd gotten into the do 'em and dump 'em game. Next you'll be telling me you bat for my bi-team. You should reply at least, tell the poor guy he's written the love of his life's number down wrong. You think he's talking about this campus?"

Shrugging, Cleo placed the phone back on the table and turned the page of her book. Try as she might to deny it, or squash it down, a small part of her yearned to have a 'normal' college experience. But her mom would kill her if she got anything less than exemplary scores in all her classes.

Unknown number: Uh… Melissa? You know
it says 'read' next to your messages, right?
Wait. Is this your calling card? Like you
leave your bra behind so I come running? A
sneaky way to make it more than a one-
time thing?

"Woman! Answer the man, jeez. Hold up – you don't think he means Melissa Ross, do you?"

Cleo must have had a blank face because Molly continued. "Cheer squad? Still not ringing any bells?"

Cleo shook her head.

"You might actually get to know people if you stepped outside of the library sometimes, you know. You should answer *The Boy*. He seems to want to get rid of that bra as a matter of some urgency."

Cleo pinched her lip between her teeth. She needed to concentrate on her assignment, and the persistence of Mr. One Night Stand was not conducive to a quiet work environment.

> Cleo: Sorry, this isn't Melissa. I hope you find your Cinderella soon, though. I can confirm the bra is not mine.

See? She could be fun. Bantering with a stranger over text was fun, right?

> Unknown number: My apologies. This was the number she gave me. The search for the owner of the over-the-shoulder-boulder-holder continues. Have a good one.

Her stomach sank at the closed nature of his reply. It surprised her. Did she want an excuse to talk to a complete stranger? A stranger who'd had a one night stand the night before, no less. No, she had no time for distractions. She would never become Summa Cum Laude if she let some asshole player take up space in her brain. Focus. That's what she needed.

"I'm heading out to the party at Beta Kappa Pi. Sure you don't wanna come?" Molly gave her shoulder a playful shove.

"I'm good, thanks."

Molly giggled. "You've reached your fill of excitement for one day. You know where I am if you change your mind."

"Be safe!"

"Always." Molly waved her rape whistle attached to her keychain and a foil-wrapped condom at Cleo before slipping them into the shallow pockets of her jeans. She left, mumbling to herself about how the patriarchy screwed women over at every turn, even when it came to their clothes.

Cleo rolled her neck and a heaviness settled on her chest. Molly was a straight-A student who loved partying. She hadn't failed a single class in her first year. She had plenty of friends, a fun dating life, and still managed to maintain high grades. She had it all.

How was it possible for Molly to keep all of the plates spinning, while Cleo had to focus all her energies on succeeding in school? Studying English Literature in the University of Minnesota had been Cleo's goal for as long as she could remember. She pursued it with fervor, but the occasional ache in the pit of her stomach made her wonder.

CHAPTER 2

Cleo

Something about the intoxicating smell of knowledge in a library made Cleo giddy. While other college students were out having keg parties or pep rallies, Cleo hunkered down in her favorite quiet space and focused on what she did best. She'd eaten an early dinner in the cafeteria with Molly hours ago, but her BFF had then abandoned her, excited about a date with an über hot dude who, she said, must have been born from a line of Greek Gods.

Cleo's back ached, and the words on the page were blurring together. *Call time. Go home, sleep, and start over in the morning.* She reached heavy arms over her head, linked her stiff fingers, and pressed her palms toward the ceiling before packing her books and pens into her backpack.

Her parents had sent her a good night message in their group chat, and Molly had texted her the address of her date and a picture of his driving license – just in case – but that was it. A pang of something she couldn't quite place volleyed to her heart at the sad state of her social life. She shook it off. School was more important.

She sent a text to tell Molly she was homeward bound, said

goodnight to the janitor who was already mopping the floor, and started the twenty minute walk home. They lived together in a shared apartment with two girls from Molly's class, Nicola and Kasia. After a year in the dorms, Cleo jumped at the chance to have a little more privacy and a little less chaos and noise around as she studied. The extra space didn't hurt either.

Despite the late hour, a group of students lingered around the social sciences building, scrolling through social media on their phones at full volume. They shoved their screens in front of each other's faces when they found something of note to share.

Her cheeks seared as she passed Lincoln Scott, who stood chatting to one of his jock friends outside the art history building. She snorted at the irony. Guys like Lincoln weren't art history kinda guys. She was glad it was dark so he couldn't see the embarrassment stamped across her hot cheeks. Clenching her teeth, she forced the mortifying flashbacks of the day they met out of her mind.

It was all Molly's fault. Wasn't everything? She'd dragged Cleo to the local sex shop, 'Good Vibes', to buy something for her birthday. As if that wasn't embarrassing enough, Cleo had attempted to flee the scene the second she completed her purchase, running – at warp speed – into a solid wall of abs.

Lincoln Scott's abs, to be precise. Hockey player extraordinaire. Well, player of all kinds if the rumor mill was to be believed.

She'd wound up flat on her back. The bag containing her shiny, new, hot pink vibrator had tumbled from her clutched fist and landed on his foot. Yup, *on* his foot. And because the universe was out to get her, the box didn't even have the decency to stay inside the bag. The jock-knight in hockey armor helped her to her feet before picking up her night stick. She still had nightmares. And, if she was honest with herself, fantasies.

She scrunched her eyes closed. The amused look on his face as he'd lifted the box and held it out to her was so burned into her brain that she was pretty sure not even a dousing with acid could have erased it.

Guys like him didn't date girls like her, and it was just as well. She had no time for hot, popular, hockey boyfriends who went to frat parties and spent most of their time at the rink. Lincoln Scott was out of her league. And even if he wasn't, she needed someone with something more than a hockey puck between his ears to fall in love with.

Lincoln Scott was *not* relationship material. But he sure was nice to look at. At least six feet tall, with broad, strong shoulders, baby blue eyes, and a strong jaw. She had no doubts that he could walk right up to the front door of an agency and bag a modelling contract for whatever company made hockey gear. And those washboard abs? Even through a loose-fitting shirt... Hot. Freakin'. Damn. Glasses-wearing book nerd she might be, but Cleopatra Isabella Martinez was not blind. The man was *fine*.

The snap of a twig broke her thoughts. She pulled her head up, and a shiver bolted down her spine. She never wore headphones when she walked at night, always kept her hands empty in case she was attacked, and stayed focused enough on her surroundings to get home without issue. Thinking about Lincoln 'Abs' Scott had taken her somewhere else, somewhere dangerous. She hadn't been aware of the tall guy with wide shoulders and his hood up, walking far enough behind her to seem innocent. But she'd heard enough horror stories of women getting attacked for her survival instincts to kick in. Slipping her arm through the loop of her backpack so it rested on both shoulders, she reached into her back pocket to pull out her phone.

She unlocked it and scrolled through her meagre list of contacts. Her parents were asleep, her best friend was busy with Mr. Right Now, and her eye doctor and OBGYN's offices were both closed. Sure, there were some friends she hadn't spoken to since high school on the list, but what would she say? "Hi, I know it's been three years, but there's a guy wearing a hoody walking behind me on the street, and I'm paranoid AF that he's going to rape and kill me. Could you keep me company for the fifteen minute walk home, please?" Right. Like that wouldn't sound at all insane. She put her phone in her front pocket and kept going.

She worried her lips between her teeth as she walked, crossing the street in a bid to put more distance between her and the North Face hoodie. He didn't cross at first, but her stomach clenched when heavy footsteps thudded across the pavement, and he joined her on her side of the street. *Text Molly.* She opened her inbox, but instead of sending Molly a text, she clicked on the unknown number of Prince Bra-ming from the night before. *What the hell?*

> Cleo: Hi, so I know we don't know each other, but as it turns out I don't have all that many friends. I know, sad, right? Anyway, not the point. I'm walking home, it's dark and kinda creepy, and there's this guy behind me who may – or very well may not – be following me home. I was wondering if you could pretend to text me a bit, just until I get home.

> Cleo: Unless of course you're busy, in which case, never mind. But if a dead body turns up on the news tomorrow, you can brag to all your friends that you knew me before I was famous.

Unknown number: Wow. That got dark kinda fast. How will the stalker dude know if I'm pretending to text you, rather than actually texting you? Do you need me to call you?

Unknown number: I could come walk you home?

Unknown number: Okay, wait. I don't even know what state you're in so you could be waiting quite a while for an escort home.

Cleo giggled despite herself, casting another glance at the man over her shoulder.

Cleo: At the risk of escaping the stalker behind me and leading another right to me, I'm in U. of Minnesota.

Unknown number: Ditto. Want me to come walk you home?

Fear seized her chest. The only thing worse than the idea of being followed home by a stranger was the idea of dragging some poor guy out of his house to rescue her from nothing more than her overactive imagination. It was why she hadn't messaged Molly. She didn't want to bother her for no reason and end up looking foolish.

Cleo: Thanks for the offer, but I could be overreacting.

Unknown number: At least tell me what he's wearing.

Cleo: I can't say I've ever had a guy text to ask me what another man is wearing. This is certainly new territory for me.

Her hand flew to her mouth with a hiccupping gasp. *Take it back!* A strangled groan escaped from between her fingers. Was she flirting with this guy? At a time like this? She never flirted. She didn't even know how.

> Cleo: He's wearing a green (I think?) North Face hoodie, jeans, and the whitest sneakers I've ever seen. It's dark out, but I'm still blinded by their brightness.

> Unknown number: LOL! I can't say I've ever messaged a woman to ask what another man is wearing. Guess this is new ground for both of us. And if he's not stalking you home, we might still need to call the fashion police for crimes against shoes.

> Cleo: I'm not sure I'm in a position to judge someone else's fashion sense. I spend my life in yoga pants and flats.

> Unknown number: Nothing sexier than a woman who isn't afraid to live her best life in a pair of yoga pants.

Butterflies fluttered in her chest. Could it be? A man on the planet who wasn't preoccupied with a woman's appearance? This guy had to be a catfish. With a wry grin, she changed his name on her phone to the all too nice Mr. Bingley, from her favorite book, *Pride and Prejudice.*

She was almost home. A quick check over her shoulder revealed she was alone and relief snaked its way through her muscles. Her mom always told her you could never be too careful. Better safe than sorry, and Cleo didn't want to be another statistic. Bad things didn't always happen to bad people, and too many rapists wandered the streets while women were called liars or told if they had dressed differently they wouldn't have been attacked. Cleo shuddered and picked up her pace. One of Molly's friends had been raped in her freshman year. The poor girl had to sit in class with her attacker every single day, knowing what he'd done to her.

Mr. Bingley: Did he get you? Or did you make it home and *gasp* discard me like yesterday's trash?

Cleo: Neither. I passed out from shock at the idea there might be a man in existence who doesn't care what women look like. I also changed your name in my phone.

Mr. Bingley: …? To what? You can't just leave it there. Talk about click bait. Also, I'm glad you weren't murdered. And it's kinda sad you have such a low opinion of men. Many of us don't care about yoga pants.

Cleo: Mr. Bingley.

As she approached her door, she tucked her phone in her pocket. She dug her key out of her backpack, before making her way up to her room.

Dropping her bag to the floor, she filled and turned on her mini kettle. She needed some decaf tea to help calm her nerves after the walk home. She'd been half-convinced she was going to die. She pulled out her mug and dropped in a tea bag before sitting cross-legged on the floor to check her messages while the water boiled.

Mr. Bingley: You're kidding, right? That bumbling idiot, Bingley? I'm low-key offended right now. Post-pride Darcy, that's what I should be under in your phone.

Cleo: Okay, now I DEFINITELY call bullshit. There isn't a man alive who loves Pride and Prejudice enough to know who either those dudes are, never mind both. I'm home by the way, and I appreciate you escorting me home, even from a distance.

Mr. Bingley: I have two sisters. Each of them prefers a different version, so I spent no less than 65% of my teenage years being subjected to countless re-runs of both the BBC version and the Keira Knightley version.

Cleo: And which did you prefer?

Mr. Bingley: A loaded question if ever I heard one. I feel like the fate of our very early day friendship might be hanging in the balance here. But I do, in fact, have strong opinions on which Darcy is better and I won't change them for any woman, no matter how charming she might be.

She tapped on her chin as the dots danced on her screen, indicating he was typing. *Wait. Did he just say I was charming?* A smile tugged at the corner of her lips and warmth seeped into her chest. People thought her aloof, intimidating, and intense, never charming. This was a first, and she wasn't quite sure what to do with it.

Mr. Bingley: Colin Firth.

Her smile grew.

Cleo: Phew. For a moment I thought I was going to have to delete your number from my phone and never talk to you again. Your answer is correct: Colin is the only Darcy.

She pulled up his contact info and changed his name to Mr. Darcy, before dropping Molly a text to let her know she was home in one piece and to make sure Molly didn't need rescuing.

> Mr. Darcy: Phew indeed. Glad you're home safe and sound, feel free to hit me up any time you need someone to pretend to text you on your way home.

Molly burst through the door in a blur of curse words and stilettos. For someone who spent more time than should be considered socially acceptable in oversized sports jerseys yelling at referees from the stands, the girl could rock a cocktail dress and killer heels like no other.

"Do I want to know why you're sitting on the floor?"

"I got distracted. Tea?"

Molly scrunched up her face. "Is it coffee flavored tea?"

"That doesn't even sound good. Date go well?" Cleo pulled herself to standing and poured the boiled water into her cup.

Her friend sighed and flopped face down onto her bed, mumbling something obscured by the face-full of pillow.

"That good, huh?"

"I mean it was fine, but he didn't get my pulse racing, y'know?"

Translation: he wasn't Finn. Molly had had a crush on her big brother's best friend Finn since before Cleo met her. Nothing had ever happened between them, and never could, but Molly spent her time trying to find a guy who made her laugh like he did. He was her yard stick, the one everyone else failed to stack up against, the one she'd steal glances at when she thought no one else could see. Molly had it bad.

"Wait. Why are you so smiley?"

Oh God. "I'm always this smiley."

Her friend's snort made her stomach drop.

"Did you break out the pink nightsaber? Is that what this is? Post screaming-O smiling?"

Cleo groaned. "No. Some dude was following me on the way home. At least, I kinda thought he was. My parents were already asleep and you were out with Jericho, or whatever his name is..."

"We need to get you more friends, girl. So what'd you do?"

Cleo turned her back to Molly so she wouldn't see her blush. She stirred her tea, plucked the tea bag out by the string and wrapped it around her spoon to squeeze a last bit of flavor into her mug before discarding it in the trash. She dropped a splash of milk into her cup, like her aunt's British husband taught her, before putting the milk back in the fridge.

"Cleo?"

"Yeah?"

"Did you call anyone to walk you home?"

"Not exactly." She picked up the spoon and gave her tea another stir.

"You've stirred it already." Molly grabbed her arm and turned her face on. "What gives?"

Cleo sipped her tea, keeping her eyes cast to the ground. "I messaged the randomer from yesterday."

"Who?" Molly tilted her head and pursed her lips. "Wait. The bra guy?" Her eyebrows shot up her forehead and her voice climbed an octave or two.

Cleo nodded.

"You didn't!"

Cleo nodded again.

"Of all the people in the world to text, you pick a guy you don't know, to save you from another guy you don't know? I mean... for a smart girl you sure do make questionable decisions sometimes. Is he even in Minnesota?"

"He is. I still don't know his name, but he's here at the U.

He didn't need to come rescue me, but we texted a bit." Cleo held her breath. Surely that would be the end of the questions. Maybe if she didn't move, blink, or breathe, Molly would forget she was even there and move on to the next thing.

"You like him."

No such luck. "I don't know him. I can't like him." Her defiant stomach flipped.

"You might want to tell your face that, Cleo, because your face says you might have a teenie little crush on the boy living in your phone."

CHAPTER 3
Lincoln

Sweat trickled down Lincoln's neck as he took the stairs two at a time up to his dorm. His legs burned and his shoulders ached, but in all the best ways. The only thing better than a rush of endorphins from working out, was the rush of endorphins from a hockey game. Well, that, and the rush of endorphins that came from doing a different kind of exercise with a beautiful woman.

"Another run?" His roommate and best friend, Russ, handed him a chilled bottle of water as he entered the room. Russ's two year old daughter was at his parent's house off campus. While they technically lived together, Russ split his time between the dorms and his folk's place. How he managed being a dad, school, and playing hockey, Linc would never know. The guy was a machine.

"Nah." Linc twisted the top off and took a few gulps. "Not by design anyway. Got chased down the street by a T-rex." He raised his bottle in salute to Russ before downing what was left, crushing the bottle like an accordion and throwing it at the trash can across the room. He missed.

"Know how I know you love me, man? When you get all

up in your sarcastic prickness." Russ winked. "No, really, it's totes adorbs. Where do you get the energy from? I can barely keep up with Coach's daily workouts and practices. And here you are, looking like, well..." He gestured an open hand from Linc's head to his feet. "Fresh as a daisy after doing your second extra run of the week."

"Third." Linc picked up the bottle and threw it in the trash can. "Hashtag humble brag." He pulled his shirt over his head, rolled it into a ball, and dropped it at his feet. "And some of us have to actually work on the ice, y'know? We don't all just cruise along the blue line waiting for the puck to come at us. Not to mention, gotta keep in shape for the ladies..." He slid his hand over his sweaty torso. "They like the abs."

Russ snorted. "What ladies? You haven't been on a date in... I dunno how long."

"It's only been days." Linc tugged off his socks and shorts, dropping them on top of the t-shirt on the floor. His phone chimed. He crossed the small space and unplugged his phone from the charger next to his bed.

"You didn't even take your phone? What kinda weirdo doesn't listen to music, or at least podcasts, while they run?"

Linc shrugged as he unlocked his phone. "It was dead, didn't have much choice. Are we..."

> Elizabeth Bennet: Thanks for 'walking' me home last night. I appreciate it. I'm sure I was overreacting, but I felt better having someone at the end of the phone.

She'd sent a gif of David Rose from Schitt's Creek with her message and the caption on it read: I might have been overreacting. He chuckled, hit reply, and sat on the edge of his bed.

Linc: Fuckin' love Schitt's Creek. Your gif
game is strong. And that's totally okay,
Eliza, you know one must be a gentleman in
such trying times for women.

She replied almost at once.

Elizabeth Bennet: My name isn't Eliza.

Linc: I know, but I figured if I'm in your
phone as Mr. Darcy, it's only fair you're in
mine as Elizabeth Bennet.

Elizabeth Bennet: Don't get your hopes up,
she's much prettier than I am.

"Who is she?"

"Hm?"

"The girl making your face do that weird lopsided, dopey smile thing. Who. Is. She?"

Linc: I feel like women are often way too
hard on themselves. My sisters are beautiful
women (in a non-creepy way) but if I had a
dollar for every time I heard them talk shit
about themselves, I'd be rich.

"Earth to Lincoln. You know we were in the middle of a conversation just then, right? You literally stopped mid-sentence. Are you seeing someone?"

"What? No!" Linc put his phone back on the bedside table, stood, pulled his boxer-briefs off and swooped his pile of damp clothes up from the floor.

"Dude. You really need to warn a guy when you're just gonna drop your drawers like that. And don't think I won't press you about this girl you're talking to just 'cause you're standing there dick-out and swingin' in the wind."

"It was a wrong number. I hooked up with Melissa the other night and she left her bra here. The number I texted to give it back wasn't hers, but some chick replied. I apologized and that was the end of it." He scrubbed a hand over his jaw and through his damp hair.

"Except you're still messaging her." Russell jerked his chin at the phone.

"Kind of. How's Jude?"

"Ha. Nice try. Jude's fine. Don't gimme that shit, man. You *literally* just messaged her. Keep talking."

"She goes here, to the U. She was walking home last night and I guess some guy was following her and she got spooked. She doesn't know many people and panicked. She asked if I'd keep her company on text until she got home. That was just a thank you message."

"Sure it was."

Linc narrowed his eyes at his friend. "It's not like that."

"Methinks the Linc doth protest too much."

Linc dropped his clothes into the laundry basket and grabbed a towel. Having a shower would keep Russ off his case about the mystery girl for a solid fifteen minutes, twenty at best, but knowing his friend he wouldn't give up until he knew who she was and how she rated.

Linc would never live it down if she was anything lower than a five, but for once, he didn't care. It was kinda nice talking to someone who had no idea who he was or what he was about. To her, he wasn't the son of an ex-NHL star, or a hot-shot hockey player. She didn't want him for his status in the team or because she thought he would look hot on her arm in a suit. To her, he was just Mr. Darcy, some random dude she happened upon by accident and maybe for once, that might even be enough.

❄

S howered and clothed, Linc's growling stomach was demanding food, but neither he nor Russ had picked up groceries the day before so he'd need to venture out into the world before he could cook anything. He grabbed his wallet and phone where a message awaited from his mystery friend.

> Elizabeth Bennet: I guess you're right. It's way too easy to be hard on yourself. Anyway, have a good one.

> Linc: Question: What are your dinner plans?

> Linc: Okay, whoa, wait. Rewind. I'm not asking you to have dinner with me, I need inspiration.

> Linc: And maybe a recipe.

Fucking idiot, stop talking. He couldn't type and walk without risking a concussion, so he sat on the floor and did some stretches while he waited for her to reply.

> Elizabeth Bennet: I'm having mac and cheese with green beans.

> Linc: Like… Kraft? I can totally do that.

> Elizabeth Bennet: LOL! No. Like, from scratch.

> Linc: Wait. You're about to blow my mind. You mean mac and cheese doesn't come from a box?

> Elizabeth Bennet: That's right, Mr. Darcy. Didn't your mom or sisters teach you how to make mac and cheese?

Linc: I make the best grilled cheese in the Midwest, but it's one of only a few dishes I've mastered. What do I need to make this bizzare not-from-a-box mac and cheese you speak of?

Elizabeth Bennet: We have to have a grilled-cheese-off some day. I make a mean grilled cheese. How fancy do you wanna go with your pasta?

Linc: How fancy are you going?

Elizabeth Bennet: Oooookay, but don't say I didn't offer you an easier way… You need to make a roux: butter and flour. You need milk, cheese (I prefer a mix of Monterey Jack, gruyere and sharp white cheddar), wholegrain mustard, panko breadcrumbs and pasta.

Linc: Miss Bennet I think you might have gone beyond my level of 'fancy', this sounds bougie.

Elizabeth Bennet: Cheese is my favorite food.

Linc: Doing my best not to make a cheese joke right now, but it's too Gouda to pass up.

Linc: You're never answering me again now, are you?

Linc: Okay, I'm heading out to the store. You're on the hook now, though. I'm going to text you around 5PM. I'll seem cool on the outside, but inside I'll be in a blind panic about how to make the bags of ingredients you're making me buy turn into real food. You have to answer and tell me how to make the mac and cheese or I'll starve and my death will be on your conscience.

Elizabeth Bennet: It's a date.

I guess it kinda is.

Linc: How was your day, Miss Bennet? I have all my ingredients set out in front of me and I'm ready to go when you are.

"I can't believe you're cooking. How long have you known this chick? Days? And you're cooking?" Russ had joined him in the shared kitchen and was heckling him from the dining room table.

"Keep sounding off, asshole, and you won't get any."

Russ dragged his index finger and thumb across his lips. "I'll say no more. But know this, I've already clocked where the fire extinguisher is, and I'm ready to dial 9-1-1 if you fuck this up and burn the place down. If by some miracle you make the freakin' pasta though, Jude will want some." He patted his stomach and licked his lips.

Elizabeth Bennet: I wasn't sure I'd hear from you again.

Linc: A gentleman always keeps his word, m'lady.

He smiled, but something about how she was speaking about herself tugged at his heart.

> Linc: You really don't have many friends, do you?

> Elizabeth Bennet: I don't, it's pathetic.

> Elizabeth Bennet: You'll wanna bring a pot of water to the boil for your pasta.

He filled the pot with water, set it on the stove and turned it on.

> Linc: It's not pathetic. It's easier to talk to me because I'm just some faceless guy on the phone. There's no judgment here. It's kinda freeing.

> Elizabeth Bennet: Is that why you talk to me? Because it's freeing?

> Linc: I can be myself.

> Elizabeth Bennet: And you can't beyond the phone?

> Linc: Not really. And I'm semi convinced I'm gonna flunk out and disappoint everyone in my life.

> Linc: This got heavy quickly, sorry. You don't need my baggage. Tell me this, what am I supposed to do with these 6lbs of shredded cheese?

> Elizabeth Bennet: No need to apologize, I get it. I feel a similar way. Not about the flunking though. If I flunked, my mom would literally disown me. I have questions about the quantity of cheese.

Linc: I figured I'd rather over buy than come up short. Size matters.

Elizabeth Bennet: Are you feeding the entire dorm?

Linc: It's a possibility.

She texted him through the various steps of creating a mass batch of mac and cheese. She never once made him feel foolish for not having an ovenproof dish to bake it in. It cooked just the same in a roasting pan he borrowed from one of the freshmen and it even resembled gooey, creamy baked mac and cheese when he served a heaped plate to himself and Russ.

Russ speared some pasta onto his fork and took a bite. He let out a satisfied moan. "Shit. I dunno who she is, man. But she sure does make a mean mac and cheese. You gonna talk to her again?"

Linc swallowed a mouthful of the most delicious mac and cheese he'd ever tried. What was the harm in talking to a girl he didn't know over text? "Yeah, I think I am."

CHAPTER 4

Lincoln

Few things in life made Linc's dick harder than a fine ass in the air. Hot damn. Whoever was attached to that ass was about to get the Lincoln Scott VIP treatment, and maybe later she'd help him out with the throbbing cock about to burst out of his pants.

"Car trouble?"

The little yelp and gasp from whoever she was made a chuckle rumble deep in his chest. He propped his forearm on the edge of the open hood and crossed his legs at the ankle as he took her in. Well-loved chucks, yoga pants hugging her thighs and the curve of her round ass, and a blue t-shirt riding up so a sliver of skin was on show. She straightened her spine as she stepped out from under the hood.

His eyes stayed glued to the still-showing strip of skin at her midriff before drifting up over her ample cleavage. Thick, wavy, chestnut brown hair was pulled into a low loose ponytail draped over her shoulder. *Oh God.* Cleo Martinez turned to face him, eyebrow arched and a smear of oil under her right cheek. Piercing hazel eyes sparkled under a deep frown. She folded her arms. At half a foot shorter than him, she was all curves and sass. Nothing good could come from lusting after that ass. That ass was out of his league. If only he could somehow tell that to the unyielding boner in his pants.

"Not at all. Sometimes I like getting all up under the hood and talking dirty to it so he stays faithful to me, y'know?"

Linc chuckled again.

The corner of her lips twitched. She swept a hand toward the engine. "I secretly love sweat trickling down my ass crack while I try to figure out what the hell is wrong with my car." She winced, as though realizing her mind-to-mouth filter was malfunctioning in the heat.

Her barbs of sarcasm warmed something in his chest. People didn't talk to him the way she did, and if he was honest with himself, he kinda liked it. She wasn't like the girls who threw themselves at him in bars. In fairness, most of the girls in his circle were puck bunnies, more motivated by a desire to meet the players and be seen on a hot guy's arm than having any interest in hockey or getting to know him.

Cleo didn't want anything to do with him at all, and that in itself was a breath of fresh air.

He hadn't noticed her until she'd dropped an eight inch, hot pink dildo on his foot at the mall, right before the semester started. The image of what she might go home and do with it, well, *that* had plagued his every fantasy for weeks. Staring into her hazel eyes, it all came flooding back to him. If it was socially acceptable to look in his pants, he'd find blue balls.

She cleared her throat, and her head jerked as if to say, 'Was that everything?' Could she somehow see inside his brain? Did she know how hot the idea of her playing with that damn vibrator was? He doubted it. She seemed oblivious to how beautiful she was. Somewhere between hot librarian, and Hermione from Harry Potter. *Shit. She's still looking at me like I'm a fucking imbecile. Say something, asshole.*

"Do you—?"

Raucous laughter interrupted him.

"You should go before someone sees." She turned, unhooked the hood strut, folded it back into its place, and dropped the hood shut with a dull thud.

His face burned. She didn't want to be seen with him. He couldn't blame her. He might not like it, but she had a point. Jocks and nerds didn't mix unless they had to, and for some unknown reason, he had 'a rep to protect'. What the fuck did that even mean? A rep to protect? Like he'd somehow be disowned by his hockey brothers if he was seen talking to a bookworm? Would he? She wiped her hands on the thighs of her yoga pants and dragged her arm across her glistening forehead. Did he care if they did?

"Ready to go, Linc?" Will Morrison, senior and captain of the Snow Pirates hockey team slung an arm around his shoulders and squeezed. "Waffles wait for no man."

Linc shrugged off his grip. "Nor beasts." He jabbed Will in the ribs.

"Touché, man. Let's eat."

His gaze lingered on Cleo who was staring at her phone as though her glare might burn through the screen. He grabbed his phone from his back pocket and pulled up the number for 'Grease Monkey' – the not very creative nickname his friend Steve went by.

Linc: Favor?

Grease Monkey: It'll cost you a signed photo for my little brother, a puck, and maybe something else depending on what you need me to do.

Linc: Silver Honda civic at the corner of 3rd and Cedar, facing the bookstore. Get her roadworthy again and send me the bill? If the owner asks, say it was a Random Act of Kindness or some shit.

Grease Monkey: You break someone's car, hot shot?

Linc: Damsel in distress. She hates my guts and would never accept help from a no-brain jock, so let's keep it on the DL, yeah?

He shuddered at the thought of what Cleo might do if she ever heard him refer to her as a damsel, and chuckled. *She'd kick my ass, that's what she'd do.*

Grease Monkey: I won't tell your boys you have a squishy heart under that hockey armor either.

Linc: You're the best, Monk.

He slapped his phone against his palm before tucking it into his back pocket and catching up to his friends. He had no idea why he was drawn to help the prickly woman with the razor-sharp tongue who seemed to hate everything he stood for, but something compelled him all the same. Maybe he was just a no-brain jock, but he was also a helper, a doer, and she was standing running her hand through her hair, hip popped, and scowling as she talked to someone on her phone.

Cleo Martinez could definitely use some help.

❄

"You should really do something with those, Linc. They're awesome." Russ sauntered into the room gesturing at Linc's bed. It was covered in half-finished sketches and art books. The edge of Linc's hand was blackened from the charcoal he was using on his current work in progress. He paused, making sure none of his sketches of Cleo were on display. Something about her had his fingers recreating the lines of her face on blank page after blank page, but he still couldn't nail her eyes.

Russ was the only person alive who knew Linc could draw. He'd come home early one night and found Linc slouched over his sketchpad, smearing pastels onto the page. Linc had expected mockery and wiseass, but Russ had only been impressed and had demanded to see more examples of his work. They'd had this argument so many times that Linc's only answer was to raise his eyebrows.

"I know, I know. Art's nothing more than a waste of time." He did a good impression of Linc's dad's gruff voice as he puffed out his chest and wagged a finger at Linc. "Gotta keep your grades up and head on the ice... but you're good, Linc. Really damn good. You could go places with this shit."

Linc stayed silent, maybe if he didn't answer, Russ would drop it for a change. He rounded the lines of the shape he was working on with the side of his pinky, blurring the edges of the charcoal just a little.

Russ stretched and his bones clicked and popped. "Who's the subject of your artistic affections today then?"

"No one you know."

"Only 'cause you haven't given her a face yet. Is she your mystery text friend?"

The idea made him laugh. The girl on the phone was nothing like the girl he was drawing. They'd been texting for two weeks and where Elizabeth was gentle and vulnerable,

Cleo was cold and unapproachable. Where Elizabeth was self-deprecating and unsure, Cleo was confident and strong. He shook his head. "Oil and water."

Russ's eyebrows furrowed and he cocked his head in confusion as Linc's phone chirped from across the room. "Speak of the devil I bet. You should meet that girl, Linc. Stop hiding behind your phone." He picked up Linc's phone and tossed it to him before leaving the room.

His comment stung because his friend wasn't wrong. Linc *was* hiding behind his screen. It was safe there. With his Mr. Darcy persona there were no expectations, no snap judgements, and no pressure.

Elizabeth Bennet: What. A. Day. Tell me something fun and happy.

> Linc: Brace yourself. What I'm about to tell you will lose me major cool points.

> Elizabeth Bennet: I'm all ears. Or fingers, I guess?

Linc chuckled and waited for the follow-up.

> Elizabeth Bennet: Oh GOD. I didn't mean… that sounds… Sorry.

Her message was accompanied by a gif of Jocelyn Shitt from Schitt's Creek saying 'I'm embarrassed by my behavior." He had to hand it to her, her gif game was almost as strong as her obsession with the show. He tucked away his charcoal, shuffled the pages into a haphazard pile that he moved into his art case and placed it on the floor before sitting cross-legged on the bed.

> Elizabeth Bennet: Say *something* Mr. Darcy. Be a gentleman and save me from my embarrassment.

> Linc: I'm laughing too hard to type. Aren't men supposed to be the dirty minded ones? It took me a minute to get the innuendo – and I'm usually shit-hot with that kinda stuff.

Her only response was a David Rose gif saying 'This is really fun for me. I'm having a lot of fun.' He snorted.

> Linc: I draw.

> Elizabeth Bennet: Like… stick figures? ;-)

> Linc: Maaaaaaan, Lizzy, you are SAVAGE! I come to you vulnerable, show you my soft underbelly and you come at me with… JOKES?

> Elizabeth Bennet: My *dear* Mr. Darcy, I do wholly apologize. I meant no ill will. What kinds of things do you draw? Can I see?

His heart thudded in his ears and his pulse raced. He should have known this was coming, prepared himself for the idea she'd want to see his work, but it took him by surprise. He swallowed down the lump of fear in his throat and pulled an art pad back out of its case, flicking through to find a nondescript drawing that wouldn't give any clues as to who he was. He snapped a picture of the sketch he'd done of the Golden Gate Bridge and hit send before he could talk himself out of it. He dropped the pad back onto the floor and pulled the quilt over his head as though it could protect him from any judgement she was about to text. Then waited.

Thankfully he didn't have to wait long. Her response came through after a few minutes. *Breathtaking, lifelike and vibrant.* Those were the words she'd used to describe his art. And when he offered an out to retract her first response and tell him it looked like something a two-year-old could draw, she had admonished him for being self-deprecating. He'd let the woman on the phone peek in behind the curtain of his soul, and she hadn't run.

> Elizabeth: Thank you so much for sharing that with me. I know you're up in your feels about it, but you have no need to be. You're *so* good, Mr. Darcy. Do you have a favorite artist? My favorite contemporary artist is Zoe Strauss. Do you know her?

A grin threatened to split his face in two at the tangible excitement radiating from her message. Nerding out over art wasn't exactly 'cool'. While he was warmed at her response to his work, sharing this piece of him with someone else, someone who hadn't made fun of him for it or told him it was worthless or pointless, was everything.

> Linc: I don't, no. I could Google her, but, to be honest, I'd love for you to tell me about her.

> Elizabeth: She's a Philly-based artist. She captures people and places that are often overlooked by society. She photographs shuttered buildings, empty parking lots and derelict buildings. She says her work is 'a narrative about the beauty and difficulty of everyday life.'

She sent him a link to her favorite photo of Zoe's, a black and white picture of a little girl standing at a protest holding a sign that said 'I am strong, don't limit me!'

Linc: Shit. That's powerful.

Elizabeth: Isn't it, though? What about you? Who's your favorite artist?

Linc: You wouldn't know him.

Elizabeth: Oh, like you knew Zoe?

Linc: Fair point.

He wiped his palm on his thigh and ran his hand through his hair. He pulled the quilt down from over his head and tucked it under his arm as he typed, lying on his side. He had no idea how long they'd been chatting, but the room was dark and his stomach growled.

Linc: I keep losing track of time when we talk. I'm starving!

Elizabeth: Nope, not letting you change the subject. Eat if you gotta eat, but you're telling me about the artist.

Linc: Fiiiiiine. Okay. He's a largely unknown Irish famine artist. Or at least, he was. He died in 2019. Self-taught, he didn't have much by way of formal education most of his life. His name was Oliver Curran. He wasn't widely known, blue mountains were his signature 'thing' and while he had a couple of exhibitions both here in the states and in Ireland, he didn't really do a lot of shows. Balloons Over France is my favorite picture of his.

He sent her a link to check it out.

Elizabeth: Wow, those blossom trees!

Linc: Right? I don't know what it is about his work, but I love it. I keep threatening to try to do one of his pictures, and then I talk myself out of it. If you can believe it, I found him on a random Google search when I was researching a paper.

The pressure of having revealed such a raw part of his soul pressed against his chest, blasting the air from his lungs. His heart thudded. He needed to turn attention from him, to put back into place the comfortable mask he hid behind.

Linc: What about you?

Elizabeth: I told you who my favorite artist is.

Linc: Nah, not art. What's the one thing that you're passionate about? That you love.

Elizabeth: Uhhhh… Reading?

Linc: I'm groaning right now. Out LOUD. I get that you love to read, Miss Bennet, but surely there's something else that you enjoy? Crocheting? Needlework? Walking through fields in the rain?

Elizabeth: I write short stories…

He rolled onto his back lifting the phone in front of his face to type. A recipe for disaster, he'd had too many instances of phone-meeting-face from a height, but he couldn't help it. He didn't want to say goodnight and stop the conversation.

Linc: Do you do anything with them? Submit them for publishing?

Elizabeth: Do you submit your art for exhibitions?

Linc: My art isn't good enough to be put on display.

Elizabeth: Neither is my writing.

Linc: Isn't that for the reader to decide?

Elizabeth: Shouldn't your work be judged by others and not yourself, too?

Linc: Touché. Does anyone know you write?

His heart thumped. She was coming at him with logic and other than a raging case of not-good-enough and 'my father might very well disown me', he didn't have a good reason why he didn't share his art with anyone.

Elizabeth: My mom. I told her once and she shut me down. She said it was a silly pursuit that wasn't going anywhere. My best friend knows too. She keeps trying to read over my shoulder when the mood strikes and she nags at me to publish. You?

Linc: My roommate. My dad thinks art is for (and I'm quoting here) 'pussies'.

Elizabeth: Ouch. I'm so sorry, Mr. Darcy, but your father is very wrong, and you have serious talent.

His face, neck and ears burned hot under her praise. It constricted his chest like a shirt that was too tight. He shifted on the mattress, unsure of how to respond.

> Elizabeth: You're freaking out, aren't you? I get it. I don't get praised much by my parents either. It's a weird feeling when someone sees the real you, isn't it? At least for me it's uncomfortable. Well, whoever you are, thank you for showing me such a secret piece of yourself, I think it's beautiful, brilliant, and brave and I hope someday you step out of whatever shadow you're living in and show the world. The world needs more art like yours, Mr. Darcy.

He blinked back tears. He read her message over three more times and still had no idea what to reply. His dad had made himself very clear on the subject, and as long as he felt that way, Linc could never step into the sun and show the world his art.

He'd have to make do with showing the girl in the phone little snippets of his soul.

CHAPTER 5

Cleo

"No."

"Ugh. You're becoming predictable, Cho-Cho." Molly flopped onto the sofa with a dramatic poof of the cushions.

"And yet I'm okay with that, Molly. I'd rather be seen dead than in a hockey stadium."

Molly groaned and pulled a throw pillow over her face before throwing it at Cleo who caught it with ease. "*Rink*, Cleo. It's a hockey rink. Or an arena, but it's not open top. It's not a stadium." She shook her head as though Cleo had committed some heinous crime. "And at this rate you're going to die from lack of fun before we turn twenty."

"So dramatic!" Cleo lobbed the cushion back at her friend. "I'm fine here. You know that, right? My books and I will be just a-okay without watching a dumb game where testosterone fueled jocks beat the shit out of each other."

Molly had set the cushion next to her on the couch and leaned forward, elbows on her knees. "*That's* what you think hockey is? Oh girl. Have you ever watched a game? It's art on ice. Six foot dudes skating... on blades... I repeat... on *ice*, trying to get a three inch disc of rubber past a guy who all but fills the goal? Skill. Nothing but skill. Fighting's part of the game, sure, but it's becoming less and less prevalent." Light danced in her eyes and her hands moved as she talked.

Cleo arched an eyebrow. "You don't need me to go with you to drool over Finn."

Molly turned red all the way to her ears. "This isn't about Finn. I'm over him, remember? School girl crush. Nothing more. William would kill both of us if he ever found out I so much as had a crush on his best friend. Nope, I'm done. Maybe I'll sleep with one of the away team to get Finn all the way out of my system, y'know, just to be certain. Plus I have an article to write. I need to be there to make sure I get all the juicy deets for the school paper."

"Juicy deets? It's a hockey game, not an episode of The Bachelor, Mol."

"I think you'd appreciate the sport, Miss Hoity Toity. And I love that you say that like you watch The Bachelor."

"You don't know what I get up to while you're out."

"This is true." She wagged a finger in Cleo's direction before pointing it at the bookshelves. "But if that shelf of llama figures could talk, they'd tell me you don't watch The Bachelor."

"They're nothing but pigs on skates."

"Talented, *hot* pigs on skates. Come on, Cleo. You're only young once, yadda yadda, all work and no play, yadda yadda yadda." Molly stood up and crossed the room to the loveseat, where she dropped herself on Cleo's lap with an ungracious plop and snuggled in.

Cleo lost her breath for a moment while Molly snaked her arms around her waist and gave her a squeeze. "Pleeeeeeease, Cleo? Do it for me. If you hate it, you never have to go again. But you can't cross 'attend a sporting event' off your college bingo card if you don't actually attend a sporting event. And then you can't win at college bingo. Didn't you know? You won't get your degree if you don't complete the college bingo minor, it's in the bylaws."

"You're sooooo good at pep talks, has anyone ever told you that?"

Molly nuzzled her head into the crook of Cleo's neck. "You mean I'm good at poking at your competitive nature. You like to come first in all things, including a made up game of college bingo. Hmmm... I can sweeten the deal, too."

"I'm listening." Cleo gave in to her friend's hug, closing her arms around her shoulders.

"I'll buy you nachos."

Cleo pursed her lips and tipped her head as though she was giving it a great deal of thought. "Okay, fine. But for the record, I was leaning toward going before the nachos."

"But only after I mentioned the bingo thing, right?"

"I really am predictable, aren't I?"

"Well, I predicted you'd hold steady and say no, so I guess you're turning over a new leaf. Before you know it, you'll be draped in a hockey jersey screaming obscenities at the referee."

"Over my dead body."

"Never say never. The hot pigs are kinda charming. They get under your skin."

Cleo wrapped her arms around her body and shivered. The chill from the ice infused the air despite the number of bodies crammed together in the stands. Molly had insisted they got there in plenty of time. She liked to try to interview some of the team pre-game, which almost never worked, but sometimes they'd throw her a quote on their way into the building.

"I told you, you shoulda brought a jacket."

"I underestimated the iciness of the ice. They aren't kidding around are they? It's like a frozen tundra in here."

"Girlie, your lips are going blue. Go out to the merch stall and buy yourself a sweater."

Cleo's mouth dropped open then snapped shut. "Hell no. You want me to wear a sports... thing?"

"I want you to not die of hypothermia before the game even starts."

Cleo clenched her chattering teeth and gave a sharp shake of her head. "I'm fine."

"If you say so." Molly turned her attention back to her notebook, scrawling in shorthand.

Cleo lasted another few minutes before the shuddering cold throughout her body and the goosebumps covering her skin drove her to buy a navy-blue sweater from the merchandise stall outside the entrance to their section. They only had one navy-blue sweater in extra-large, which was fine, until the lady behind the counter held it up. It read: My Heart Belongs to a Snow Pirate and had a puck in the middle of a heartbeat printed on the chest. Cleo groaned, paid for the hoody, and grabbed a coffee before returning to her seat just as the lights were dimming.

"Is it the dull light in here or does it say your heart belongs to a Snow Pirate across your boobs? Did I fall unconscious? How long were you gone for? Which of the hot pigs has your heart? I have questions Cho-Cho. *So* many questions."

Cleo's cheeks burned. "Shhh... stand up, the anthem's starting." Cleo had to admit the set up was impressive. Someone in an oversized pirate costume was working the crowd, and both teams had skated onto the ice and lined up along the painted lines. The fans went wild as the puck hit the ice for the first time.

"If you have questions, ask them, 'kay? You can't learn unless you ask, and I can multitask."

Cleo recognized many of the player's names on the back of their shirts, Molly's brother Will wore the number eighty-two on his back and a 'C' on his chest. "Does that mean Will is the captain?"

Molly beamed, and nodded, pride radiating from her like a beacon. "Yeah, it's pretty cool. Finn and Austin are alternates. That means they serve as captain if Will is on the bench, injured, or in the penalty box. Uh... Finn is number fifteen and Austin is – to absolutely no one's surprise – sixty-nine." Molly pointed to the different men on the ice.

"I don't know what that means."

"You will. It's the worst kept secret on the team." She dropped her voice to a loud whisper. "He's basically a sex god."

Cleo rolled her eyes but sought out the numbers on the shirts passing by in a blur of clicking sticks and grunting. "It's so fast!" Her heart was racing.

Molly grinned again. "Told you. They're badass athletes. Okay, so they're douche waffles sometimes... Fine, a lot of the time, but they're talented as fuck."

She was only half listening to her friend, her attention was glued to the guy skating in their direction wearing a blue helmet. He'd broken away from the rest of the pack and was moving toward the goaltender. He was faster and more elegant on the ice than a man of his size had any business being. The goaltender had skated out from his net. He was squatting – presumably in preparation to meet the fast skater, in a bid to foil his attempt at scoring.

She shuffled to the edge of her seat, leaning forward to get a better view. Would the skater crash into the goaltender? Into the net? He'd stop before he got there... right? Her breath caught as he barreled toward the goalie.

Excitement crackled in the stands as the fans cheered him on. The player skated left and drew back his stick, the goalie flinched right, and without a millisecond of hesitation, the player with the blue helmet smacked the puck into the back of the net. Cleo was on her feet cheering and clapping before her brain caught up. She ignored Molly's piercing stare, heating up her cheeks, and kept her eyes on the ice and dropped back onto her seat.

The goal scorer skated toward his teammates. They surrounded him and clapped on his back with gloved hands. She could make out his number – thirteen – and when the crowd of players around him dispersed, the name above the number read *Scott*. Lincoln? The towering, broad-shouldered, graceful guy on skates was Lincoln Scott.

Her stomach flipped. She didn't know anything about anything when it came to hockey, or any other sport for that matter, but scoring a goal was a good thing, she knew that much. She tilted her head and squinted, his grin was infectious, even if his teeth were hidden behind a mouth guard.

He turned toward the bench, scanning the crowd as he passed. When his eyes traveled over her, she held her breath. His face remained impassive, as though he didn't recognize anyone, but when his brows twitched she shrank into her seat and pulled her arms around her. Could he make out who she was from all the way down on the ice?

Molly cleared her throat. "Huh."

"Hmm?" Cleo dragged her gaze from the ice and found Molly with yet another stupid grin on her face.

"Nothing but pigs, eh? Looks to me like someone's got a wicked craving for some pork."

CHAPTER 6
Cleo

Despite Lincoln's exciting goal, the Snow Pirates lost two to one. The disappointment around the rink was palpable, but it didn't come close to the gloominess curling in her stomach. Mr. Darcy hadn't replied to any of the three messages she'd sent throughout the day.

Maybe he's found a girlfriend.

Maybe he died. Christ that's dark, Cleo. Could you be any more dramatic?

Maybe he's just busy and you're overreacting just a teensy bit?

Frustration, sadness, and anger pressed heavy on her shoulders as she left the rink with a dejected Molly to hit the coffee shop next door. Most of her anger was directed at herself. What had she expected? To talk to the stranger on the phone forever?

Maybe?

Did she think he would never date or find anyone else?

I mean, I'd kinda hoped he wouldn't.

They hadn't set down any expectations of exclusivity. She snorted aloud, drawing a raised eyebrow from Molly that she dismissed with a shake of her head. They'd never even met, they'd only been trading texts for a few weeks, and she had no right to be upset that he hadn't replied to her messages.

Except she was. And she was mad about the fact she was upset.

The Sugar Bean opened late every evening and served the best hot chocolate she'd ever tasted. Tonight was a hot chocolate kind of night – fully loaded with cream and marshmallows – she couldn't feel her toes but was desperate to remove the hockey team branding from her body before anyone else saw her.

She shivered, unsure why it bothered her so much. It was just a sweater. It wasn't as if her grades would tank from one night out at a hockey game, and it wasn't as though the fabric of the team sweater would suck out her intelligence. Plenty of smart people watched sports, Molly being a prime example. So why did the collar feel as though it was closing around her throat?

"Wanna talk about it?" Molly picked up the two drinks from the end of the counter and followed Cleo to a small two-seater table tucked in the corner.

Cleo slid into the seat facing the entrance and accepted the brimming mug of hot chocolate from her friend. "Talk about what?"

"Oh honey, we both know this..." She waved a hand in front of Cleo's face. "Isn't because the Pirates lost. What gives? Why so sad, Flower? Trouble in phone-boy-land?"

Her breath stopped in her chest. "We're not... I don't even know him, Mol. Can you not? Please?"

Molly's eyes widened. She plucked a marshmallow from her drink and popped it in her mouth. "Yeah, okay. So you're not at all having any feelings about this boy at all, right?"

Cleo wasn't going there. "Oh hey, I was meaning to thank you for calling *AAA* for me. The guy who came out to fix my car was super nice. I dunno how you got him to come out so fast, every number I called couldn't fit me in."

"Nice try. Deflecting from your feels by thanking me for something you know I didn't do."

Cleo's head snapped up from her mug, confusion creeping up her spine. "What? You didn't? Then who the hell fixed my car? He wouldn't take any money and I figured it would go through insurance. I hadn't gotten around to asking my folks about how it all works since I've never needed to get my car fixed before. If you didn't do it, then who did?"

Molly shrugged her shoulders. "Not it. Also not an issue since the car is fixed and it didn't cost you anything. Take the win, girlfriend. Now, back to the Phone Boy..."

The tinkling of the bell above the door bought her a moment to think about the answer. Lincoln, Will, and two guys she assumed were also on the team, walked into the coffee house.

A blast of cold air passed through the café, taking her higher brain function with it. Was she drooling? Why were they wearing suits? Why was her mouth drier than the desert? Why couldn't she peel her eyes away from the... shoulders? Good lord, had he always had those shoulders? That was one fine group of men standing at the counter.

Lincoln stood, dragging the pad of his thumb across his bottom lip as he stared up at the menu.

Cleo chewed the inside of her cheek as she trailed her eyes across his chest, and all the way to the floor. She swallowed hard, and squeezed her thighs together. *When did it get so warm in here?*

She squeaked as a giggling Molly pinched her thigh.

"You're getting drool on the table, Cho-Cho. Damn. People will think you've never seen a post-game hockey player before."

Mute. Cleo couldn't form words and she hated herself for

it. She'd always judged the women in books and movies who lost the capacity to speak at the sight of a delicious man, and yet here she was, barely able to remember her own name and drowning in her own drool.

Stop staring.

She plunged her teeth into her lip and turned her attention back to her hot chocolate, which, despite being hot enough to scald her tongue, didn't come close to the burning she was feeling in other parts of her body.

Stop it.

"He has that effect on a lot of women." Molly's murmured hush was loud enough for only Cleo to hear.

"Who?" Was that her voice? That raspy, croaky noise? Cleo cleared her throat and took a sip of her drink.

"Well I sure as shit hope you're not jizzing your pants over my big brother or I'll have to kill you in your sleep."

Cleo laughed at the same time she was swallowing, causing a marshmallow to lodge in her airway. She coughed into her elbow, her sight blurring and eyes stinging as she choked. Molly cracked open the bottle of water from the bag at her feet and handed it to Cleo who grumbled a thanks and gulped down the cool relief.

"Ladies." Molly's brother saluted the two women as he passed, followed by Linc, whose impassive face Cleo couldn't read.

Cleo's face burned hotter. Not only was she mortified to be seen at a hockey game, but to choke on her own tongue at the sight of a jock in a suit was shameful. She managed a small smile and a nod at Will, as the two other players walked past. *Pull yourself together, woman!*

Someone behind her sniggered. "As if any of the Pirates would want *her* heart."

It was almost word for word what Archie Abram, her high

school crush, had said to her when they were fifteen, in front of all their friends.

I'm not saying you're fat, but it looks like you were poured into your clothes and someone forgot to say "when".

A gasp lodged in her chest and unshed tears burned her eyelids at the memory. The barbs about her appearance had started in high school, but they never stung any less, no matter how often they were thrown. Molly's fist clenched on the table and her jaw was firm-set. Cleo gave her an almost imperceptible shake of her head. Causing a scene would only make it worse. Experience had taught her if she didn't react, they'd stop eventually.

Cups and spoons clicked and rattled behind Cleo, followed by the dull thud of a thump. "Shut your fucking mouth, Johnny. Why do you always have to be such an asshole?" Will's defense of her against the stranger did little to uncoil the anxiety and self-loathing pooling in her stomach. She couldn't bring herself to look at Lincoln. Did he feel the same as Johnny?

"Let's go."

Molly didn't object. She had to know Cleo well enough to know this wasn't the time to make a stand.

It was time for Cleo to go home, set fire to the dumb sweater, and cry where the asshole jocks couldn't see her.

Cleo's chair screeched against the wooden floor as she pushed back from the table. Cheeks on fire, she grabbed her purse before standing. She straightened her spine and raised her chin. She'd be damned if she let that asshole see he'd hurt her. Something ignited deep inside her and she spun to face the now quiet table of men who wouldn't meet her gaze, Lincoln included.

"Hey, asshole." She bent to the floor, stood, and held out an empty hand toward the guy who was rubbing his bicep, she assumed from the thump Molly's brother had given it. "I found your nose, it was over here in my business."

Will sniggered, Lincoln's face split into a wide grin, and Johnny mumbled something under his breath.

"Sorry, what did you say? I don't speak idiot." She didn't wait for a reaction, but Will gave her a reassuring nod as she turned and left the café.

They walked home in silence, Cleo stewing in her thoughts and Molly typing on her phone. Shame and embarrassment crawled over Cleo's body, but the cold was bone deep and she couldn't tear off the sweater encasing her in her mortification. As soon as she crossed the threshold into their apartment, she yanked it off, balled it up, and threw it at the trash can.

Molly swooped in to rescue it. "No ma'am. Not happening. You can purge your rage on that one, singular asshole, but you're keeping the hoody, just in case."

"In case what?"

Her friend shrugged. "You decide to go back."

Cleo snorted. "That is also not happening, my dear, sweet, and optimistic as fuck bestie. Hockey sucks and jocks are assholes."

"Don't hold back, Cho-Cho, tell me how you really feel. What about Phone Boy?"

"What about him? Foolish crush on an imaginary person. Nothing more."

"Still hasn't replied yet, huh?"

Cleo clenched her jaw and narrowed her eyes at her friend who held her hands up in surrender.

"Wine?" Molly made her way into the kitchen, while Cleo sank onto the sofa and tucked her knees under her chin, wrapping her arms around her shins.

"Wine doesn't cut it. I need to stop the emotional hemorrhaging."

"Okay, drama llama. Tequila it is."

Cleo ignored the magnetic pull of her phone for the rest of the evening, not wanting to be disappointed by a blank screen and no notifications, but she couldn't avoid the discontent lying heavy in her stomach. Climbing into bed, tears brimmed as she rolled onto her side. She'd get some good sleep and wake up not caring about Lincoln Scott and his jock friends, no matter how breathtaking he was in a suit.

She wouldn't care about Mr. Darcy, hockey, or anything outside of school. She'd retreat back to her comfort zone. Books couldn't hurt her. Assignments couldn't hurt her. And since jocks didn't generally frequent the library, she wouldn't get called out for being fat and unlovable in public again.

Her phone vibrated on the nightstand. Nope. She wasn't going to look. She scrunched her eyes closed and pulled the quilt over her head to ignore it.

What if something was wrong with her parents?

Sighing, she threw the quilt from her face and turned toward the offending phone. Four messages, all from Mr. Darcy. Her traitorous heart twitched and the ball of anxiety loosened in her stomach.

Mr. Darcy: Sorry for the radio silence, I've been slammed all day.

Mr. Darcy: I hope you're okay. Call me creepy but you usually at least read your messages faster than this.

Mr. Darcy: Eliza? Can you at least let me know you're okay before you go to bed, please? I know you don't owe me anything, but I'm kinda worried.

Any lingering anger fizzled away at his words.

Cleo: Sorry, I was with friends this evening after the game. It was… something. That's for sure. I'm not sure how I feel about the display of testosterone on the ice.

Mr. Darcy: You were at the rink? Like, the ice hockey rink? You like hockey? I feel like I'm going to need a moment to process this information Miss Bennet.

Cleo: Take all the time you need. Maybe my fingers will defrost before your shock wears off.

Cleo: Are you sporty? Do you… do sporty things?

She groaned at her lack of knowledge about anything athletic.

Mr. Darcy: You could say that, yeah. I like to keep fit.

This would never work. If they ever took whatever they were cultivating away from screens into the real world, it couldn't work. She was so far from fit it wasn't even funny.

Mr. Darcy: That wasn't a come on by the way. But I do work out.

Tears trickled down her cheeks. Of course it wasn't a come on.

Cleo: Didn't think it was. I'm gonna go to bed, early start tomorrow. Goodnight Mr. Darcy.

Mr. Darcy: Goodnight, dear Elizabeth. For what it's worth, I missed you today.

You wouldn't have if you knew who I was.

CHAPTER 7

Lincoln

Cleo Martinez was fury personified. Waves of irritation and contempt rolled off her from across the room. Mrs. Kelly had put them together for a group project in English class, and if the folded arms, furrowed brow and scowl on Ms. Martinez's face were anything to go by, she was less than thrilled at the idea.

Seeing her at the game with his team branded across her chest had given him a hard on right there on the ice. He'd thought he was seeing things, and almost didn't recognize her without a book in her hand, but it was definitely her. Not only that, but she cheered when he'd scored – which had given him a warm feeling he was actively avoiding identifying.

He didn't have those kinds of feelings for Cleo Martinez. His fickle cock had other ideas and was thrilled at the idea of working with her for the project. He chuckled.

Her lips were set in a thin line, and if he listened hard enough he might have heard her teeth grinding.

She hated him; hated all jocks, though after Johnny's behavior in the coffee shop the other night, he couldn't blame her. Brotherhood had been the only thing preventing him from breaking the asshole's jaw after what he'd said to her. If Will hadn't reacted and thumped Johnny, Linc would have said something.

While he hadn't seen her face, the changes in her body were subtle enough that those paying less attention might not have noticed. But her confidence had seeped out of every muscle, her shoulders curled forward and her head drooped. He'd expected her to cry, but when she stood tall and threw shade right in Johnny's face, Linc had never been more turned on. She might have been broken and miserable on the inside, but she didn't show it. She had steeled herself and made Johnny look every ounce of the prick he was.

As though she could feel him staring, she tossed him some wicked side-eye. If looks could kill. He clamped his lips between his teeth, fighting the laugh rumbling in his chest. Fuck, she was sexy as hell when she was mad.

A blush stained the apples of her cheeks, but Linc was no fool. That was not an embarrassed woman, and while he wasn't a mind reader, murder was most definitely on that Latina's mind. Namely, his.

The bell chimed, punctuating the end of class with a shrill peal. She shoved her belongings into her backpack, her wild waves falling into her face, and strode over to him. "I'm not giving you my cell number." Her nostrils flared and he itched to reach out and tuck her unruly hair behind her ear.

"I didn't ask. But don't we need to communicate for the project we're working on?"

She mumbled something half under her breath about how God hated her and paired her with him as punishment. They were the only 'group' in the class that had two members instead of three.

"I won't do your work for you."

"I didn't ask you for that either. Seems you're making a lot of assumptions here, Cleo. Here..." He pulled his notebook out of his backpack, scribbled his email address, tore the page from the book and handed it to her. "Why don't you decide what you think I'm capable of contributing to the project and let me know, yeah? I mean, you've already written me off as a dumb jock. And you said you're not going to do the work for me, so maybe when you email you could use small words, and write in short sentences so my tiny, athlete brain understands what you want."

Her jaw twitched, and her eyes widened under raised eyebrows. She snatched the notepad and pen from him, wrote her email address, and gave it back to him. "I don't like to give out my number."

"I bet your friends have it."

A flush crept up her neck reaching all the way to the tip of her ears. "They do. My roommate keeps getting dick pics. I don't want that shit near me."

He snorted. "And you think I'm not only stupid, but that I want to send you pictures of my cock?" He folded his arms and tapped a finger on his jaw. "Interesting. Though, for the record..." He leaned close. She smelled of strawberries and something sweet he couldn't place. "Everyone knows you're more into books than dicks. If I were the type to send dick pics, I wouldn't waste them on you."

"Good." She squared her shoulders. "'Cause I'd block and report you, but not before screen-shotting it and sending it to everyone you know on social media."

He failed at schooling his face, it broke into a smirk.

"You don't believe me?"

Something in her challenge made him want to back her against a wall, thread his fingers into her hair and kiss her till they both got dizzy.

Down boy. She was off the table; not at all interested in him. Not to mention he shouldn't be interested in her. Jocks and Nerds, right? Then why was the scent of strawberries and the look of fire and 'fuck you' in her eyes sending all the wrong signals to his stiff-as-a-rod dick straining against his pants?

The woman would be the death of him. *But what a fucking way to go.* "Oh, I have no doubt you'd do just that."

Glaring, she plucked her phone from her back pocket, unlocked it and left without a backwards glance. She was clearly done entertaining him.

It might have been a few minutes, or an hour later, but his phone vibrating against his ass cheek dragged him out of the post-Cleo stupor. He shook his head. She was not the right girl for him. And yet part of him, a part growing louder by the day, wanted him to act on the lust boiling him from the inside.

But what about Elizabeth? Guilt at lusting over Cleo while talking to Elizabeth doused his desire like a storm on a wildfire. Maybe the girl in the phone didn't look as beautiful as Cleo, but did he care? She spoke to him on a level, *got* him on a level that no one else did. She talked to him because of who he was, not where she thought he could get her, that counted for way more than a smoldering gaze that said 'I'm going to murder you in your sleep, jock boy.'

He needed to put the beautiful brunette from his mind and focus on the girl in the phone, maybe he could coax her to meet him in person. Maybe she'd be even more gorgeous than Cleo. He snorted and his dick twitched.

"Yeah, yeah, I know, not likely." He unlocked his phone and clicked his message icon.

> Elizabeth: My roommate wants me to go to a party tonight and I'd rather boil my face in vinegar. What excuse can I use? I tried to tell her I need to work on a group project for school but she says that excuse is wearing thin.

> Lincoln: Wow. Talk about graphic. Tell her you have a date.

> Elizabeth: She'd know I'm lying. She's my best friend, she knows everything.

Lincoln: You won't be lying. You'll be on a date with me, Miss Bennet.

She went quiet. He shoved his notebook into his bag, slung it over his shoulder, and left to find food. An hour later, she still hadn't replied.

Lincoln: Elizabeth?

Lincoln: Is this cause I suggested a date? We don't have to go face-to-face if you're not ready. To be honest I'm not even sure if I'm ready. I just thought it might be fun. If you'd rather stay home, in our separate houses, we can do that too. We'll pick a movie, order pizza and text. It can be a virtual date night. If you want to, we can call each other. Or not. I dunno, I kinda like the mystery, but I'm happy to do whatever you're comfortable doing.

Jesus Linc, shut the fuck up.

> Elizabeth: Are you nervous, Mr. Darcy? You're not normally so... babbly. That's my territory. I'd love a virtual, text date. Someday we can meet, sure, just... not today. I'm not ready.

Lincoln: You know I don't care what you look like, right?

> Elizabeth: I'd love to believe that. With all my heart I would. Maybe someday.

Lincoln: Someday suggests a future, Miss Bennet.

She went quiet again, and he scolded himself for being a dick.

> Lincoln: What about we order pizza for seven?

> Elizabeth: Sounds like a plan. What's your favorite pizza topping?

> Lincoln: Buffalo chicken, bbq chicken, meat, more meat... I'll eat anything really.

> Elizabeth: But it needs to have meat.

> Lincoln: I feel like we should have talked about this sooner but please don't tell me you're a vegan. I don't think my heart could take it.

> Elizabeth: LOL! All this talk of your heart... a girl might think you're emotionally invested, Mr. Darcy.

> Lincoln: And what if it's the truth and that's what I want her to believe?

Shit. Abort mission. Reverse thrusters. Stop talking. His heart thundered in his ears. He had somehow made it back to his motorcycle in the parking lot, but he hadn't moved. He leaned forward over the handlebars texting, breath caught in his chest, waiting for her to reply.

> Elizabeth: This is a very dangerous conversation.

Fuck it.

> Lincoln: Is it though? We've been talking a
> lot, and for weeks. Call me crazy, but I'm
> feeling real feels here, Lizzy. If it's just me,
> then say so. But I really do like you,
> Elizabeth... whoever you are... I'd like to
> take you on a real date someday.
>
> Lincoln: Like, in public, a nice meal, mini
> golf, hiking up a mountain with a picnic... I
> dunno, even Dave and Busters – y'know, to
> fuel your competitive nature...
>
> Lincoln: Okay, this is awkward. It's just me,
> right? You're quiet 'cause you're
> embarrassed and don't want to hurt my
> feelings?

Shit. He wasn't used to the insecurity churning in his stomach.

In his everyday life, he was confident and self-assured. He could often tell by looking at a woman's face whether she was attracted to him or not. But he'd told Elizabeth things he'd never told anyone, he'd let her into a corner of his life that only Russ had ever seen.

Panic crept into his chest, prickling through his lungs. What if he'd let her in and she'd been humoring him this whole time?

> Elizabeth: Okay, stand down crazy boy.
> You're not alone. I have... feelings... too. It
> feels, I dunno, weird? Foolish? Stupid? I
> don't even know who you are. You could be
> anyone and in your first text you were
> looking for another woman 'cause she left
> her bra at your place. I mean... it's hardly
> the most romantic of meet cutes, is it?

Lincoln: We didn't bump into each other reaching for the same box of cereal in Target, so what?

Lincoln: I need to drive home before people call the cops on the crazy lurker who's just sitting with a dumbass grin on his face. And to be honest, I'm kinda afraid of being a douche goblin and scaring you off by saying something I shouldn't.

Elizabeth: You're adorable when you're flustered.

Lincoln: Don't tell anyone, I have a rep to protect. Pizza. 7pm. I'll pick the toppings, you pick the movie?

Elizabeth: Oh, Mr. Darcy, that was a rookie mistake, but you're committed now and can't take it back.

Elizabeth: Also: I'm not a vegan.

CHAPTER 8
Cleo

Cleo had never completed an assignment so fast in all her life. She'd hurried home, finished her essay and had a bubble bath in preparation for her date with Mr. Darcy. Despite it being virtual, and off camera, butterflies flapped in her stomach and her head buzzed with excitement. She even shaved her legs, laughing to herself at the lunacy of it all.

It wasn't as though she didn't know the dangers of the internet, but so far this guy hadn't done anything other than talk to her. He hadn't asked for any information, and she hadn't seen anyone following her at school or behaving weirdly, so why shouldn't she indulge in a little fun?

At some point she'd convince him to watch the BBC version of *Pride and Prejudice* with her, but not tonight. After twenty agonizing minutes of scrolling through Netflix with sweaty palms and a racing heart, she couldn't decide on a movie, so he suggested a 'light hearted chick flick' with Chris Evans called *What's Your Number?* She had to admit, Captain America *was* easy on the eye so she'd said yes.

She'd opened a bottle of Cupcake Moscato as the perfect

pizza accompaniment and a mixture of quiet contentment and wine warmed her cheeks as they texted.

> Cleo: Are you gay? Is that why you picked this movie? To tell me you're gay?

> Mr. Darcy: I think every man alive could be gay for Chris Evans. But no, not gay. What do you think of the buffalo chicken pizza?

> Cleo: It's perfect.

She took a bite, closed her eyes, and moaned at the explosion of flavor on her tongue before wiping her chin and greasy fingers.

> Cleo: The neighbors probably think I have male company with all the sounds I'm making right now.

Embarrassment mixed with the pizza and wine in her stomach. "Oh God." Her cheeks flared hotter, and when her phone chimed she half expected a dick pic waiting for her on the screen.

> Mr. Darcy: Kind of sad I'm not there to hear that.

Her breath hitched, somewhere between a gasp and a hiccup, and a small squeak escaped her. Was he flirting with her? People didn't *flirt* with *her*. She had no idea if he was flirting or not, and Molly and the girls were out at the party so she couldn't ask for best friend guidance on best practices for flirting.

> Mr. Darcy: I can almost hear your brain whirring from across campus. Yes, I'm flirting. Yes, I like you, and if you were here, I'd absolutely kiss you right now, even if you do have strings of cheese dangling down your chin.

Her hand flew to her face on instinct, but there was no drippy cheese. Her shoulders sagged with relief, and she giggled. Would he really kiss her if he was there?

> Mr. Darcy: If I need to dial back the flirting please say so. If I need to dial it up so it's more obvious and something you can more readily identify, I can do that too. But I like you Miss Bennet and I would absolutely be kissing the hell out of you right now if you were beside me.

> Mr. Darcy: I'd probably try for more, but only after washing my hands. Hot sauce on the nether regions isn't fun. Take it from someone who learned the hard way.

She snorted. She loved how he could make her heart quicken and heat pool between her thighs while also being able to make her laugh. Maybe it was okay to let him into her heart – just a little. Maybe he truly was as good as he seemed.

> Cleo: I'd let you.

> Cleo: Once you washed your hands, of course. I mean nothing would kill the evening more than a spicy hot va-jay-jay.

> Mr. Darcy: LOL!! Well. I can say with certainty that I hadn't expected to snort milk out my nose this evening. Part of me is kind of glad you're not here to witness this.

> Cleo: Part of me wishes I'd been brave enough to say yes to an in person date.

> Mr. Darcy: Well, Lizzy, you just made my whole damn week. The milk-snorting was worth it. We'll both be brave enough someday.

> Cleo: I hope so. I kinda want my kiss.

> Mr. Darcy: You'll get it.

She got up off the couch and put the now-cold pizza in the fridge. She refilled her glass of wine, made her way to her room, and got ready for bed.

> Mr. Darcy: Did I spook you? You went quiet.

> Cleo: No, I'm getting ready for bed.

> Mr. Darcy: Oh man. I was hanging in there just fine until you mentioned bed.

> Cleo: What do you mean?

> Mr. Darcy: I'm a red blooded man, Lizzy. I might not know what you look like, but knowing you're getting undressed and climbing into bed...

> Mr. Darcy: Don't panic, I'm not going to send you dick pics or anything. I just wish we were in the same space, that's all.

> Cleo: 'Cause you'd kiss me?

> Mr. Darcy: More, if you'd let me.

Sliding between the sheets, she plopped her head back onto the pillow. She would absolutely let him. She couldn't remember the last time she'd even flown solo, let alone had someone else get her off. Pressing her thighs together, she rolled onto her face with a frustrated groan. She propped herself up onto her elbows and typed out an answer.

Cleo: You're killing me.

Mr. Darcy: At least we'll die together, eh?

Cleo: I don't think you quite understand.

Mr. Darcy: My blue balls beg to differ, Miss Bennet.

Cleo laughed. Her whole body radiated heat, her clit throbbed, and her nipples could cut glass. It was going to be a long night if she didn't let off some steam. She rolled onto her side, pulled open her bedside drawer and hunted for her vibrator. It was time to see just what it could do... other than fall on the foot of one unsuspecting hot hockey player. Sliding the vibe below the band of her pants her tense muscles loosened. A message startled her, she left the toy on her stomach while she read it.

Mr. Darcy: Penny for your thoughts.

Cleo: You don't want to know.

Mr. Darcy: Well now I absolutely want to know.

Her chest heaved. She took the phone with one hand, and put the vibrator next to her on the bed with the other. Swallowing down her shame and fear she snapped a picture and hit send, chewing on a thumbnail while waiting for his reply.

> Mr. Darcy: Fuck. You're not playing fair Lizzy. I'm trying to be a gentleman here.

> Mr. Darcy: Okay, I know the blue ball comment wasn't gentlemanly, but Christ. I'm trying.

> Mr. Darcy: So, I'm not normally this needy, and I kinda hate myself for asking, buuuuut… that's for me, right? I mean, because of me? Or did a nekkid Chris Evans singing and playing the guitar drive you to getting off?

> Mr. Darcy: No judgement, I almost blew my load when he started playing that guitar too. ;-)

She'd expected judgement, not wisecracks. His insecurity was alluring and intoxicating. The fact he was trying to confirm he'd made her want to touch herself drove her crazy. The fact the idea of her touching herself turned him on, drove her even crazier.

> Cleo: Can you stop talking about Captain America when I have this thing between my thighs please? I mean, he's hot and all but he's not who I want to have in my brain right now.

> Mr. Darcy: At the risk of sounding like a conceited prick: who do you want in your brain right now, Miss Bennet?

> Cleo: Why, you, of course, Mr. Darcy.

Her stomach clenched. She'd never been this forward with a man before, but hiding behind her cell phone it was easy to be brazen, to pretend she was confident and sensual, even if it made her cringe a little inside.

Mr. Darcy: The relief I'm feeling right now is really somethin'. I can't compete with Cap. I know my limits. I do not have America's ass.

She giggled.

Cleo: I appreciate the lols. I'm nervous. I don't really do this kind of thing.

Mr. Darcy: Masturbate? Phone sex? Or both?

Swallowing hard she typed out her reply.

Cleo: Both. I'm not very experienced.

Not like Lincoln Scott and those asshole friends of his, anyway. Or you, Mr. You-left-your-bra-here.

Mr. Darcy: Despite the Brinderella (Bra plus Cinderella – I think that's a catchy name right there) I'm not all that experienced either. Just relax. You don't have to do anything you don't want to.

She scrunched her eyes closed at the throbbing between her legs.

Cleo: Oh… I want to, alright.

Mr. Darcy: Tell me? I really don't want to spook you, and I don't know where the line is.

Swallowing again, she sucked in a deep breath, steadying herself. She could do this. She could tell someone what she wanted... how she felt. She typed out a message but couldn't bring herself to press send. She deleted it and tried again.

> Mr. Darcy: Get out of your own head, Lizzy. Press send.

> Cleo: I want you to feel how wet I am for you. It won't go away. I'm always fucking wet, it's embarrassing. My nipples are constantly hard and pressing against my bra. I want to curl into you, breathe you in, hold you while I drag my nails and tongue over your skin. I want you, Mr. Darcy. All of you.

With a trembling hand she hit send.

> Mr. Darcy: Fuck. I know it's not at all gentlemanly but I'm touching myself, Miss Bennet.

> Cleo: Because of me?

> Mr. Darcy: Because of you.

She slipped a hand up her shirt and squeezed her hard nipple, a soft moan escaping her lips. A shot of desire travelled south and she couldn't wait another moment.

> Cleo: I'm sliding it inside me.

> Mr. Darcy: Christ, Lizzy. What's it like?

> Cleo: It's about six inches long, and has a clit attachment

> Mr. Darcy: Lube?

> Cleo: LOL! You're adorable. I definitely don't need it.

She sucked in a sharp breath as she slid the toy inside her with ease. Her hips raised to meet it as she inched it deeper. "Fuck." She dropped the phone onto her chest. "Shit."

Mr. Darcy: Not to sound like a broken record, but: fuck. So hot.

Cleo: I'm turning it on.

Mr. Darcy: I've been turned on for a while, Miss Bennet. Catch up. And while it's much less sexy to talk about cock, in case you need assurances, mine is hard as fuck, and ready to come.

The vibrations started deep inside her and tingled against her clit. It wouldn't take long. Between Lincoln Scott looking all fuckable around school, and Mr. Darcy caressing her very soul, she had been primed for a while. Lincoln Scott. *Nope.* She needed to put him out of her head and focus on Mr. Darcy.

Cleo: Close.

Typing one-handed while your body was responding to a vibrating object against your most intimate parts wasn't easy.

Mr. Darcy: I won't come till you do.

Cleo: Such a gentleman. What if I take an hour?

Mr. Darcy: Then I wait an hour. But I warn you. It wouldn't take an hour if I was there. Teasing your nipples between my teeth and fingers, kissing your neck...

She moaned again and closed her eyes. Having no idea

what the Mr. Darcy in her phone looked like she conjured Colin Firth in her mind as her hips raised again to meet the buzzing toy between her legs.

The image of Colin Firth was replaced by a pair of strong shoulders. Shoulders she'd come to obsess over. Shoulders belonging to one Mr. Lincoln Scott. Try as she might, she couldn't shake the picture of him lying naked on top of her with her nails sunk into his delicious shoulders, kissing her with the fire she'd seen flickering in his eyes.

Cleo: So close.

The wave crested and right as she was about to crash into her climax, the vibrator stopped dead.

"Mother fucker!" She pulled the toy out and pressed the buttons. Nothing. She opened the base of the toy, took the batteries out and changed them around as though that would magically breathe life into them. Still nothing. She had no spare batteries. She threw the damn thing on the floor.

Cleo: My mother fucking toy died.

Mr. Darcy: Shhhhh… Just use your fingers. Close your eyes, small circles, imagine I'm lying beside you, kissing you and rubbing your clit in slow and measured circles.

She closed her eyes and did as he suggested, panting harder with each circle she drew on her throbbing clit. The orgasm that tore through her ripped a ragged scream from her chest as she shuddered and twitched. With shaking hands she picked up her phone.

Cleo: I made a mess. Don't leave me messy alone, Mr. Darcy.

It was a couple of minutes before he replied.

> Mr. Darcy: Your wish is my command,
> milady. Fuck. Thank you, I needed that.

She smiled, muscles heavy, and a wave of contentment rippling through her.

> Mr. Darcy: Don't move if you don't have to.
> Stay here and close your eyes. Sleep, Lizzy.
> I'll be here in the morning.

His reassuring nature fed her insecure heart. It was as if he knew what she was thinking and feeling without her having to say anything. And instead of calling her out on it, he'd tailor his texts to soothe her anxiety. Her sigh turned into a yawn. *Shit. My assignment.*

Guilt pounded in her temples. She opened her email to send a message to her professor and paused. She'd need her laptop.

Throwing back the blanket, an email caught her eye. Linc had completed the part of the assignment she was planning on turning in, and had submitted it on time to the professor.

She scoffed, pulled the blanket back over herself and clicked on the attachment. Her jaw dropped open. Not only had he done the work, but he'd done it better than Cleo had attempted to.

Something dark and bitter twisted in her stomach. Jealousy? Anger? She couldn't place it, but knew it was irrational. She should be glad he'd done a good job and submitted it on time. But it whipped up her mind as she struggled to settle for the night.

> Mr. Darcy: You okay?

Cleo: I am, thank you. Sleepy, keep yawning, but my mind is busy so I'm too awake.

Mr. Darcy: Tell your beautiful mind to pipe down. I'll talk to you in the morning, okay?

Cleo: Promise?

Mr. Darcy: I promise, pretty girl x

Her heart squeezed. Lincoln Scott might have game in the classroom and on the ice, and, okay, fine, in a suit, but his cocky jock-ass wouldn't ever make her heart race the same way Mr. Darcy did.

Cleo: Can't wait x

Lincoln

He couldn't remember who the fuck had convinced him that a doing a kissing booth was a good idea but he was going to kill them with his bare hands. Sure it was for a good cause but that didn't mean he had to like it. This shit belonged in high school with wedgies and prom.

One of the guys on the team had broken his leg pretty badly at a game a couple weeks back and needed a ramp installed at the house. The team were raising funds to make it happen, anything over and above what they needed for the ramp would be donated to the local women's shelter that Molly and Will's mom helped out at.

In the stands, the hockey team weren't as popular as the football team, but the based on the steady stream of women throwing money at them for kisses, they still had some lookers among them – those who still had all their teeth, anyway.

As usual, Russell and Austin were the most popular, something about their tall, dark, and brooding nature appealed to the ladies. Linc finally 'got' the draw of being mysterious. Lizzy's mystery had him tangled up in knots, even when he stood kissing randomers in full view of anyone who passed by.

His line had died down long enough for him to text Elizabeth back. It had been a few days since their virtual date and he was still riding the high.

> Elizabeth: I took anal for two hours again today! Felt awesome.

What. The. Fuck? His stomach dropped and an unexpected burst of jealousy slapped him like a cold shower.

> Linc: Uhm. Excuse me?

> Elizabeth: O.M.G. A nap. I took a fucking nap for two hours today.

> Elizabeth: Fuck. Shit. Mother fucking fuck. A nap.

> Linc: Autocorrect strikes again.

> Elizabeth: I'm pretty sure there's a drunk elf in my phone trying to be 'helpful'. It comes out as auto-incorrect more often than not.

"What's so funny?" Russ elbowed him, craning his neck to look at Linc's screen.

Linc pulled the phone against his chest, still chuckling. "Autocorrect."

"From our mysterious Miss Bennet I presume?"

"You presume correctly."

His friend's sharp elbow jabbed him again. "Don't look now. Hurricane Cleo, two o'clock."

Her hips swayed as she half stomped, half glided, toward him. He couldn't read her rosy face, but it didn't have her usual 'Death to Lincoln Scott' glare.

"Ms. Martinez." His voice was steadier than his heart, hammering against his ribs. What was it about this girl that got his pulse thundering and his dick stir on sight? He shifted in his chair.

"Mr. Scott." She glanced at Russ who busied himself with the tin of money on the table in front of him.

Linc smirked. Dude was a terrible bluffer. He was eavesdropping like a Southern granny at a funeral.

"I imagine you're not here for the kissing."

"The... what?"

He pointed both index fingers to the sign above his head with a grin, enjoying the blush spreading across her cheeks. He'd never seen a more beautiful woman when she was embarrassed.

She pinched her bottom lip between her teeth and rolled it a bit before shaking her head. "I... no. I'm not. I came up to say thank you, for getting that report—"

"You're holding up the line, Martinez. Monopolizing one of our most lucrative kissers isn't good for business." Russell shook the money box at her.

"What are you? His fucking pimp?"

Linc arched an eyebrow and shrugged. He fucking loved her sass. He expected her to turn on her heel and take off in a bluster of attitude. When she pulled her wallet from the side pocket of her bag and threw a ten dollar bill on the table in front of Russ, his dick strained against his pants. Russ's jaw was hanging open like a barn door. Linc shifted his weight on the chair.

"Can I talk to him now?" She widened her eyes and popped her hip.

"This ain't a talkin' booth, princess. Kiss the man."

Why the hell was Russ pushing this so hard? Hard was the operative word. He cleared his throat and leaned forward over the table, hoping she wouldn't see the tent he was pitching in his pants.

"Oh. You read the room wrong, man. She hates my ever-living guts. She won't kiss m—"

Cleo clutched the front of his shirt, yanking him up off his chair as her soft lips landed against his. When his eyes met her heated gaze, it stoked the flames of lust swirling in his chest.

She eased the pressure off his mouth, pulling back, but he wasn't done. If this was the only time in his life he was able to kiss Cleo Martinez, he would make sure she never fucking forgot it.

He cupped her chin. Sliding his fingers into her thick hair, the smell of strawberries wafted towards him. Her shampoo? Lotion? Her eyes narrowed, but she didn't move. Dragging the tip of his tongue along the seam of her mouth, an almost inaudible gasp parted her lips, and she accepted his invasion. Her kiss tasted of like sweet cinnamon with a faint hint of mint and he struggled to remember ever having touched skin so soft. Her eyes flickered closed as he tilted her head back to deepen their kiss.

His left hand traveled the length of her back to join his right, cupping her face. He didn't want to stop kissing her but the wolf whistles and howls surrounding them suggested it was time.

With anyone else he wouldn't give a shit, and he'd kiss her until they ran out of breath but with Cleo... he didn't want to die. She pulled back, lips swollen, eyes filled with confusion, lust and desire, and her hair, mussed.

He fought every urge to sling her over his shoulder and find a dark janitor's closet to continue their kissing and discover if the rest of her body was as soft as her lips. He was glad to have the desk between them to steady him. Was he still standing? Where had this woman been his whole life? Was that what kissing was supposed to feel like?

Her brows pulled into a frown over her tumultuous hazel

eyes, and she touched the side of her thumb to her mouth as though she was having similar questions roll through her mind.

The whoops and teasing softened into a low din over the group that had gathered in line for both Linc and Russ.

"Fuck." Russ's voice sounded miles away, and Linc refused to break eye contact with the smoldering woman standing in front of him until he absolutely had to. "I think I just came. That was hot as fuck. I feel like I need to pay you both for what I just witnessed."

Every guy has *that* fantasy where a stunning woman grabs their shirt and stops them with a kiss. That kiss was better than all his fantasies combined. Would kissing Lizzy feel like that? Guilt stewed in his stomach.

Johnny's cruel, hard voice broke the spell. "Well, well. Looks like our chica gordita found a way to get her rocks off with a Pirate after all. Hope she enjoyed it since the only way any of us would touch her with a fucking barge pole was if she paid us."

Raw agony flickered in her eyes for a beat. Her jaw twitched, she blinked, and when she reopened her eyes there was nothing but cool indifference. She tilted her head, as though waiting for Linc to defend her honor, but before he could move, or think, or breathe, she turned on her heel.

"Pendejo."

Fucker.

Did she mean Johnny? Or was she talking about Linc? If he reacted, it would put Cleo on Johnny's radar even more. He'd know she was a soft spot to press when he wanted to get at Linc. But could he live with himself if he let the asshole get away with calling her fat once again?

He didn't have time to mull it over before Russell had Johnny pinned against the wall. "Once was bad enough, but twice? What the fuck is your deal?"

Linc hadn't seen Russ so mad in a long time.

"Do you want to bone her? Is that your deal? She said no, and now you're fucking butt hurt?" He pressed his arm against Johnny's throat. "'Cause let me tell you man. God help the man who ever calls my fucking daughter fat. I'll tear him limb from limb with a smile on my face." He leaned his weight against his arm.

"Russ, that's enough." Linc reached out to touch his shoulder, and Russ yanked out of his grip, releasing Johnny.

"Do you know the kind of shit women deal with about their weight? That woman has probably beaten herself up enough about it over the years. Maybe she got bullied in high school. Hell, maybe she's happy as can-fucking-be and doesn't give a shit what you think of how she looks. That *still* doesn't give you the right to say a goddamn word to anyone about their appearance." He jabbed a finger into Johnny's pale face. "It's pieces of shit like you that make people like her depressed, suicidal, or develop fucking eating disorders. Watch your fucking self, asshole."

Linc's stomach dropped and fear seized his chest at Russ's words.

"All right guys, let's break this party up." Finn stepped forward and clapped his hands. "We're going to take a short break, but we'll be back later for more smooches."

The women in the line stepped forward one at a time, dropping their money on the table where Russ had sat. Some said thank you, some mouthed it, and some merely met his gaze with sad eyes. Russ's nostrils flared and his jaw and shoulders were taut.

He was right. When stories came out about people taking their own lives it often stemmed from bullying. Johnny was toxic and a bully. Linc had seen the deep-seeded pain of trauma flare in Cleo's eyes before she took off.

He mentally smacked himself for not acting faster. For

being concerned about Johnny picking on her further. If he'd stood up for her the first time, maybe Johnny wouldn't have breathed a word to her again. Except Will had told him to knock it off and he'd continued regardless. *Shit.* He raked a hand through his hair. He had no idea where she'd run off to, but he needed to find her. He needed to make sure she was okay. And he made a mental note to check in with Miss Bennet later, too. Just in case.

CHAPTER 10
Lincoln

er message stared at him from his screen. Was he okay? Guilt and discontentment swirled in his stomach threatening to bring his late dinner up. While he didn't regret kissing Cleo, his growing fondness for Elizabeth tugged at his chest. Not to mention Russ's words about the consequences of fat shaming women had Linc worried about every woman in his life.

He'd spent the evening in the rink training with the team, but not even ice time with his brothers managed to pick up his spirits. He should be honest with her, she hadn't yet run at the glimpses of his squishy insides, maybe if he let her in a little more she'd stick around.

As soon as he pressed send he itched to take it back. He rubbed the back of his neck and loosened his jaw.

Elizabeth: What's up? Something in the air today, I'm having a funky kinda day.

He tugged the towel from his waist and ran it over his hair before collapsing into bed.

Elizabeth: It's okay if you don't want to talk about it. I just… I'm worried about you. It's not like you to be 'off.'

Linc: I don't usually talk to people about my feelings.

He tucked an open palm behind his head and typed with one hand.

Elizabeth: Me neither. I've let you in more than anyone else. Except my best friend, obviously. You can trust me, you know. Even if I knew who you were, I wouldn't go telling people things you've told me. I'm trustworthy.

Linc: I know, and I feel safe talking to you. Guys aren't supposed to be mushy on the inside, y'know? We're supposed to be like Elsa.

Elizabeth: Elsa?

Linc: Oh man. You haven't seen Frozen? Have you been living under a rock? She has these like freezing capabilities, but she's taught 'conceal don't feel' her whole life. That's what men are taught. If not by their families or friends, by society.

Elizabeth: That's so sad. I kinda know how it feels though.

Linc: Women have it way worse.

If he could steer the conversation away from himself, he'd be safe. While he trusted her, something still tugged in the back of his mind, telling him not to let her in, not to let her see the real him. But another part of him, a bigger part, was screaming to let her in.

Linc: I'm kind of glad we don't know who we are outside of our phones.

Linc: I don't mean that in a shitty way.

Linc: There are no expectations. We're safe to be who we really are.

Linc: I'm not happy with my life as it is. I'm suffocating. My dad… he's…

He scrubbed a hand over his face and shook his head. "Can you maybe try coming out with a complete sentence, Lincoln?"

Elizabeth: Is he hard on you?

Linc: He's trying to extend his youth by living it through my life. Or something.

He let out a frustrated growl and covered his face with his palm.

Linc: I don't want to be who he wants to be.

Elizabeth: Who does he want to be?

Linc: An athlete.

Elizabeth: Who do you want to be?

Linc: An artist. What do you want to be?

Elizabeth: You're the only person who's ever asked. I've never questioned what I was doing until lately. I just followed what my mom wanted for me 'cause she knew best, right?

Linc: And now?

Elizabeth: Now I'm not so sure I want to do what my mom does.

Linc: Same. Do you think we can get out from under their shadows?

Elizabeth: Y'know, when I talk to you I think maybe. It's possible. You make me feel like I have something more to offer the world than what my mom wants me to give.

Linc: Shit, Lizzy. That's deep AF. FWIW you make me feel the same way. Like I could walk right up to my dad and say, 'this is what I want' and it would be okay.

Linc: I'm falling asleep my dear Miss Bennet, I'm sorry. It's been a long day and I don't have any gas left in the tank. I'll talk to you on the morrow. Maybe we won't feel so glum with the rise of the sun.

Elizabeth: You should add wordsmith to your list of mad skills, Mr. Darcy. Chin up. As Elizabeth Bennet herself said: My courage always rises with every attempt to intimidate me.

Linc's courage always disintegrated every time his father spoke. Oh, to be as brave and strong as his own Miss Bennet. Maybe then he could live the life he wished to.

❄

At ass-crack-of-dawn the next morning, four art history books lay open at various pages in front of him in the library. Half written notes were scattered across the table, and a pen was tucked behind his ear. The squeak of a chair being dragged across the floor made him lift his head. A wincing Cleo was slinking onto a chair, clutching her backpack against her stomach.

His pulse quickened. Her hair hung loose around her face and his fingers twitched with the urge to tangle his fingers in it once again. When their eyes met, he threw her a small smile which she returned.

He was three paragraphs from finishing the notes for his assignment. No matter how beautiful Cleo was, he had to focus. He turned the page on the last of the art history books he'd snagged from the shelves, and scribbled more notes. It was a popular myth that van Gogh had only sold one painting during his lifetime. Well, the sources littered across the table proved that wrong – he'd sold at least three other pieces before *The Red Vineyard at Arles (The Vigne Rouge)*.

Rolling his neck he locked eyes with Cleo. Was she staring at him? Did she have the same burning ache to repeat their kiss that he did? She turned her attention back to the pages on the table in front of her, but he didn't miss her tongue snaking out to wet her lips. Fuck. This wasn't good. No matter how many times he repeated Lizzy's name in his head, he couldn't pull his eyes away from the woman in front of him.

It took him forty five minutes to finish his notes, and throughout that time, he'd caught Cleo staring at him with a bemused and curious expression, three more times. Her tongue poked out from the side of her mouth and a frown creased her forehead as she wrote. Tucking his pages into a folder and sliding it into his bag, he stood. He grabbed the stack of books and made his way to her.

She looked up at him, eyes widening and a flurry of quick blinks, her frown of concentration turned to bewilderment. Tilting her head, she pursed her lips.

"Hi." He kept his voice quiet. It was still too early for anyone else to be around, but something about being in a library called for hushed whispers.

"Hiii...?"

"I know this is weird, but I wanted to check in with you after that thing with Johnny yesterday."

Her eyes dropped to her paper and she chewed on her lip.

"I tried to find you after, to make sure you were... I dunno, okay. I mean I know we're not friends or anything but—"

"I don't need your pity Lincoln." Her voice was so quiet he almost missed it.

"Good cause you don't have it."

Her hazel eyes met him from behind the curtain of hair in front of her face. Flecks of gold dancing in the early morning light. Somehow he was reaching out and tucked the loose strands behind her ear and tipped her chin so she'd look at him. Her breath hitched and she swallowed.

"I'm not pitying you, Cleo. I just wanted to make sure you were okay. Johnny is an asshole. That's no excuse for what he said to you, either time, but he doesn't speak for the team, and he certainly doesn't speak for me."

Unshed tears brimmed in her eyes.

"I just wanted to make sure you were okay. That's all. I have no ulterior motive."

When she didn't answer, he sighed and turned to leave.

"Why did you kiss me yesterday, Lincoln?"

"You kissed me." He spoke over his shoulder, if he turned back to face her, he might be the one to kiss her first this time.

"I did, that's true." She chewed on the end of a pen for a

moment. "But when I stopped, you…" She shook her head as though trying to dislodge the memory. Her voice dropped to barely a whisper. "You kissed me. Why?"

"When a pretty girl grabs you by the shirt and lays one on you, it's only right to do your level best to make it a good one." He rubbed a thumb along his bottom lip as he resisted the desire to see whether she still smelled of strawberries.

A smile tugged at the edges of her lips, and even in the low light, her cheeks darkened.

"Don't let the bastards get you down, Cleo." He rapped a knuckle on the nearest desk and left.

One thing was for certain, kissing Cleo Martinez had only served to make him want her all the more. From her folded arms and the narrowed glare on her face as he walked away, something told him it would be easier to learn how to wrestle an alligator than convince her to let him kiss her again.

CHAPTER 11

Cleo

"Sí, mamá." Cleo folded a pair of pants and placed it on top of the pile of clean laundry. Her phone was sandwiched between her ear and shoulder as she worked. For as much as her mother was listening to her, though, she could have left the phone in the kitchen next to Simon the cactus and Mamá Martinez wouldn't even have noticed.

Every week Cleo called home, and every week her mom gave her the same spiel. "Necesitas trabajar duro hija..." You need to work hard. "No tienes tiempo para distracciones..." You have no time for distractions. "¿Cuáles fueron tus calificaciones esta semana..." How are your grades this week?

Dread curdled in Cleo's stomach. It would be the first time she tried to skirt that last question. She'd slipped in English, and but for the excellence of Lincoln's piece of the project, she might even have slipped lower. She winced. Maybe she couldn't have it all, the fun and the high grades. Maybe she could only have one, an either or kinda deal, and if that were the case, it wasn't a choice for her: school would always win out.

"Es importante que personas como nosotros consigamos buenos trabajos..."

It's important for people like us to get good jobs.

"Sí mamá. Lo sé."

Cleo sighed. What mamá wasn't saying out loud was that she didn't want Cleo to have the same *type* of job that her *abuelos* had. Cleo's grandfather was a gardener and her grandmother was a cleaner.

To mamá, this wasn't enough. She wanted Cleo to do more, to *be* more. But she never seemed to care about what made Cleo *happy*. Just what she *should* do as a Latin American woman.

If mamá ever asked, she'd know that Cleo was fiercely proud of her grandparents. No one could landscape or get plants to grow quite like her abuelo. She hadn't inherited his green thumb, but she'd been so jealous of how it seemed he could talk to plants and get them to bloom bigger and more vibrant than she'd ever seen.

And so what if *yaya* had been a cleaner? Cleo had never met a happier woman. She often had captivating stories to tell about her clients, and they always treated her with kindness and respect. Right before she died, yaya told her, *persigue tus sueños, nieta mía.*

Chase your dreams.

So Cleo did. She got into a good school to do what she'd always thought she wanted, become a professor.

Just like mamá.

The longer she was in college, and if she was honest with herself, the more she spoke to Mr. Darcy, the more she wondered. Was she really chasing her own dreams? Or at some point along the way had her mother's dreams become hers? What would her own dreams be if her mom had no influence over her choices?

That was where she'd stop. Going down the path of

'shoulda, coulda, woulda' was as dangerous as it was fruitless. What did it matter what her dreams might have been? Teaching was her dream and she needed to work hard to ensure it happened.

Her mother was still talking. "Sólo queremos lo mejor para ti, Cleo." *We only want what's best for you, Cleo.*

An unexpected barb of bitterness curled in her stomach. "Mom, I have to go, I'll talk to you next week, okay? Te amo."

She didn't wait for a response before pressing the button to hang up and throwing her phone onto the bed. Hot, angry tears streamed down her face as she slid onto the floor next to the bed. She dropped her face into her hands and tugged on her hair with a frustrated growl.

A month ago, everything was fine. A month ago, she had no men in her life, and her eye on the prize. But she'd somehow let Mr. Darcy get in her head, and Lincoln-fucking-Scott under her skin.

How had this happened? And how could she make it un-happen? She ground the heels of her hands into her eyes.

She needed to refocus, to stay the course.

Everyone's parents were full on. Mr. Darcy's parents had no idea he liked to draw. They were controlling too. It was just parents being parental, right? And wasn't that the whole point of college? For shiny, new and interesting things to pop up and try to distract you from what you really wanted out of life?

She wanted to be a professor of English. She *did*. Lots of kids wanted to be like their parents when they grew up, it was normal to follow in the footsteps of those you were closest to.

It was also customary to question your life choices every now and then. At least that's what she told herself as she dragged herself from the floor and dusted off.

And even if she did want to dip her toe further into having more fun, Mr. Darcy didn't want to meet her, and most days, she couldn't blame him.

"Normal. How can it be normal?" Molly pulled the thermometer away from Cleo's forehead, turning it so she could see the result. "You're not sick. Okay. Sure. Fine. Whatever. Uh... abducted by aliens? Temporary insanity?" She grabbed Cleo by the shoulders and shook. "Who are you and what have you done with my best friend?"

Cleo laughed, but she had no answer for her.

"Cleopatra Isabella Martinez doesn't just go around kissing jocks in front of the whole damn school!"

Cleo shrugged, idly touching her lips as though she could still feel the scorch of the best kiss of her life lingering there.

"Oh girl. You not only kissed him, you *liked it!* It was hot, right? Lincoln Scott has that look about him. Like he could make a party in your lady pants with even a peck. Was it a peck?"

Cleo stiffened.

Molly gasped. "Ohhhhh lord, it wasn't a peck, was it? Never play poker, Cleo, your game face is awful. It's written all... over..." She pointed at Cleo. "Shit. Hot damn. Did your lady parts have a party, Cho-Cho? I'm your best friend. I am entitled to this kind of information."

"It doesn't matter. I'm done with all this dude-shit."

"Done?" Molly crossed her arms, pursed her lips and squinted one eye. "Like, done, done? Or like I'm done with this crush over Finn-fucking-O'Brien, done? And no!" She held up a hand to stop Cleo from pursuing that line of questioning. "We aren't talking about me right now. So which is it? Are you done? Or do you just wish you were?"

"I'm done." Cleo hoped her firm nod was convincing enough, but from the wry smirk pulling at her friend's mouth, she'd failed.

"So... you're done with entertaining the... uhm..." Molly

waved a hand as though she was searching for the right word. "Penis-distractions, but you went and got yourself a job at the coffee shop? I mean... sounds to me like you're trading one distraction for another."

Cleo swallowed her bite of fish taco. Wiping her hand on a napkin she held it up. "Don't. Okay? I know it doesn't sound like it makes sense."

"But? I mean you don't owe me an explanation, or justification. I just... can't figure out why you'd want to go get a job and take time away from school." She pursed her lips and narrowed her stare. "Mamá Martinez have anything to do with this?"

Cleo took another bite of her taco and pointed at her mouth as if to communicate that she couldn't answer because her mouth was full.

Molly popped her hip, planted her hands at her waist, and arched an eyebrow. "Mmhmm. Nice try. I can wait all day for an answer, girlfriend."

"Ugh. Fine. Yes. They want me to appreciate the value of money and hard work – because for some reason they think I don't? I dunno. Anyway, sure they give me an allowance and I have my student loans, but it's *just* shy of what I need."

She picked at the slivers of cheese dangling from the remains of her taco. "During our chat a couple weeks ago they sent me a spreadsheet mamá created to help me 'understand my finances'. They calculated that I could work for ten to twelve hours a week somewhere like the coffee house without it adversely affecting my studies."

"Huh. Nice of them to do the math for you and everything. Did they apply for the job for you too?"

Cleo winced at the sarcasm dripping from Molly's words.

"Sorry. That was harsh. I'm menstrual."

"Harsh but fair. I mean I know they love me and want

what's best for me. I know they want me to be successful and respected..." She sighed.

"Buuut?"

"But it's stifling, you know? All I feel is pressure... and it's not like I don't put myself under plenty of that as it is."

"So of course you went out and got yourself a job to... add... *more*... pressure?" Molly's screwed up face made Cleo giggle.

"Ironically it takes away some pressure. It gets them off my back about something so I can focus without worrying that I'm gonna get nagged every week."

"Damn girl." Molly crossed the kitchen and pulled a pint of Ben and Jerry's from the freezer. Grabbing two spoons, she yanked off the lid, dropped herself onto the seat next to Cleo and offered her a spoon. "I'm not sure Ben or Jerry can fix this, but it can't hurt to try. My parents are pains in the cooch sometimes, but I think I'd buckle under that kind of parental pressure."

"Your folks aren't like that?" Cleo speared her spoon into the solid ice cream, not waiting for it to melt a little. She jabbed at the chunk of cookie dough embedded near the top.

Molly hissed. "We gotta get you laid, amiga. The frustration is seeping from your every pore. You don't gotta get all stabby on the ice cream! What did it ever do to you?" She snatched the tub from the table and pulled it close to her chest, whispering sweet nothings at it before shoveling a heaped spoonful into her mouth and moaning. "So. Good."

Waving her spoon at Cleo, she continued. "No, my folks aren't like that. I mean, they care, and they're invested, and have opinions... but spreadsheets and that level of strict? Nuh uh. Not even with Will, and he was their first child. Parents are generally more over protective of their first, right? I guess my parents might be easygoing? Certainly by comparison to yours. What does Mr. Darcy say?" She dug in for another spoonful of ice cream while Cleo pulled out her phone and brought up his messages.

"He told me he picked up a minor he's keeping secret from his parents."

"Wow. What are the odds that both of you have strict AF parents? Wonder if he's getting a job at the coffee shop too."

"It's weird not knowing who he is."

"And he still won't meet?"

Cleo shrugged, and sank her teeth into her lip. She didn't want to tell her best friend about how obnoxious the demons in her mind were. How they screamed at her that he wasn't meeting her in public because she wasn't enough for him. She wasn't in the mood for one of Molly's pep talks.

"I bet he's scared."

Yeah, of me being a friggin' ugly whale.

"I saw that look. This has nothing to do with whatever just went through your mind. You said yourself, there's something freeing about talking to him about whatever you want to without fear of judgement."

Cleo nodded. "You're right, I'm just..."

"Self-loathing? Self-deprecating? Self-destructive?"

"Yes."

"Well, knock it off. Be nicer to my bestie, or I'll be forced to beat you. You're pretty awesome and he'd be lucky to have you on his arm. You hear me?"

Cleo nodded, fighting back tears. If that was true, wouldn't he want to meet her? He hadn't brought up the idea again. In fairness, neither had she, but she was scared. Was he scared too? Or was something more than fear holding him back?

"Maybe it's what's-her-face with the nose ring?" Finn shot the puck down the ice at the freshman goaltender, Sébastien.

"Lucia?" Austin accepted the puck back from Seb and lined up a shot.

"Yeah, maybe it's her."

"It's not her." Russ put himself between Austin and the goal, skating backwards in an attempt to block the shot.

"How do you know?"

Linc groaned and covered his face with his glove at Will's voice joining the conversation.

"Are we talking about Linc's mystery phone chick?" Johnny skated past him, joining their group and accepting a pass from Austin.

"Who the fuck told him?"

No one spoke. Somehow everyone knew about Elizabeth, and they'd been talking shit about her for the last forty minutes of practice. He'd hoped they'd lose interest at playing 'guess the girl', but the names kept coming.

Johnny took a shot and skated back toward them along the boards. "I bet it's a dude."

Russ slowed as he passed Johnny, threw him a glare and jerked his chin toward the locker room. "Go hang out with people who, for whatever reason, like you. This doesn't concern you."

"Ah! Stewart's still on his period." He held his hands up and skated away from them toward the tunnel. "No one's good enough to join the secret seven, eh?" He pulled off one of his gloves and flipped them the bird before leaving the ice.

"On n'est que six." Sébastien squirted water through the grill on the front of his helmet.

"I think he's trying to be funny." Will turned to face Linc and patted him on the chest. "We'll find out who your Cinderella is, Prince Charming."

"No. Don't do that. Absolutely, do *not* do that." Linc's jaw ached from clenching his teeth.

"We gotchu, boo." Finn skated up behind Linc, slinging a heavy arm over his shoulders.

"No. I don't need getting. Go find someone else to annoy the shit out of. I'm good."

"Nuh uh. We're the Hardy Boys, we solve mysteries. We'll get to the bottom of this." Will fist bumped Finn.

Finn pointed finger-guns back at Will. "Dude's right. Detectives 'n' shit."

"Someone put me out of my misery and kill me right fucking now."

"I have never seen this guy so bent out of shape over a chick before. For all he knows she's Uncle Fester, but he's smitten as fuck. Attached to his phone 24-7 these days." Russell, the traitorous bastard, picked up the spare sticks lying at the side of the rink, skating off toward the tunnel.

Linc shot him what he hoped was a withering glare, but

his friend simply chuckled in reply. "I don't want this to be a thing."

"You know better than to keep secrets from your brothers, man." Austin was the last to leave the ice, and was grinning like the others. "But I feel for you. They're not gonna let up till they figure out who the hell she is. Isn't it driving you fucking crazy?"

"To be honest, it's kinda nice being anonymous sometimes."

"I get it. With big skates comes big responsibility."

Linc nodded, and prayed his teammates wouldn't find out who she was, at least not yet. It wasn't that he didn't want to know who he'd been talking to, he just wasn't ready to accept the rejection when she found out who he was.

"Your party is already seated." The server tucked two menus under her arm and led him through the restaurant.

Will had asked him to dinner. Linc had said yes under the assumption that it was a team thing, but the waitress led him to a two-seater table, with a woman sitting with her back to him. *What, the fucking fuck?*

Linc slid onto the seat facing the woman who gave him a shy smile. She had long, wavy black hair, the darkest brown eyes he'd ever seen, and her sandy complexion, smooth and tawny was flawless. If she wasn't a model, he'd eat his shoe. "I'll give you a minute to look at the menus. Drinks?"

She ordered a Dr Pepper and he asked for an iced water with lemon. Who was this girl? Why was he here?

"Mr. Morrison asked me to give you this." The server handed him a menu with a folded sticky note stuck to the front of it. He unfolded the sticky note. *This one isn't Miss Bennet, but she's gorgeous, and in-the-flesh. You're welcome – Will.* Linc tried to stop his eyes from rolling. *P.S. Dinner's on me.*

The food better be good. He'd never tried the Ethiopian restaurant before, but he was going to order one of everything on the menu just to get back at his interfering, Cupid-wannabe captain.

She tilted her head and pursed her lips. "I'm not what you expected, huh?"

Linc's face burned with embarrassment. Blind dates were awful at the best of times, but when it was a surprise blind date... it was a new level of mortification that Linc had been unprepared to face when he woke up that morning. "You could say that. I thought I was meeting the team for dinner."

Her jaw dropped open, and a small giggle escaped her as she clapped a hand over her mouth. "Oh no. They didn't."

If the ground opened up and swallowed him whole from his humiliation it would be a mercy killing. "They did." He groaned, hanging his head in his hand. "I... never mind."

"If you wanna leave, we totally can. I don't mind."

"Oh hell no. We're eating this place out of all the food they have. Will's paying."

Her grin was infectious. But it didn't set his heart on fire. His fingers itched to pull the phone from his pocket and message Elizabeth. They ordered sambusas and curry – vegetarian for her – and Linc asked for a refill on his water.

"What were you going to say? Why do your friends hate you so much they sent you on a surprise blind date?"

"You don't wanna know." His cell phone buzzed in his pants, and a bolt of joy struck him straight in the chest. He was a goner.

"Sounds like exactly the kind of story I want to know." She sipped her Dr. Pepper. "Actually, hold that thought. I need the restroom – be right back."

He gave her a small smile, pulling out his phone before she'd even turned her back to him, but his stomach sank when it wasn't Elizabeth. The message was from Will, asking what he thought of Sabrina. Sabrina. He hadn't even asked the woman's name. Because she wasn't Elizabeth.

Linc: You doing okay, milady?

Elizabeth: Why, Mr. Darcy, I thought you had forgotten me.

Linc: Never in a million years.

This girl had worked her way into his life and he had no desire to shake her loose. Not even for the striking beauty walking toward him from the bathroom.

"Okay, whoever *she* is, you should be with *her* right now, not me."

"Hmm?"

The server placed the plate of sambusas between them and poured a refill of water for Linc.

"Whoever it was who made you smile like that. Why aren't you with her?" She picked up a sambusa, the crisp filo pastry crunched as she bit into it with a moan. "These are so freakin' good."

Linc picked up one of the triangles and took a bite, spice-scented steam hitting his nose the moment he did. "You're right, these are pretty damn tasty."

She took another bite and gestured for him to continue.

"No judgement..."

"Well, I can't promise that. But I'll try." She smiled, and for some reason he trusted her. Or maybe he needed to tell someone how he was feeling.

"I guess that's good enough." He took another bite while she picked up a second one and tucked in. "I don't know her name. I don't know who she is. I just text her. It started as a wrong number but now..."

Sabrina regarded him thoughtfully and nodded, pursing her lips. "And now you're falling for her."

Linc laughed, but it was brittle. "I can't fall for someone I don't know."

"And yet, you're not denying it, my doomed new friend. So your hockey pals thought you could get over the girl on the phone by throwing you at me for dinner?" She shook her head, tossing him a world class eye roll. "Men."

"Tell me about it."

"What are you going to do?"

"About my team setting me up on a blind date with you? I'm probably going to put super glue on their sticks, or itching powder in their jockstraps and helmets."

"Uh... okay, sounds like we definitely have some rage issues to work through here, but I meant your lady friend." She popped the last of the appetizer into her mouth, wiped her hands on her napkin and folded her arms.

"What am I going to do? Nothing. Why? What do you think I should do about her?"

"Christ. Will said you were smart. But for a 'smart guy', Lincoln, you really are dumb as rocks about this one, aren't you? Meet her, idiot. You absolutely, positively, need to meet that woman."

Linc dropped his forehead onto the table so hard the silverware clinked. "I was afraid you were gonna say that."

CHAPTER 13

Lincoln

Linc: How was your day, Miss Bennet?
Sorry I've been quiet. I've had an…
interesting evening.

Elizabeth: Oh? Pray tell.

Linc: My friends set me up on a blind date.

The screen said 'read' under the message, but she didn't reply right away. He sat up in bed to ensure he didn't fall asleep.

Linc: Noooooooo. Please don't freak out. It wasn't an actual date. I had no idea it was happening. I thought I was meeting my friends. When I got to the restaurant there was a woman waiting for me. She was attractive, but I made sure she knew pretty quickly that I… uh, kind of have someone already.

Had he crossed the line? Was she not on the same page as him? Uncertainty clogged his throat as he swallowed.

Elizabeth: Who do you kind of have, Mr. Darcy?

Linc: Oh, no. I've had a night of full-on mortification, I'm not spelling it out for you Miss Bennet. But I will say I spent the whole meal wishing it was someone different sitting across the table from me.

Elizabeth: You kind of have me?

Linc: I'd like to all-the-way have you.

Elizabeth: When you say things like that it gives a girl ideas.

Linc: Would it be so bad for her to have those kind of ideas? I feel like it wouldn't. I like you, Lizzy. I'm scared of you seeing who I am too.

Elizabeth: 'Cause you're a jock? You have to be a jock. No one spends that much time in the gym and isn't a jock.

Linc: LOL! Guilty as charged. I am a jock.

Elizabeth: So I know all the worst parts of you already.

Linc: And you think seeing what you look like will be the 'worst part' of you?

She didn't answer once again. She was probably staring at the screen figuring out how to get herself out of the situation she'd landed herself in. Answering yes would mean she'd open herself up to him giving her a talking to about her self-perception. Answering no meant she had no reason left to decline meeting him face to face.

Elizabeth: I'm not fishing for compliments.

Linc: I didn't think you were. I think you have a deeply skewed opinion of yourself and it has you scared and ready to run. We're all self-conscious about our bodies, Elizabeth. Even jocks. Obviously I'm not going to push you or try to force you into doing something you aren't ready for but I really do want to meet you.

Linc: Look. I'm throwing down where I'm at, okay? If it freaks you out, I'm sorry, but I can't keep it to myself anymore. I can't stop thinking about you, Lizzy. I enjoy 'talking' to you. I want to spend time with you 'IRL' so we can see where this goes. I know we started out by accident, but my days don't feel complete unless I've at least checked in with you to see how you're doing. I know I probably wasn't supposed to, but I care and I feel like if I don't tell you that I care, you're going to remain oblivious and whatever this is, whatever this could be, will end up passing us by.

Elizabeth: You're just saying that because it's mysterious and exciting.

Linc: I'm saying this because I enjoy your company and I really want to kiss you.

Elizabeth: Mr. Darcy...

Linc: Shhhh. Don't say anything tonight. Think about it, okay?

Linc: But it's good to know you think I'm mysterious and exciting! ;)

He reached onto the floor and picked up his sketchpad.

He flicked it to the vibrant, colorful, almost cartoon-esque self-portrait he'd drawn in chalk and snapped a photo. It wasn't an accurate likeness, in fairness it could have been anyone, but he wasn't ready to out himself to someone who might as easily walk away knowing so much about him. He pressed send.

He silenced his phone, turned off the lamp next to his bed and turned onto his side, pulling the blanket up to his chin. When he woke up in the morning, he'd either be met with deafening silence, or she'd answer, maybe even with a picture of her own. He could only hope.

"You see who's in the stands with Will's lil sister again?" Russ skated up behind him as the clock on the big screen counted the final few seconds to zero then reset to twenty to count down to the start of the game.

Linc had in fact seen who was in the stands, but he wasn't going to give Russ any additional ammunition. "Huh? Who?" He forced his face to stay impassive and his voice to stay level and cool.

"Nice try, asshole. You missed two easy shots on an empty net during warm up because you were... let's just call it distracted." Russ led the way to the tunnel and extended his stick for Linc to go first. "We both know you clocked her. We both know you wanna make sweet, sweet love to that woman, Linc. What's stopping you? Is it what Johnny said about her weight? Because—"

"Easy there, tiger." Linc patted his chest with a gloved palm. "That's not the why. She despises me and everything I stand for. I'm trying to convince her I'm not a no-brain jock by pulling my weight on this project, but she's not giving me an inch, man. She's just..." They trudged through the corridor toward the locker room. "Cautious, I guess. I can't blame her really. Not after that shit Johnny pulled."

"Rumor has it that asshole is bound for 'Bama."

"No shit?"

"Truth. We'll see if anything comes of it though. Also, you missed a reason. We both know that girl on your phone has you in your feels so you're not entertaining anyone in-the-real-world, not even our sassy Ms. Martinez in the stands. What is it about a beautiful woman enjoying sport that's hot as fuck?"

Linc erupted into boisterous laughter. "Dude. I think you're overstating it, just a little. Did you see her face? She'd rather be having a colonoscopy right now than be at this game. Molly must have something on her to convince her to come back here."

"What's that about Molly?" Will shuffled his way over to sit between them on the bench.

"Scotty here was just commenting on how your sister had brought her brunette friend with her to the game again."

"Cleo?" Will's accusatory stare fell to Linc. "What about it? Are you...? Do you...? Lincoln Scott you surely don't..." Realization dawned on his face as hit eyebrows shot up his forehead. "Ooooooh boy."

"You did a thing all by yourself there, man. You didn't finish a single sentence."

Will dropped his voice to a quiet murmur. "No, no, no. Stick with the phantom girl on the phone, man. Cleo Martinez is not the girl for you. Nuh uh. She'd chew you up, spit you out, and not even break a sweat."

"Plus, it seems her heart doesn't belong to a Snow Pirate anymore. She's not wearing that sweater tonight. Or even our colors for that matter. Guess the pirate lost her heart..."

Linc groaned. "You're both shitheads, you know that, right?"

Will grinned. "You sure know how to pick 'em, Linc." He shook his head. "I mean, you're a good guy and all, but..."

"She's outta my league."

Will's brows pulled into a deep frown as he shook his head. He opened his mouth to speak but was cut off by Johnny yelling that it was time to hit the ice.

"**Y**our skates on fire tonight, Linc?"

He wasn't sure which of the guys crowded around him had shouted, but Linc had just scored his second goal of the game and had two assists under his belt too. He couldn't remember the last time he'd played so well.

But that wasn't even the best part of his night. The game was made all the more interesting when one Miss Cleo Martinez jumped to her feet at his second goal, cheering as though she'd been a hockey fan her entire life. Her face broke into the most beautiful, contagious smile, and she threw her arms around Molly whose eyebrows almost disappeared into her hairline with shock.

We could make a fan out of you yet. He almost convinced himself she probably had no idea who had scored. To newbies, hockey players all looked the same from the front. He pulled his helmet off, tucking it under his elbow while he wiped the sweat from his forehead and raised a questioning eyebrow at her once he'd caught her gaze.

Her face flushed as red as her sweater – which also happened to be the same color as the away team, giving him all manner of feels he wasn't thrilled about. She pulled her plump lip between her teeth and offered a half-shrug before Molly followed her line of sight to the ice and jabbed her elbow into Cleo's ribs. Cleo's blush darkened as guilt swelled in his stomach.

There'd be no way in hell he could convince Elizabeth to even watch a game with him on the TV, let alone persuade her to come and watch him play. While she enjoyed literature and art, she'd made it clear she didn't enjoy working out or watching sports.

He'd dated a fair number of girls throughout high school and in his first year of college but kept them all at arm's reach. He couldn't be with someone who might have enjoyed sport, but who couldn't appreciate his love of the arts. Could the reverse be true? He might not want to play pro-hockey, but he'd never give it up. Could he freely and entirely love someone like Eliza? Someone who encouraged his artistic side but who'd never be part of his athletic life?

CHAPTER 14

Cleo

Cleo stepped into the Minneapolis Institute of Art at 10.05AM, precisely five minutes after it opened. Her car still wasn't fixed, she'd left it back in the shop and taken a thirty minute bus ride from the university campus across town to enjoy the peaceful Sunday morning stillness. It was her favorite time to visit. At least once a month since she'd moved to Minnesota, she took a trip to the Institute of Art. Even if she'd seen an exhibit before, doing another pass brought with it a depth of understanding and added an extra dimension to her enjoyment.

"Hello there, Cleo, how are you?" Bright eyes peered at Cleo over the top of a pair of cat-eye shaped glasses.

"I'm okay thank you, Miss Lola. I see someone beat me to it; that's one shiny bike sitting outside."

Lola leaned forward and spoke behind the back of her hand as though she had a huge secret to tell. "He's a handsome one, Cleo. If I were you, I might find myself staring at that young looker as much as the exhibits."

Cleo giggled, shook her head, and threw a small wave at Lola before entering the exhibit hall. She'd arrived with every intention of viewing "Unexpected Turns: Women Artists and the Making of American Basket-Weaving Traditions" but her feet piloted her to "In the Presence of Our Ancestors: Southern Perspectives in African American Art". She'd been to the exhibit three times before, but it called to her again. Her phone vibrated in the pocket of her pants.

> Mr. Darcy: Good morning. Maybe one of these days we could do something fun on a Sunday morning? It's my 'me' morning and I always find myself doing fun things by myself.

> Mr. Darcy: Shit. Not *those* fun things. I just mean things around the city.

As she rounded the corner, nose buried in her phone replying to Mr. Darcy, footsteps to her left startled her. They moved into the next space. Had she found the mysterious biker so soon? She craned her neck to try to see if Lola was right about him, but he moved too quickly for her to get a good look.

> Cleo: That sounds like fun. It's my favorite time, too. I love exploring the city.

She tucked away her phone and studied the exhibit, taking in every detail as she moved from one picture to the next, getting sucked into her surroundings.

Over two hours later her stomach growled as she exited the building, pausing to collect some fliers on the way. She said goodbye to Lola, who gave her a homemade cupcake from behind the desk and told her she'd see her next time.

Cleo made her way to the bench facing the park and the spires of downtown Minneapolis and peeled off the cupcake wrapper. She split the cake part in half and put the bottom of the cake on top of the icing, turning it into a kind of sandwich.

"I thought that was you." Lincoln Scott dropped onto the bench beside her. "I didn't want to interrupt your art enjoyment, however I had no choice but to come over and see what the hell kinda crime against cupcakes you're committing with that thing."

Her brain scrambled to marry up Lincoln Scott the jock with Lincoln Scott the guy who was at the Institute of Art first thing on a Sunday morning. Had she entered the twilight zone?

"Don't knock it till you try it." How her voice sounded so calm when her stomach was tangled in knots, she had no idea. He wore blue jeans which hung like they were custom made and a plain black t-shirt hugged his torso. Looking that good should be illegal. She broke the cupcake in half and offered him one piece. "It's better this way. A more even cake-to-frosting mouthful. It's easier to eat, too, less messy."

"Messy can be fun." His lazy smile almost undid her. The mischievous twinkle in his eye as he leaned forward and took the entire half-cupcake in his mouth, right from between her finger and thumb, had her pressing her thighs together. It was as though he moved in slow motion, never breaking eye contact.

Was she dying right now? Were hearts designed to beat this fast? How was a fully dressed man eating a chocolate cupcake so Goddamn sensual?

Flames of desire lapped low in her stomach and searing heat torched her from the inside. His tongue snaked out to grab some frosting from his bottom lip. Was it possible to orgasm without being touched? Would she ever be able to eat a cupcake again without thinking about Lincoln Scott's tongue and his chocolate covered mouth?

"You're staring." His voice was husky and laced with amusement.

"You... uh... chocolate." She gestured to his mouth. Pointing was easier than speaking. Her arm moved without her telling it to and her thumb swept along the curve of his lip, gathering up the chocolate.

He caught her by the wrist, an intense, smoldering stare from under low brows punched the air from her lungs. He raised an eyebrow.

Was he asking permission? For what? Did it matter? She volunteered as tribute. She nodded, biting the inside of her cheek so she didn't let out the moan ricocheting in her chest like a pinball in a machine.

His tongue darted out and licked the chocolate from her thumb as a small squeak escaped her. She couldn't move. She couldn't breathe. Time stood still. There was only Lincoln Scott, holding her by the wrist, and his wild blue eyes pinning her with unbridled want. He'd somehow made her mute and paralyzed. Did she want to flee? No. She shamefully wanted to offer him the other half of the dessert so he'd do it all over again.

A knowing smile tugged at the corner of his lips. "You gonna eat that?"

She nodded, taking a small bite. Why did some people get to make being a messy eater so sexy and hot while the rest of the world looked like Shrek?

"You want a ride back to campus? I don't see your car."

"I... uh. I grabbed the bus." She glanced around him to the bike standing outside the entrance to the Institute. "I've never ridden before."

He snorted.

"A bike, Lincoln. I've never ridden a bike before." She shoved the rest of the cupcake in her mouth before she said anything else stupid.

"Not to get too Aladdin on you, but you can trust me. I won't let you fall." He reached out an open palm and she somehow found her hand in his.

She followed him to the bike. What was she doing? This was not who she was. What if someone saw when she got back on campus? What if Johnny was there? Would the bike even move with her weight on it? So many questions rattled through her brain as he pulled out a helmet and offered it to her.

She opened her mouth to speak but he covered her lips with his finger.

"Don't overthink it, just go with it."

She closed her eyes while he reached around behind her and pulled out her hair tie; her hair fell onto her back. He slipped the helmet onto her head and, placing a finger under her chin, tipped her head back enough so he could clip it into place.

Her stomach lurched. There wasn't much room on the bike, she'd have to sit close to him. She'd have to *touch* him. Would he feel how hot and wet she was after That Cupcake Thing?

He swung his leg over the bike and shuffled forward on the seat. He reached behind him and patted the padded space. "I've got you."

Something squeezed in her chest at how genuine he sounded. She climbed on and rested her palms on his hips. His body vibrated with a chuckle as he reached both hands back, cupped her ass and pulled her toward him so his perfect, sculpted hockey ass was pressed tightly against her core. "I'll only bite if you ask me to, Cleo." He took her hands from his hips and wrapped them around his waist, tugging her body flush against his back.

Could he feel her heart hammering?

He started the bike and took off slowly. She gasped,

squeezing her eyes closed as they picked up speed. Every fiber of her body wanted to splay her hands on his stomach and run them up the length of his torso to feel each chiseled muscle under his shirt. She groaned.

"You okay?"

She nodded, afraid if she opened her mouth a bug would fly in or a request for him to pull over and ravage her against a tree might slip out. Minneapolis blurred past in a haze and they arrived at her apartment before Cleo had fully relaxed into the ride. Once the bike was turned off she held onto Linc for a beat longer.

His palms covered the backs of her hands and he squeezed. "Told you I wouldn't let you fall."

She nodded against his back. Reaching up to unclip the strap under her chin, she tugged the helmet off with trembling hands.

"Was that so bad?"

She pulled her leg over the bike, a little wobbly on her feet. Linc leaned on the handlebars, intensity blazing in his eyes. She folded her arms around the helmet, clutching it to her chest. "I think it would take a little getting used to."

"Happy to give you a ride anytime." He nodded down at the machine between his thighs. "On the bike."

She clamped her lips between her teeth to stop from grinning. "Thank you." She offered the helmet back to him, but he reached beyond it to tuck her hair behind her ear as he'd done in the library, before taking it back. Her pulse raced as sparks of desire... anticipation... need crackled between them.

"Like I said, any time. It looks good on you."

Her heart swelled. It wasn't the first time he'd paid her a compliment, and he always sounded so genuine and sincere when he gave them. There was no trace of teasing or malice in his tone. How could a man who looked like him think she was in any way pretty?

She stumbled backwards away from the bike toward her door, not wanting to take her eyes off the beautiful man smiling at her as though she lit up his world. Was this a dream? A cruel joke? She tried pinching her palm but didn't wake up.

"You gonna stand out there drooling on the sidewalk all afternoon, Miss Thang?" Molly appeared next to her, giving her a gentle hip bump. "Thanks for bringing her home, Linc."

"Any time, Miss Morrison." He nodded. "Thanks for the cupcake."

Did he wink at her?

"Did he wink at you?"

The bike roared to life and Linc pulled away from the sidewalk.

Molly's fingers snapped in front of her face. "Earth to Cho-Cho. Blink once if you can hear me, blink twice if you need medical assistance."

"What the hell just happened?"

"Girl, you were there, not me. What the hell *did* just happen? It looked like you got up close and personal with Lincoln Scott's fine ass."

She turned Cleo around by the shoulders and led her inside. "Did you kiss him again? Did you grope his butt on the bike? You're gonna need to give me something more than this vaguely-traumatized stare you've got going on. Did he hurt you? Is this a good stare? You've got just-fucked hair but you *did* ride a bike home so that's probably where that came from, but he was abso-freakin'-lutely eye-fucking you when I walked out. Like, I need a shower to scrub you guys' smut off me."

"We didn't kiss again, but we shared a cupcake."

"And that traumatized you?"

"I've never been more turned on by a cupcake in my entire life."

Molly cackled. "Girl, is this our new code for Linc's dick? When you fuck him – and believe me when I tell you – you *will* fuck him, you just gotta text me 'cupcake' and I'll have the 4-1-1."

Cleo covered Molly's face with her palm and pushed her away. "Shut up. That's never going to happen."

Molly waggled her eyebrows. "Never say never, girlfriend."

She left her friend making kissing sounds, and made her way to her room. Pulling her phone out of her pocket her stomach dipped, with guilt, and disappointment at the lack of messages from Mr. Darcy. She'd have to choose, and soon. The tug of war in her chest over the two men in her life was dizzying. Stress squeezed her shoulder blades. How was it possible to be so fond of two men?

She unfolded the fliers she'd picked up at the Institute and snapped a picture of the one that talked about a local art competition. The first prize was a small, short-run exhibition in one of the local art galleries. She sent it to Mr. Darcy with a text.

> Cleo: You should totally enter this competition. You'd be great at it! Feel the fear and do it anyway, Mr. Darcy. Do the scary thing!!!!

As she pressed the send button she couldn't help but feel somewhat hypocritical. Pressing him to do the big scary thing with his art while she kept herself at arm's reach from considering what she wanted to do for herself. The more she pushed it away to convince herself she wanted the same things her mother wanted for her, the less sure she felt in her decision.

Reaching under her bed she pulled out a tatty shoebox of notebooks, grabbed her laptop, and sat against the headboard of her bed. She flipped open the cover of the oldest notebook in the pile, fired up her laptop, and started typing.

CHAPTER 15

Cleo

Cleo was going to kill Molly. It had only taken a split second. She had taken leave of her senses for just a moment and Molly had pounced, making her agree to attend a blackout party across campus.

Where Molly was now was anyone's guess. Making out with the guy who made a beeline for her as soon as she arrived, no doubt.

Why did she need Cleo to tag along if she was only going to abandon her as soon as they got there? An excellent question she'd be asking later, if she ever found her again.

She leaned against the wall, sticking close to where it met the hallway leading into the kitchen. The lack of light was disorientating, and while a few people had worn white clothing, and donned glow sticks and UV paint over their bodies, visibility was still low. She cradled her red solo cup in one hand and her phone in the other. The more she tried to ignore the tug in her chest to Mr. Darcy, the stronger it pulled.

Cleo: I hate my best friend right now.

> Mr. Darcy: What's up? I might be slow to reply, I'm at a party with some of the team, but I'm around. It's kinda lame here.

Her eyes flitted around the room, straining against the darkness. Could he be at the same party? She shook her head, pinched the edge of the solo cup between her teeth and typed out a reply with both thumbs.

> Cleo: Ditto. She dragged me to this dumb party and then ran off with LITERALLY the first dick to sidle up and smile at her.

She tucked her phone back into her pants and sipped the last of her drink. A chime came from her butt pocket almost right away. Followed by three more in quick succession. She hadn't expected him to message back so soon and even over the din of the party her ringtone was still audible. Another chime sounded as she was pulling her phone back out, already giggling at the onslaught of messages.

> Mr. Darcy: Wait.

> Mr. Darcy: If some dude's dick is smiling you need to go save your friend.

> Mr. Darcy: I'm not kidding.

> Mr. Darcy: That dick needs medical attention.

> Mr. Darcy: Miss Bennet, I do believe we're at the same party.

She gasped, dropping her empty cup. Pushing off from the wall she took two steps forward and gnawed on her lip. The phone weighed heavily in her palm. Her instincts told her to flee. As she started to move, a firm hand gripped her right hip, and a phone appeared next to her left arm. A hand, *his* hand. Whether she was ready to meet him, or not, Mr. Darcy had his hands on her. She swallowed and sucked in a few deep breaths as a thumb typed.

> Don't freak out, Lizzy.

> You don't need to turn around, just...
> please, don't leave.

She relaxed against the warmth of his hand on her. He rested his head against the side of hers, stepping closer to.

> Do you want to leave? I won't stop you.

Careful not to shake him off, she shook her head slowly. Her chest heaved from the strain of forcing breath into her lungs as her heartbeat thudded in her ears.

> Do you want me to leave?

Her right hand covered his and she squeezed, shaking her head again. She tugged his fingers from her hip and slid his hand onto her stomach. He rested his chin in the crook of her neck and inhaled, his chest rising against her back. The warm air on her neck making goosebumps spread across her skin.

He stepped back against the wall, pulling her with him.

> Can I kiss your neck?

Scrunching her eyes shut, she sucked in a steadying breath. She had no idea who this guy was, but every piece of her wanted his lips on her skin. Tilting her head so her ear touched her shoulder, she hoped inviting him with her action was enough because all of her words had evaporated.

Lincoln

Cleo-fucking-Martinez.

There was no doubt about it. That's who he had his hand on. Those hips pressing against his as she stood with her back to him… the smell of strawberries radiating from her long, wavy hair.

His hand was on Cleo Martinez's stomach, and it felt *right*.

No matter how much he willed his dick to stay still it stirred against her perfectly plump ass. Her tiny gasp was adorable, and barely audible, but did little to ease the hard-on straining against his pants. He tucked his phone into his pocket and linked his hands together on her stomach.

Her hand trailed along the side of his neck as he brushed his lips against her soft skin. He smiled at the shiver that rippled through her muscles. Her fingers curled into his hair at the nape of his neck and he kissed her again. She arched her back into him, pressing him against the wall and his pulse quickened. Intoxicated by the smell of strawberries, he dropped his head to her shoulder.

"Cleo, you're killing me." He gritted his teeth. The truth

was out in the open, hanging between them. He prayed she wouldn't bolt.

Her body stiffened in his arms.

"Lincoln?" Her fingers clawed into his before she flinched and loosened her grip.

He'd never before heard his name said with such emotional weight. One simple word was tangled in confusion and longing, but if he wasn't mistaken it was also mixed with relief. Her body softened against his. He nodded his head against her shoulder, afraid to speak again in case she got spooked.

"Y-you're my Mr. Darcy?"

He moved his lips so they were close to her ear, but not quite touching. "Yes, Lizzy. I am most definitely *your* Mr. Darcy."

Tiny shudders raked through her body. "Lincoln." She hiccupped and a hand flew to her mouth.

Ice chilled his veins at her misery, but something drove him to slide his arms tighter around her middle. "So, tears tell me you're unhappy, but my arms don't want to let you go. Please tell me what you're thinking. If you'd rather I leave you to figure out your thoughts, I can do that too. I just heard your phone and couldn't help myself."

She turned her head, if he lowered his just an inch, he could kiss her. But he needed her to come to him. They both did. She trembled in his arms.

"Do you need time?"

She shook her head.

"Do you want to leave? We should talk, right? I feel like we should talk."

She turned her body around so she was facing him, her head hung low and her hands planted flat on his stomach. She must have felt his heart thumping wildly in his chest. Would she reject him now she knew who he truly was? That he was the same hockey playing jock from her English class?

He slipped a knuckle under her chin and tilted her head so he could see her face. A door opened, sending a beam of light over her face. Tears glistened on her cheeks and she had her top lip pinched between her teeth. He dropped his hands to his sides, this had to be her choice; he'd already made his.

Her face was unreadable in the dim light, but she slid her hands up his chest until they rested on his shoulders. She ran a finger along the collar of his shirt, gripped the fabric in her hand and tugged him toward her.

She was clutching the collar of Lincoln Scott's shirt. Had part of her suspected all along?

As his lips moved toward hers, she had to wonder. Relief had flooded her veins at the sound of his voice. He'd been her Mr. Darcy the whole time. She didn't have to choose between the man on the phone with a warm spirit and a gentle heart, and the guy on the ice with a smile that could melt butter. They were one and the same.

Their lips crashed together. Cleo let go of the fabric of his shirt and slid her hands behind his head, running her fingers through his hair and pulling him against her.

She was kissing Lincoln. Again. And she never wanted to stop. Her heart raced.

Her hands roamed his broad shoulders as he cupped her ass, picking her up and wrapping her legs around his waist. He turned, crashing her back against the wall. His lips left hers and found their way onto her neck. She tipped her head back, giving him space to drag his mouth along her skin and moaned as his tongue traced the line from her collar bone to her ear, nipping at her lobe. His rock-hard dick pressed against her core. Her forearms rested on his shoulders and her hands linked behind his head. Wasn't he getting tired from holding her against the wall?

"Linc..."

In the dim light, his brows pinched with confusion and his eyes searched her face. "Do you want me to stop?"

She could almost reach out and touch the pain of rejection blinking back at her in his eyes.

"No... I..." She shuffled her weight in his hands until he put her down. "I don't want to do this *here*. Can we...?"

He brushed her cheek with the back of his knuckles. "Absolutely." He leaned forward, kissed her forehead, and lowered his mouth to her ear. "Lemme just give Russ a heads up that I'm leaving, okay?"

She nodded and settled back against the wall, her body jolted when he slid his hand into hers and gave a small tug.

"If you think I'm leaving you here to let your mind talk you down you have another thing coming."

She smiled. This was going to be a thing now. He knew her. She'd let him know her and more than that, she kinda liked it. Holy shit. Mr. Darcy and Lincoln fucking Scott were one and the same. And she'd just had his hands over her body and her tongue in his mouth.

In the next room, someone had lit candles. Cleo wasn't convinced that was the smartest thing for a group of drunk college kids to do, but they were well enough out of the way that they shouldn't cause any problems.

The guy who had been with Linc, Johnny, and Will in the coffee shop was sitting on the floor playing spin the bottle – a sight which must have been unexpected to Linc, who burst out laughing. He waved hello to someone in the circle he called Sabrina who gave Cleo a shrewd smile. Linc tapped the guy on the shoulder. "Russ."

Russ stood. "Linc, my man. Where'd you disappear off

to?" Russ peered around Linc's shoulder. "Ah. Never mind. Dumb question. It's about fucking time." He patted Linc on the chest. "You leaving?"

Linc nodded.

"You kids have fun, yeah?"

Cleo's cheeks burned in the dim light as Linc turned to leave.

"And Linc?"

Linc paused. "Yeah?"

"You know Morrison will kill you if you hurt her, right?"

"Will can stand easy, I won't hurt her." Linc squeezed her fingers still-wrapped in his, he might as well have held her heart with his bare hand.

"I meant the *other* Morrison."

Cleo bit back a giggle. "He's not wrong. Molly is *way* scarier than Will. Shit! Molly!" Cleo reached into her pocket and slipped out her phone.

Russ pointed at the phone. "Yeah, you better tell her where you're going, or she'll torture everyone in here until she gets a location of your whereabouts."

She followed Linc outside, pausing next to his bike. Her brows pinched in confusion.

"I didn't drink anything." He handed her a helmet. "Did you message Molly?"

She shook her head, unlocking her phone.

Cleo: Cupcake.

"Cupcake?"

She gasped. He was staring at her screen, eyebrow raised in question.

"I'll explain later."

Her phone pinged right away.

Molly: I FUCKING TOLD YOU SO.

Molly: If you're going home, leave a sock on the door so I don't come home and try to be the big spoon on Lincoln's nekkid ass.

Lincoln cleared his throat. "She knew from one word who you were with and what you were doing? That's some next level girl talk right there."

She laughed, tucked her phone away and climbed onto the bike. Linc stretched his arms back and pulled her toward him just like the first time. She wrapped her arms around his waist, rested the side of her head on his back and smiled.

Lincoln fucking Scott. Who'd have guessed?

CHAPTER 16

Cleo

"Did you freak out on the bike ride?" He reached out to take the helmet from her.

"It wasn't as bad as last time." She handed it to him and stepped back from the bike, waiting for him to dismount.

"I didn't mean about the ride itself."

She cast her eyes to the ground, shrugging.

"I figured that might happen." He swung his leg over the bike and turned to face her, still leaning against the seat. He picked her hand up from her side, threaded his fingers through hers, then pulled. His hands rested low on her back, just above the swell of her butt.

"Cleo?"

She focused her eyes on his lips. Maybe he wouldn't notice she couldn't bring herself to meet his stare. Anxiety stabbed in her stomach and fear crept along her spine. Lincoln Scott, jock and popular guy, had his hands on her body.

"Cleo?"

Her shoulders sagged on a sigh as she tipped her head back, just enough.

"We don't have to do anything you don't want to do."

"I know that."

"Then what is it?"

"I..." Her forehead dropped against his chest. "I just don't know why you'd want to do anything with me."

Instead of recoiling in horror at the realization she was right and he was insane for wanting to touch her, he spread his knees, tightened his arms around her and pulled her closer against him. He nestled his cheek into her hair. "Even after all we've shared with each other you don't trust the fact that I might find you attractive? I know you have demons, Cleo, I think everyone does. But this isn't a joke or a game to me."

He cupped her jaw. "I care about you. I like you. I enjoyed talking to you in texts, and I want us to explore what this is between us. Not only all of that, but I think you're beautiful, inside and out. If all you wanna do right now is walk in that apartment alone, I get it. I won't pressure you. I'll ride home and text you when I get there. If you want to talk out here, or want me to come inside and just talk, that's okay too."

Cleo pulled out her phone and tapped out a message. Linc's phone chimed in his pocket and he cocked his head, a smile dancing on his lips.

> Elizabeth: I'd like for you to come inside with me, Mr. Darcy.

> Mr. Darcy: What my lady wants, my lady gets.

She giggled at his reply, took his outstretched hand, and led him into her building. Side by side in the elevator, their arms touched. Her stomach flipped. She was taking Lincoln Scott up to her room. Whose life was she even living?

"I can hear your thoughts from here, *preciosa*." He

bumped his hip against their clasped hands dangling between them.

Her heart stumbled in her chest. The only thing more of a turn on than Lincoln eating a cupcake was hearing Spanish tumble from those full, kissable lips.

"Don't get excited. It's literally one of the only words I know and only because Google told me. I could be saying something rude and offensive."

The complex knot of anxiety and fear loosened in her stomach. She prompted herself to breathe. All she had to do was remind herself that this was Mr. Darcy, the guy from the phone, with the face of Lincoln Scott and maybe she'd calm down. Maybe her stomach would stop doing that flippy thing it kept doing when she caught him staring at her, or when their skin touched.

"It's not offensive. Just... unexpected."

He slid his arm around her as they walked along the corridor to her door. She pulled out her keys and let them inside.

"Tea?" She made her way to the kitchen. It was safe there, neutral territory that wouldn't cause her lady-parts to ignite and demand she jump into bed with him the second he closed the door behind him, right?

Heat radiated through her clothing as his hands traveled down her arms to her hands. He shook his head against hers. "No tea, thank you. And if it's okay with you I want to stay close while you make it."

"I d-don't want tea either."

"You don't?"

She shook her head.

"Then why are we in the kitchen?"

Because I'm afraid of you seeing me naked?

She turned to face him, placing her hands flat on his chest.

Christ alive he was built. "I guess I'm trying to reconcile the guy on the phone with the guy in front of me."

"It's okay that you need time, we can sit and talk, have some face-to-face time that isn't you scowling at me from across the room and take our time."

"That's just it." Her voice was barely a whisper. "I don't want to take my time. I look at you, and damn if I don't want to..."

"What do you want, Cleo?" He dropped his forehead to her forehead and rubbed his nose against hers.

"You're going to make me say it out loud, aren't you?"

"Would you believe me if I said my ego needs to hear you say it."

She laughed, her nose bobbing against his. "I think your ego is just fine, Lincoln."

His sigh vibrated in her soul. "I love how you say my name. And with everyone else out there, sure." He jerked a head to the door. "But with you? You make me feel..." His eyes swam with an emotion she couldn't pinpoint.

"What do you feel?" Her breath caught around the shards of self-consciousness in her chest as she spoke. She stroked his cheek with her thumb, closing her eyes, as though it would somehow shield her feelings, keep them away from him.

"You make me feel like I want to be better, Cleo."

Her eyes shot open and met his. "I... how? We barely spoke before the... shopping incident. Better than what? I don't understand."

"Honestly? I thought you were way out of my league. You're smart, funny, you radiate a confidence that says 'don't fuck with me, I have my shit all figured out' and sure, it's a little intimidating but it's also hot as hell. I didn't think I had anything to offer. Plus you were scowly as fuck."

"And now?" She was no doctor but the amount of heart racing that had happened since Lincoln walked into her life was unnatural – and perhaps going to cause her untimely demise.

"And now I still think you're this incredible, beautiful woman and I'm just hoping you can see past my irritating jock-ness to something deeper, something we can maybe build on. Your turn. You didn't answer my question."

"What question?"

"Qué quieres?"

"You said you didn't know Spanish."

"Qué quieres, preciosa?"

Her cheeks flared with heat. Embarrassment, desire, and proximity to him had her body screaming at her to act. "You, Lincoln. I want you." She trailed her fingertips along his jaw and into his hair. "I'm just not sure how. It's not that I've never..." She closed her eyes.

"Open your eyes, Cleo. Don't hide from me." Concern radiated from his gaze when her eyelids flickered open. "This is new for both of us, we can figure it out together, but not if you keep closing your eyes or burying your head in my chest every time we hit on something uncomfortable. I mean, don't get me wrong, I like the head on the chest thing, but I can't see your eyes and you have such pretty freakin' eyes that say so much."

"What do they say?"

"Right now..." He cupped her face. "They're saying you're scared to let me in. But we both know you did that the day you answered my text. I'm in, Cleo."

She rolled forward onto her tiptoes and placed a chaste kiss on the corner of his mouth. He turned and met her lips with his, returning her kiss, slowly at first, his hands snaking around her waist and travelling up her back until his palms lay flat against her shoulder blades. "Lincoln..."

Their kiss turned from sweet to heat in an instant. Her hands slipped from the sides of his face onto his shoulders, where she curled her fingers into his shirt and dragged her nails down his chest. She was in, too. She had no idea how things would work between them, but the aching between her thighs, and pounding of her heart, demanded she try.

A low growl rattled in his chest and she nipped at his bottom lip before stepping back to catch her breath. She tucked her hair behind her ear, took his hand in hers, and led the way through the house.

Her body was on fire. Her inner demons were yelling that a girl like her had no business being naked with a guy like Lincoln, but she pressed down the self-deprecation. It was his choice to make as much as hers, and he'd made it.

She sucked in a cleansing breath and pushed open the door to her bedroom.

CHAPTER 17

Lincoln

Even from three feet away with her back turned to him, her discomfort was obvious. The way she held her body, shoulders curled forward, head down, arms wrapped around her middle... it ripped at his heart.

What could have happened to her that was so bad she didn't want him to see her body? Who had made her feel so awful about how she looked that even after he'd told her she was beautiful, she wanted to hide?

He couldn't stay three feet away, he needed her in his arms. He needed to do whatever he could to convince the vibrant, strong, and incredible woman who was tangled in her own self-perceptions, that she was everything. If that meant cuddling on the bed until day break while his raging boner pressed against the seam of his jeans, he'd do it.

He closed the space, slid his arms along hers, and pulled her back against his chest. Her muscles were tense and rigid. "I know I said it already but we really don't have to do anything you're uncomfortable with."

She nodded against his chest. "I know." She turned to face him. "I just need to get out of my own head."

"That can be hard to do."

"You say that like you understand." Her quiet voice shook as she spoke.

He kissed her forehead. "Not everyone has the same hang ups, Cleo. I might not understand exactly what you're going through, but I do understand."

"I'm sorry, I didn't mean…"

He stopped her sentence with a kiss. If he couldn't explain to her how he was feeling, maybe he could show her. He teased at the seam of her mouth with his tongue, and she softened in his arms. She tipped her head back, slid her hands behind his head, and deepened the kiss.

He stepped forward, holding her tight to his chest, until they reached the edge of the bed. The mattress caught behind her knees and she dropped onto the quilt. "I'm not saying I don't want to see you, but if you'd feel better with the light off and the lamp on, I'm okay with that."

Indecision flickered across her face, heat flooding her cheeks before she shook her head.

Lights on it is.

Maybe if he got naked first she'd be more at ease. Or maybe she'd feel more self-conscious. Her head was tipped in curiosity as she leaned up on her elbows.

Fuck it.

Reaching behind his head, he tugged his shirt off by the collar, dropping it to the floor before shucking his jeans. He trod on the toes of his socks to remove them one at a time. Leaving his boxers on, he picked up her feet, dangling off the edge of the mattress, and peeled off her wedge sandals. She wore Capri jeans which hugged her hips, and a flowy red shirt dipping just enough at her cleavage to send bolts of desire to his dick. He lay next to her, propping his head on the heel of his hand while she dropped from her elbows, flat onto her back.

She reached a tentative hand to touch his chest, the tiny trembles vibrating against his skin. Leaning over her, he kissed her forehead, dotted another on her nose, and another on her lips. She pulled his head lower and kissed him, melting beneath him, as though her decision had been made. Her rigid muscles, softening under his touch as he dragged his fingers down her sternum, running them along the bare strip at her waist from where her shirt had ridden up.

He kissed her cheek and nibbled on her ear. "Do you remember the day your car broke down?"

She nodded.

"When I saw you..." He caught the fabric with the tip of his finger and pushed it above her belly button. "You were bent over the engine, ass in the air, and your shirt had slipped up your back just enough to drive me insane. I wanted to reach out and drag my fingers over your skin." He trailed his fingers down her stomach to the band of her jeans and back up, taking the fabric higher each time.

"That was ages ago." Her breath caught as his fingers reached the band of her bra.

He pushed the fabric over the swell of her breasts before running an inquisitive finger along the edge of the lace fabric on her bra. Her chest rose and fell with shallow breaths. "Cleo, I've wanted my hands on you since the moment your shiny, pink vibrator landed at my feet."

"You h-h-have?" Her voice stuttered as he slid the cup of her bra aside. Jesus fucking Christ she was perfect. He blew on her already hard nipple.

"Mmmhmm." His tongue darted out and teased her nipple. Her back arched; he took the opportunity to slide his hand behind her. After struggling one-handed with her bra, he swore under his breath and she reached around to help, giggling.

If nothing else, his incompetence had made her laugh. She

sat up as he dragged her shirt over her head and pulled the straps down her arms, discarding the clothes on the floor over the edge of the bed.

Perfect. She was completely perfect. He cupped her breast and squeezed, running his thumb over its peak. A moan escaped her. How was she so clueless about how beautiful she was?

How was she so clueless about how beautiful she was? He'd just have to show her. He needed her to see herself the way he saw her. He rolled over on top of her, thighs on either side of hers. Kissing her neck, he nipped at her skin, dotting soft kisses as he trailed his tongue down her collar bone, along the curve of her breast, and her nipple. He continued across her chest, and repeated for the other side before moving down her stomach.

He unbuttoned her jeans, tugging them along with her underwear. She covered his hand, forcing him to pause for a beat. "Please, Cleo." Relenting, he continued his journey further down her body. Her skin was creamy and smooth, and when he got to her ankle he changed to her other leg, kissing his way back up. He pressed her knees apart. She wrapped her arms around her middle and his body stilled. Dragging his tongue along the inside of her thigh he reached up with both hands, slid his hands into hers, and locked their fingers together. He moved her arms to her sides, giving her palms what he hoped was a reassuring squeeze.

Nudging her thighs further apart with his chin, he inched closer to her glistening pussy. He let go of one of her hands and dragged a lazy thumb to brush over her clit as he slid two fingers inside of her, curling them forward to her g-spot. She half-stifled a moan with her hand. Spurred on, he pumped his fingers twice before spreading her lips wide and blowing on her clit.

At the cool air hitting her sensitive bundle of nerves she

gasped. "You don't have to…" She had let go of him and was leaning up on her elbow, cupping his head and tugging at his hair.

Sliding his hand onto her stomach, he pushed her back onto the bed before covering her clit with his tongue. He hummed in satisfaction, enjoying the shiver that rippled through her body in response. Sliding his fingers in to massage her g-spot, he worked his tongue and his fingers in tandem, relishing every single gasp and pant and moan that escaped her. Her fingers threaded through his hair, gripping at his head.

As she got closer to her orgasm, her thighs clenched and twitched against his shoulders. Her breaths came in short, gasping pants as his tongue swirled her clit.

Come on, Cleo. Let go.

Her muscles tensed before a scream broke from her chest as she came. "¡Dios mio! *Fuck*!"

"I hope that's a good thing?"

She giggled as he kissed his way up her body, pausing over her. Her cheeks were rosy, and her eyes heavy. She nodded, kissing him, pulling him against her. She hooked an ankle behind his calf and raised her hips against his erection.

"I don't have protection." Frustration coated his gruff voice.

She kissed him. "Molly." She kissed him again. "Does." Her teeth nipped his jaw between kisses. "Bathroom cabinet." She moved to get up, but he stopped her.

"I got it. No one's home?"

She shook her head. Her gaze burned into his ass with every step he took. She hadn't moved an inch when he returned. Her mussed-up hair cascaded over the blanket, her lips were puffy, and her eyes on fire with lust and want. Legs spread and ready for him, Linc wasted no time in tearing the foil wrapper and sheathing himself before climbing onto the bed, pausing to drag his tongue over her clit one last time before lining himself up with her entrance.

Her nails dug into his ass cheeks, pressing him against her as her hips arched to meet his. He kissed her neck, enjoying the tiny moan she gave. "Are we a little impatient, Cleo?" He slid his cock through her wetness and she shivered beneath him.

"Please, Lincoln..."

"Why Miss Bennet, all you had to do was ask." He inched into her. Pausing in an attempt to compose himself so he didn't disappoint both of them, he sucked in a shaky breath. She clenched her muscles around him when she'd taken his length.

"Fuck."

She clenched again.

"Shit, Cleo, you're going to make me embarrass myself if you keep doing that." He slipped all the way out and back in again, his breath stuttering at how well they fit together.

She tightened her grip around his shoulders and their hips found a slow and languid rhythm. He'd never been so aware of the woman in his arms. Every sigh and muscle twitch, the sweet scent of her hair, the softness of her skin, how her hips tilted just so to meet his, how snugly he fit inside her, and how their sweat-slicked bodies molded into each other.

Slipping a hand between them, he circled her clit with the pad of his thumb. Her teeth scraped across his shoulder as she tightened around him. His pulse thundered as salty sweat trickled down his forehead.

"Don't stop. Close." Her plea made him only more intent on getting her to come first. He kissed her, driving deep inside of her, and circling the tight bundle of nerves causing her to tremble beneath him. He swallowed her scream with a kiss as she came apart in his arms. She gripped him like a vise, twitching around his cock as she climaxed. He couldn't fight his own release building and came with a deep grunt and her name on his lips.

He collapsed next to her in a tangle of sweaty limbs and satisfaction. Dotting kisses along her jawline, he sighed as his muscles sagged with tiredness laced contentment. He peeled himself from her, removing the condom, and tying it off. "I'll be right back."

She nodded, but didn't move.

"Unless you'd rather I left?"

"Stay."

He smiled at her sleepy lack of inhibition. When he returned from the bathroom she'd made her way under the covers and turned back a corner so he could join her. She hadn't put clothes on, but she'd scooted as far away as she could. He slipped into the bed, pulled the cover over himself and extended an arm toward her. "Are you not a snuggler?"

"I can snuggle."

"Then why's your ass glued to the wall? Get up in here." He patted his chest and she obliged with a smile that made her tired eyes sparkle.

"You don't have to stay, you know."

"And you, Miss Cleo, don't have to keep telling me all the things I don't have to do. I'm not here because I have to be, I'm here because I want to be. And when you wake up in the morning and find my naked ass in your bed, please don't freak out. It's what people in relationships do." He smothered a yawn with the back of his hand.

"Is Lincoln Scott asking me out?"

"If we're being honest, he's more asking if he can eat you out than take you out, but he'd happily do both. Every day."

She tipped her head back, gawping at him open-mouthed. "You have a filthy mouth on you, Mr. Scott." She pursed her lips, eyes narrowing. "I think I like it."

"You only think you like it? Shit, I'll have to try harder

next time." He kissed her forehead before she settled against his chest. There was no way in hell they'd wake up curled up together like something out of a movie, but he'd be lying if he didn't admit to how right everything felt to finally have her in his arms.

Cleo Martinez.

Eliza Bennet.

One and the same.

Regret tugged in his chest. He could have been with her weeks ago had he been brave enough to let her see who he was.

Her chest rose and fell, slow and even. His fingers itched to draw her as she slept. Her creamy, flawless skin, her kissable lips, those perfect, almond shaped eyes and a button nose. Little did she know, he had an art pad full of sketches of her. He brushed his nose into her hair, inhaling the sweet scent of her shampoo. He could definitely get used to this, but could she?

CHAPTER 18
Cleo

"You're telling me Lincoln Scott is asleep in your bed right now?" Molly poured a cup of coffee and offered the carafe to their roommate Kasia, who hugged an empty mug with both hands and nodded.

"He *was* asleep in my bed, yes. But since you have a voice like a fucking foghorn, he'll be joining us momentarily."

Molly scrunched up her face. "Blah, blah, blah. So." She dropped her voice. "Tell. Me. Everything."

"That's my cue to leave." Kasia grabbed a pancake from the stack.

"You don't wanna hear all about Cleo's romp in the sack with the God on skates? Your loss."

Kasia rolled her eyes with a shake of her head, shoved the pancake in her mouth, and left.

Molly turned back to Cleo. "Again I say... tell. Me. *Everything*. But don't stop the pancake production to do so." She winked and took a huge bite before gesturing at Cleo to continue.

Cleo's face burned hotter under her friend's questioning

than from drizzling batter into a hot pan. She kept her back to Molly as she flipped another pancake.

"I haven't heard many rumors about Linc in the sack, or anywhere else, really. He's got the goods on the ice, and it seems he doesn't get around much. Keeps both his nose and his dick clean, I guess. What's he like? Other than STD free I'm assuming?" She leaned forward, chin on the palms of her hands, elbows planted on the table. "At least tell me... is he good in bed?"

"I'd love to hear the answer to that." Lincoln was standing in the doorway, a grin teasing at his lips, and his fingers gripping the frame over his head. He'd borrowed a pair of her pajama pants which were about a foot too short in the leg and hung low on his hips, the band of his boxers from the night before peeking over the top of the pants.

Good Lord, that was one delicious Adonis belt. And what was it about men with bare feet that turned women to a molten pile of want?

"You went through my drawers?" She slid a pancake onto the pile and returned the pan to the stove.

"Not quite. Pile of laundry on top of your chest of drawers. But let's not change the subject. Molly asked you a question, Ms. Martinez." He crossed the room and placed his hands on her hips as she poured some batter onto the hot pan. He kissed her cheek and spoke into her ear. "Aren't you going to tell your friend how I rated in bed?"

"I hate you both." She flipped the pancake and turned to face him.

He leaned down, covering her mouth with his and gave her a gentle kiss. "Good morning to you, too."

Molly giggled. "Gag. You're gonna make me puke my breakfast before I even eat it. That's how vomiticious you two are. It's oddly... intimate for two people who just hooked up." She tapped her empty fork on her chin. Her eyes brightened and her eyebrows jerked as though she'd clicked a piece of a puzzle together. Jabbing her fork in Linc's direction she shrieked. "Is he… are you…?" She didn't complete her question, but Cleo could all but see the cogs turning.

Linc didn't answer the half asked question, but his cheeks darkened.

"He is, isn't he?"

"You realize you haven't actually asked a question yet, right?"

"Cho-Cho so help me, I will stab you with this fork if you keep dancing around the point."

"He's the guy you've been texting?"

Cleo rolled her lips between her teeth and nodded, willing Molly not to make a scene. Mercifully she didn't, mostly because her mouth was hanging open. "Well. That's going to need unpacking later. But for now, fend for yourself in this house, Linc. Coffee's in the pot, juice is pre-poured over there on the counter, and if you're a tea weirdo like Cho-Cho, there's hot water in the kettle. Pancakes, bananas, bacon, whatever your jock-heart desires. And I'm with Linc." She turned toward Cleo, raising her voice. "I think you should answer my question. It's my duty as a best friend to make sure he performed to satisfactory levels."

Cleo swallowed a mouthful of tea on a snort, glad it didn't squirt out her nose. She glanced between her best friend, and the God among men whose tongue had ravaged her clit, before quirking an eyebrow. "Satisfactory." She folded her arms.

Molly's braying laugh and Lincoln's indignant "What the fuck?" made Cleo giggle so hard she could hardly breathe. "Okay, fine. Cuddly. He was cuddly in bed. Happy now?"

Molly stabbed a piece of pancake with her fork and flapped it at her friend. "This isn't over."

"I like to cuddle." Linc shrugged, picking up a plate,

moving some pancakes onto it from the stack next to Cleo. "I was very disappointed I woke up alone." He lowered his mouth to her ear. "I woke up wanting a very specific something for breakfast."

His quiet voice shot heat straight to her core, she squeezed her thighs together and bit her lip.

"You'll wanna flip that, Lizzy." He gestured at the pan with his elbow and grabbed a glass of orange juice.

Molly let out a dramatic, dreamy sigh, but stayed otherwise silent, watching the exchange with a smirk playing on her lips.

She tossed the pancake, swearing at the burnt underside. "Quit distracting me, Darcy."

"Oh no." Molly waved a piece of bacon between Cleo and Linc. "Please continue distracting her. This is hot as fuck. Totally here for it."

Cleo giggled. Molly was unrelenting, but Linc wasn't fazed, and the fact he'd both borrowed her pajama pants, and walked into the kitchen as though he owned the place somehow drew her to him all the more. He was comfortable in her space.

Linc sat next to Molly at the table, untangling some bacon from the pile on the table in front of him. Molly mouthed "Oh my god" and Cleo nodded, pinching her lips between her teeth again, afraid if she opened her mouth, words might come out. Staring at the hot, shirtless blond guy sitting at her breakfast table like he'd been part of their routine forever, she wasn't sure she had any sensible words.

Throwing a lazy half-smile across the table at her, his heated gaze told her in no uncertain terms he'd rather be eating her for breakfast.

Was it getting hotter? Was it considered rude to fan yourself, to stick your head in the freezer, or disappear for a cold shower because you thought you might spontaneously combust from nothing but a stare?

He smirked as he chewed. "Breakfast is the most important meal of the day, Lizzy. I can recommend the pancakes, they're delicious."

They were doing this, then. Pretending as though it was normal for him to be half naked around her, in her space, and it was not at all as though she might swallow her tongue if her eyes lingered on his six pack for one more second.

Cool. She could do that, right?

"Cleo?" Molly was snickering behind the rim of her mug.

"Mmm?"

"I asked what your plans are today. I asked twice in fact. Seems you're a tad distracted, though I can't, for the life of me, imagine by what."

Lincoln turned to Molly and shook his head. "At the risk of getting a black eye, you're very like your brother."

It was Cleo's turn to snicker as she sat, slicing into her fluffy pancakes with a satisfied nod. "She gets that a lot, and as you can see, she loves to hear it."

Molly folded her arms, and a deep-set scowl crept onto her face. "And for a moment there, I was cheering for you, Linc. Why d'ya gotta disrespect me like that?"

Linc's chuckle was warm and melodic. "You are a most individual, badass goddess who doesn't need her brother's stinkin' shadow anyway."

Molly's face softened and a smile ghosted her lips, threatening to overpower her resting bitch face. "That's more like it. I'm back to 'you can keep him'."

"Thanks, Mol. You know I can't function without your approval on every area of my life."

"It's a heavy burden, but someone must carry it."

Lincoln watched the exchange with mirth in his eyes as he

finished his food and reached for a second glass of orange juice. "So what *are* you doing today, Cleo?"

She swallowed a mouthful before answering. "Class, and work at the coffee shop later." She'd gotten the job and was already a few shifts into her training. It wasn't something that stoked a fire in her belly by any means, but it was decent hours, decent pay, and kept the parentals off her back – which was worth every dirty mug and crappy tip.

"So... You have some time before class?"

She was on fire. Molly raised an eyebrow and widened her eyes. The look said 'answer the man, you dumb shit.'

"I do." Cleo's mouth was dry and her tongue heavy. She dropped her fork onto her plate with a shrill clang.

"Then I'll get started on the dishes, so we don't waste any time when you're done eating."

"Next you'll be telling us you cook as well as do dishes, Linc!" Molly finished the last two sips of her orange juice, got up from the table and placed her glass next to the sink. "I'll do the dishes. Y'all go... do... each other."

Lincoln didn't even blush at Molly's words, which probably made her all the more eager to cause him embarrassment. It would come back at some point to bite him in his perfect butt. Cleo stuffed the last forkful of bacon into her mouth, handed her dishes to Molly who gave her an exaggerated wink, and followed Linc back to her room.

He stripped off the pj pants he'd borrowed, along with his boxers, and tossed them aside before climbing back into bed. "Thanks for breakfast, it was delicious."

He expects me to talk about breakfast when he just flashed me his perfect, naked body? Speak. He's doing that smiling like he knows what you're thinking thing.

"Any time."

"I wasn't kidding though. I wanted you for breakfast."

She had no idea how he could speak like that without

dying from embarrassment. Telling her what he wanted without stuttering or his face going on fire was both impressive and attractive. Could she be that comfortable and confident some day?

"Lizzy?" Lincoln had rolled onto his side, facing her, head propped up on his elbow. "You gonna stand there all day?"

She took two steps toward the bed.

"...Or can I convince you to come sit on my face?"

Her jaw dropped open. Did he just...? He couldn't possibly mean...

"Okay, wait, woah. Whatever horse left the stable in your brain right now, can we lasso it back? What are you thinking?"

"I'd suffocate you!" Her hand fluttered to cover her burning face as she groaned.

Mortified. She mentally willed Molly to trigger the fire alarm so she could escape the humiliation smothering her in the room.

When she dared to peek, he was in front of her, reaching out to stroke her face.

"You won't." His voice was as calm as his features and showed no trace of humor. He wasn't mocking her. Did he really think she could sit on his face and he wouldn't die? Surely, not.

She leaned into the warmth of his palm cupping her face, and sighed.

"If you really don't want to try it, or don't like it, that's okay. But if it's something you enjoy, or haven't ever tried and would like to, I'm not going to accept 'I'll suffocate you' as an excuse not to give it a go."

She blinked. Who was this guy? Did they come more perfect? Sure he chewed a little loudly, but that couldn't be the end of his annoyances, right?

Maybe he had ugly feet and she hadn't noticed, what with all the ab-staring she was doing. Maybe he smelled bad...

except he absolutely did not smell bad. He had to have something *wrong* with him, didn't he?

Maybe this was simply the honeymoon period, she was a novelty to him. She'd been a secret kept from him for so long, that him knowing Elizabeth and Cleo were one and the same was new and fun. It would wear off. There was no way he could be this... interested, all the time... right?

"Let me put it another way. Did you like it when you came on my face last night?"

Good Lord, this man would be the death of her. She nodded.

"Would you like for me to do it again?"

She nodded again. How flames weren't bursting from her cheeks she had no idea.

"Do you want to try it standing up before you sit on my face? Like, leg over my shoulder?"

"Why are you so intent on doing this?"

"Little known secret, some guys fucking love going down on their girl. I happen to be one of them. I had you last night and it wasn't enough, and while I'll be disappointed if you don't wanna grind on my tongue, it's absolutely your choice."

She was soaking wet. He was talking right to her clit and it wasn't listening that she could suffocate the man. It just wanted his tongue.

Why was she second guessing this? He was confident he wouldn't die and the heat pooled between her thighs reminded her she was aching to come again...

"Okay."

His answer was silence and a wolfish grin before he slid his hand behind her neck and pulled her in for a deep kiss. He ran his free hand over her shirt, and her nipple strained against the material. She shuddered. He trailed down the curve of her hip and ran two fingers along the inside of the band of her pajama pants. Her breath hitched as he cupped her crotch.

"So wet." He ground the heel of his hand against her sending vibrations of pleasure rippling through her body. She shifted her weight from side to side, hoping the friction would be enough to send her pants to the floor, leaving nothing between his hand and her aching core.

No such luck.

She pressed against him, deepening their kiss. Her heart raced. Not long ago the idea of kissing Lincoln Scott had been terrifying, but with their lips locked, and tongues crashing together, she never wanted to stop.

He slid his thumbs into the band of her pants and tugged. When they hit the floor, she stepped out of them, kicking them toward Linc's discarded clothes. Scrunching her eyes closed she willed the voice in her head to stop. He thought she was beautiful. He wanted this. And the needy ache radiating from her core was driving her to desperation at the memory of his tongue.

He grabbed her hand and pulled her toward him, sitting on the bed when his knees hit the edge of the mattress. Scooting back fully onto the bed, he tugged her arm. Taking a slow, shaky breath she pressed down her self-consciousness, and climbed on top, straddling his waist.

He cupped her ass with both palms and slid her toward his face, causing her to lose her balance. A nervous giggle-shriek exploded from her as she leaned forward, bracing her hands on the headboard to right herself.

"Are you sure?"

"You're killing me, Lizzy. Let. Me. Taste. You."

What would Molly say? 'Mount that fucking tongue and stop keepin' that boy waiting!'

She shifted so her center was lined up with his mouth. Firm hands grabbed her hips and brought her down onto his face with a jerk. Her nerve endings exploded like fireworks on the fourth of July as his tongue met her clit. "Fuck!"

"Mmmmmmm, you taste so fucking good, Cleo."

His eyes showed nothing but glee as he lapped at her clit between her legs. Her fingers curled around the edges of the headboard as she fought the urge to ride his face. Waves of pleasure crashed into her as her knuckles turned white.

He paused. "Stop. Holding. Back."

"Fuck." She let go of the headboard, scratching his scalp as she sank her fingers into his hair. His growl of satisfaction vibrated deep in her core as her eyes rolled back in her head. She moved her hips, slowly at first, but the hum of approval from between her legs soon had her grinding her clit against his hungry tongue, chasing her fast-approaching ecstasy. She screamed, and her thighs tightened around his face as her hips bucked with wave after wave of blissful release.

Muscles pulsating, limbs shaking, and damp with sweat, she crumpled into a heap next to him, slinging an arm across her forehead. "Fuck."

He licked his lips, reached across to pluck two Kleenexes from the bedside table, and wiped up her wetness trickling down his chin.

"Let me help." She took the tissues and wiped his glistening chin. Dotting a kiss on his cheek, she finished, then threw the tissues into the garbage can next to the bed.

She flopped onto the bed and let her head lol onto his chest which rose and fell with a contented sigh. "Anyone would think it was you that screamed the house down."

His arm tightened around her waist, drawing her closer. "I'm just glad you got out of your own head and gave in. I know the physical thing is new, but we've been talking for a while. We've done the hardest part of getting to know each other; the sexy times are the easy part. And since you're not fighting it anymore, you can admit we've always had chemistry." He kissed the top of her head.

He was right. There'd been a spark from the moment her

vibrator landed at his feet and she's squashed it down assuming she never had a chance. The clock told her it was almost time to leave for class, but her chest tightened at the thought.

In her room they were in their bubble of bliss. Out there she was reminded that her mom would flip her shit if she found out about the delicious hockey player she was spending time with. Out there, would he pretend he didn't know her? Would they hide their relationship from the world? Or worse still, people would find out and wonder what the hell a guy like him was doing with a girl like her.

CHAPTER 19

Lincoln

"Finally got the girl, eh?" Russ handed Jude a plastic, pink, princess cup, and turned to Lincoln. His friend being ordered around by a tiny, two-year-old spitfire was one of the highlights of Linc's day. She kept handing him little toy cups and plates demanding he eat and drink her imaginary offerings.

Did he have her? He wasn't sure. He wanted her, but she'd been keeping her distance since the morning she sat on his face. Unless she was a Hollywood actress, it couldn't have been because he sucked in bed. Right? An unfamiliar feeling of uncertainty and self-consciousness seized his chest.

"I dunno about 'got.' She acted like she didn't know me in class yesterday afternoon. We spent the whole morning in bed, but in English class she arrived at the last minute and bolted as soon as class was done. It's like she doesn't want to be seen with me."

"Or..." Russ raised a hand. "And just hang in there with me for a moment. Maybe it's not about you. Maybe she doesn't want you to be seen with her."

"Huh?" Linc folded his arms and leaned against the doorframe. "Wait, what do you mean it's not about me? Isn't everything about me?"

"Stop deflecting with humor, asshole—"

The little girl dropped her plastic plate and wagged a finger. "Daddy! Daddy naughty!" Her face twisted in a deep and angry scowl.

"Sorry princess. Daddy's sorry for saying a naughty word." He rolled his eyes at Linc who stifled a chuckle behind his fist. "It's time to be real – you said she's self-conscious, right? Not overly comfortable with her size? So maybe she's trying to 'save' you from being seen with her by the skinnier, more popular girls that tend to gravitate toward jocks. Maybe *she* thinks *you* don't want to be seen with her, and she's making it easier for you by giving you space in public."

"Damn. When did you get so smart?"

"I've always been smart. I hide it under tiaras and super-hero costumes."

"Unca Lin!" Jude's held out a purple teacup on a mint green saucer. "Eat!"

"You mean drink." He smiled and stepped forward to accept the offering but she snatched it away with a giggle at the last second. Her ice blue eyes twinkled with mischief behind her dark curls. Linc had never known the child's mother, but she was every bit of Russ to look at.

"Scamp!" Linc ruffled her hair, and she giggled again. "Maybe you're right, R. Maybe Cleo thinks I'm ashamed to be seen with her or something, and she's preempting that by flee-ing. I mean based on the *one* class we had together yesterday, I think you might be onto something."

"You know what you gotta do, right?"

Linc groaned, throwing a palm over his face.

"You gotta Lloyd Dobler that chick." At what must have been Linc's confused face, Russell continued. "Oh man, we gotta watch *Say Anything*. You really have no idea what I'm talking about? Iconic grand gesture. Dude, a boombox blasting some Peter Gabriel... You'll prove your point in no time."

"Cleo isn't a grand gesture kinda gal. I think if I did that, she'd not only plot my murder, but she'd go right out and kill me. Are you trying to get me dead, man?"

Russ chuckled and handed his cup back to Jude who pretended to refill it. "Then what *are* you going to do?"

Shrugging, Linc slid onto the floor to work out some tension in his muscles with some stretches. Maybe he could work out the tension in his brain at the same time.

"You have class again this afternoon, don't you?"

"Yeah, maybe I need to take her on a real date. She'll see I'm not afraid of who sees us together and hopefully that'll help."

"Sounds like a plan. Where are you going to take her?"

"Dude, I've done the hard work of realizing I need to take her on a date. Don't tell me I gotta work out where we're going, too?"

Russ rolled his eyes. "'Fraid so, bro!"

Groaning, Linc slumped onto his back. "Fuck."

Linc walked into class with butterflies warring in his stomach. Nerves weren't something he often suffered with, but when it came to Cleo, everything was different. What if Russ was wrong and she didn't want to be seen in public with him?

As he approached her in the classroom, her neutral face shifted to a scowl. "Lose your way, Lincoln?" Her voice might have been cool, but there was fire in her eyes.

"Not at all, Cleo. I don't think a guy can be blamed for wanting to sit next to his girlfriend." Ignoring a small gasp a few rows back, he slipped into the seat next to Cleo, leaned over and pecked her cheek, hovering for just a moment longer than he needed to. "Let me take you out." He kept his voice low.

"People will see."

"I don't care who sees. Are you ashamed of being seen with me?"

Something he couldn't identify flashed in her hazel eyes. "What? No. Of course not. I just—"

"Then you have no reason to say no to a date. A real, in person date."

She opened her mouth to protest, but he covered her lips with his index finger, and gestured to the teacher clearing her throat to begin the lesson. "You can argue with me later, Lizzy, but for right now, learn all the things."

A smile teased her lips as she turned her attention to the teacher.

He spent the entire class fighting the urge to reach out and touch her. He wanted to tuck the stray lock of hair behind her ear and run his finger along her neck and collarbone.

He had no idea what the teacher said, he was too busy being bewitched by the beautiful woman sitting next to him. Her brow furrowed in concentration as she chewed on the end of her pen, and he'd never known anyone to have such perfectly organized, color coordinated notes, and index cards.

Once.

She looked at him once throughout the entire class, and her pale cheeks flamed when she caught him staring.

Not that he was trying to hide it. Now he was sure she liked him too, he didn't give a shit who caught him looking at her.

Shifting in his seat, he tugged his pants away from his hardening dick. His fingers twitched and he curled them into his palm. He wanted to reach out and touch her, to drag his lips and tongue across her skin. He'd had his fair share of lovers, but none of them had ignited the primal need to have his hands on them like Cleo did.

Was she indifferent to him?

Did she have the same pulsing desperation thrumming through her core that kept his dick impossibly hard? How was she able to concentrate on their class while he was in such close proximity?

She drove him crazy. If she agreed to let him fuck her where she sat, he'd already be balls deep inside her and wouldn't give a shit who watched.

The bell rang signaling the end of class. "Could you be any more obvious?" Her piercing eyes pinned him as she turned to face him.

He shoved his books into his bag. "I don't know what you're talking about."

"You burned a hole in the side of my head that whole class, Lincoln." She tucked her belongings into her backpack before standing and wagging a finger at him. "How do you expect me to concentrate on... well... anything? When all I wanted was..." She cleared her throat and slung the bag onto her shoulder.

Maybe she did feel some of what he'd felt. He tipped her chin so their eyes met. "When all you wanted was what, Miss Bennet?"

The side of her bottom lip disappeared between her teeth, and she shook her head, checking over her shoulder to see who else was lingering in the hall. "No. I'm not... nuh uh." She turned away.

He slid her bag from her shoulder and pulled her back a half-step, so her body was flush against his, pressing his erection against her ass. She relaxed against him on a soft "Oh."

"Please tell me I'm not suffering alone here, Lizzy." His voice was rough and so thick with desperation, he was almost embarrassed, but the throbbing in his pants gave him no choice but to be honest.

It wouldn't take much for him to blow his load right there, and part of him was even tempted to dry hump her just to get some relief.

She shook her head. "Definitely not suffering alone." Her ass cheeks clenched against him. "But we're also not doing anything about it here and now."

"Dinner?"

"Dinner. What should I wear?"

"Jeans and flats, or yoga pants and flats, whatever's more comfortable."

She spun to face him, brow pinched with confusion. "Where are we going?"

"Dave and Busters."

"What made you pick here for our first date?" Cleo sipped her Coke Zero and regarded him in the dim light. They sat in a booth, her body tucked against him as his arm stretched out along the back of the seat.

"You don't strike me as someone who lets herself have a lot of fun, Cleo. I figured this would be fun for both of us."

"That's it?"

"That... and the fact I know you're competitive as fuck and will play 'cause you want to win. Aaaand their mac and cheese – I really like the mac and cheese here."

Her melodic laugh vibrated against his side. "How do you know I'm competitive as fuck?"

It was his turn to chuckle. "Other than the look on your face when we were put onto a group project together? That 'this dumbass jock is gonna tank my score and I might get a 95 instead of a 99' look? Oh, I dunno... lucky guess?"

The server brought their spinach dip and napkins, and Cleo thanked her before taking a bite. Her eyes rolled back and a sinful moan escaped her. "This... damn. So good. I love spinach dip."

"Tell me I'm wrong, Miss Bennet. Tell me you're not competitive."

She waved a chip in his direction. "Why do you keep calling me Lizzy, and Miss Bennet? We know who we are now – we don't need to use those names anymore."

"I can't help it. I used Lizzy for so long and it's kind of adorable, so it just slips out I guess? Do you hate it? I can try to stop my mouth from saying it if you'd rather?"

She swallowed her mouthful of food and shook her head. "No, I just... I mean I like it, I just... I don't think I've ever had anyone other than Molly call me a pet name before. Cleo's a pretty short and sweet name..."

"It's how we started. It's something that's 'just us,' y'know? I like how it makes your cheeks go pink." He stroked his thumb across the apple of her cheek. Leaning closer to nip at her ear lobe, he enjoyed the small shiver that rippled through her. "Are you a competitive person, Lizzy?" He kissed her neck just below her ear.

She licked her lips, nodding, and wiped her fingers on the napkin draped over her thigh before jabbing a finger into his chest. "Yeah, I am. And I can't wait to kick your ass."

CHAPTER 20

Cleo

Cleo dipped the scrunched up napkin into the iced water and dabbed it on the buffalo sauce on Linc's shirt. He chuckled, eyes lighting up with amusement. "You know this is it now, right?"

She frowned. "What is?"

"This happens at every meal. Without fail, something lands on my shirt. If you start mopping me up now, you're going to have to do it forever."

Forever.

Her heart juddered. Did he just say forever?

He barely knew her. He had to be joking but she couldn't bring herself to meet his stare and find out. She hadn't ever given much thought to being with someone *forever*.

School preoccupied most of her thoughts, and when she allowed herself to daydream about the future she was always alone. Sure, she had the same binder of wedding designs that every other little girl dreamed of, but she hadn't pictured *the* guy standing next to her.

Surprisingly, the idea of a long-term thing with Linc didn't traumatize her.

"Forever's a very long time, Lincoln. Let's try getting through this semester first, yeah?"

His smile was genuine and warm. "Sure, but I can already tell you, a semester won't be enough."

The wet napkin rested on her thigh, seeping through the fabric. "Awfully deep conversation for a first date, wouldn't you say, Mr. Darcy?"

A server came to clear plates and presented Linc with the check. She fought to pay her way but he didn't relent. "I guess I don't feel like this is a first date, Miss Bennet. We've been talking for a while now. We've had virtual dates. I know you. I know I want to be with you."

The server took the check away, leaving them to finish their drinks. She pulled a leg up on the bench of the booth and tucked her left foot against her right thigh, creating space between them as though it would help her think straight. She wasn't usually one to be affected by proximity to a boy, but heat crept across her chest and up her neck and she was suddenly parched.

"What do you know about me?"

"I know you're a Sagittarius, birthday's November 24th. Favorite color: red. Favorite food: caldo del res. Favorite drink: tea. Favorite snack: Sour Patch Kids. You're right handed and have a very peculiar obsession with stationery. You have the biggest collection of notebooks, a bunch of that tape stuff..." He clicked his fingers and scrunched his face up.

"Washi tape?"

"Yes! You have more washi tape and journals and planners and pens than I've ever seen. Like there could be a stationery apocalypse someday and you might need to provide the entire universe with supplies lest they perish. But they are 'too good to use' so you just stare at them with lust in your eyes rather than cracking one open to write in it." He picked up her hand and laced their fingers together.

"You love cats, not dogs, you like to cook, but can't bake for shit. *Pride and Prejudice* is your favorite book. There's only *one* Mr. Darcy – on pain of death – and it's Colin Firth. You secretly love romantic fantasy books and your favorite author is Clare Sager. I can see why. Vice is a badass. I know you write stories that you think suck. Your mom is a history professor at the U, your dad's a dentist, and you're an only child. You told me once you're an enneagram one-wing-two, but I have no idea what that is, only that enneagram is a hard word to say, so you better be giving me bonus points for that shit."

Her brain raced as quickly as her thumping heart, trying to process everything he'd said. Warmth spread through her as she held up a hand. "Wait... you... read *Vice?*"

He opened his mouth, sucked in a dramatic deep breath after talking so fast, snapped it shut, and nodded. "Was I not supposed to? I got curious. You're so..."

She steeled her spine and clenched her teeth, readying herself for whatever derogatory thing was about to come out of his mouth.

"Serious? Guarded? When you said you read romantic fantasy it piqued my interest. What could draw this mysterious and scholastic woman out of her thoughts and into a realm of magic and fae? I wasn't at all surprised to find the kick-ass pirate queen. Though let's be honest, Barnacle is totes my favorite character."

Her breathing returned to normal. "I feel like I'm being punked right now."

"I *know* things about you Lizzy, and I know you. What's more, you not only *know* that I know you, but you know me too."

"That's a lot of knowing."

"My point exactly."

Damnit. She'd walked right into that one. The obnoxious roar of gamers in the arcade interrupted the moment.

"Come play games with me, I'll kick your ass, then we'll blow all our tokens on something outrageous and gaudy in the store and I'll give you a ride home like a proper gentleman."

She arched an eyebrow and pursed her lips. "Are you goading me into a competition, Mr. Darcy?"

"Why Miss Bennet, I would never." He extended his hand to help her from the booth and offered his elbow. She slipped her arm through and they walked through the corridor leading to the games area.

Linc charged up their power cards with twenty bucks a piece while Cleo turned in a slow circle taking everything in. There was no overhead light source, but vibrant lights flashed from every direction. Kids and adults alike giggled, playing games and taunting and shoving each other in playful competition.

"Anything catch your eye?"

"Is that... Whack-A-Mole?"

His mouth twisted, as though fighting a grin. "You like Whack-A-Mole?"

"Betchurass I do, jock-boy. I wasn't raised in a cave, you know. I have a pretty good Whack-A-Mole game." She brushed her shoulder off twice with a flat hand.

He chuckled and shook his head. "Prove it."

She rolled her neck and shoulders as they walked to the game. Flexing her fingers she nodded at him to swipe the card to put credit on the machine and picked up the mallet.

Excitement bubbled in her stomach. She hadn't played Whack-A-Mole in a decade, at least, but that rush of anticipation and nervous energy crashed into her as soon as the first mole poked his head up from his hidey hole.

With the clock taunting her, counting down the seconds,

moles popping up and down, and Lincoln's eyes on her, she swung the hammer again and again.

A short time later, she tore the tokens from the machine and crammed them into her paper cup. "Thirty three, not bad."

"You're a machine, Cleo Martinez. How did you get thirty three?"

"Told you, I gots wicked Whack-A-Mole skills." She laughed, throwing a nonchalant shrug for good measure. "You wanna go for a third time, don't you? I can see the need to beat me written all over your face."

She grabbed his arm. "C'mon, Lincoln. Let's go find something athletic for you to kick my ass at."

He won at Skeeball and shooting hoops. They kicked ass in the four-player Mario Kart against two strangers. And they tied in air hockey – a game apiece – much to Lincoln's chagrin.

Gold Fishin' was a favorite. It had about fifty tiny glass 'fish bowls' lit in pink, purple and yellow, and they had to throw small rubber balls into the bowls. As much as she enjoyed the game itself, hearing Linc grumble and grouse at how much he sucked at something tickled her. They saved Pac-Man and the slot machines until last.

"Oh man, look at that."

"At what?" Cleo turned but there was nothing behind her.

"Your cup of tickets."

"What about it?" She tipped it so he could look inside.

"Our cups say everything anyone needs to know about our personalities, Cleo. Yours are all neatly folded and tidy, enclosed within the cup. Mine's crammed in any old way, bits sticking out everywhere, and I keep losing containment."

She giggled. "Do you need me to help save you from the explosion of tokens?"

Linc curled his arm around his cup, as if to protect it from her. "I'm good with my messy self, thanks. Hey, you wanna put all these tokens onto one card and save them for next time? Then we can get something bigger or two somethings so we can each have one."

"Wow, you've done some wicked token math haven't you? What do you have your eye on?"

"I dunno, maybe an oversized stuffy for you to cuddle at night when you're desperately missing me? Matching Dave and Busters hoodies? Maybe I just want a hundred Nerd ropes?"

"Dang. How's a girl to compete with the allure of a hundred Nerd ropes?" She handed him her cup of tokens.

He gave both cups, and one of the power cards to the woman at the checkout. "All on one card is fine, thanks."

When the woman had weighed their tokens and loaded them onto the card, he handed it to Cleo.

A flicker of hope stirred in her chest. "Giving me the power of the Nerd rope? Wow. You seem awfully confident we'll last, Mr. Darcy."

"You have bewitched me body and soul, Miss Bennet. Body and soul."

"He quoted *Pride and Prejudice* at you?" Molly swooned, the back of her hand over her forehead, collapsing onto the couch. "And he dropped you off at the door? No sexy times? Just a chaste kiss? Who the fuck is this guy? And why didn't you grab him by the shirt and haul his ass up to bed?"

Cleo groaned against her forearm on the table. "I know. I have regrets. I'd say my vagina is weeping but that just sounds gross. Do you know how hard it is to ride that damn bike pressed up against his... his..."

"Everything?"

"Yes! Fuck! It's awful."

"And yet you sent him home."

"Ah, ah, ah. I did no such thing." Cleo lifted her head and wagged a finger at her friend. "I just didn't jump his bones at the door when he dropped me off."

"Booty call."

Cleo cringed, though her lady parts were in full agreement with Molly. She pressed her thighs together. "I am not booty calling Lincoln Scott."

"Right, you're not. You're booty calling your boyfriend. That's kind of their job."

"I don't think that word means what you think it means."

"This isn't about me, Miss Cleo. This is about you. And if you don't booty call that boy you're going to need to take some batteries with you to bed for BOB. I mean, that's an option. Just grab one of those pirate romance novels you love and use that for inspiration."

"Excuse me?" Cleo's face heated.

"Oh, dial back the outrage. I'm on to you, girl. Thar be smut in those pages, arrrr!" Molly held a hand over her eye.

"You make such a sexy pirate, Mol."

"Don't I though?" She pointed an accusing finger at Cleo. "Don't change the subject. I was tidying up the kitchen the other day and found one of your books lying open so I took a look. What kind of monster leaves the characters mid-romp? I rescued them, I read a few pages until they got past their orgasms, so they're feeling better now. But girl..."

She fanned her face. "That. Shit. Is. HOT. I thought you were reading like... Lord of the Rings, or some kind of adventure fantasy stuff... that... well, that's certainly an adventure. I need to find a Knigh of my very own so he can do to my pearl what that Knigh does to Vice's." She gave Cleo an exaggerated wink. "Know what I mean?"

Cleo held up both hands in surrender, her already burning cheeks getting hotter. Why was Molly so comfortable with all this *stuff*? A better question was probably, why was Cleo so *un*comfortable with it all. "Please stop talking about your pearl."

"Only if you call Linc to come play with yours."

"Oh God." Cleo dropped her head onto the table with a thump when her phone chimed.

Lincoln: Just home. Hopefully a real life, in the flesh date wasn't as bad as you expected it to be.

Molly stood a few feet away, hands on hips and an eyebrow arched in challenge. "If you don't message that boy, I will."

Cleo: So, on a scale of one-to-pissed where would you fall if I asked you to come back?

Lincoln: What's wrong? Are you okay?

Cleo: Yes! Sorry. Please don't worry, I'm fine.

Lincoln: I'm on my way.

Cleo: I feel bad asking.

Lincoln: Fifteen.

The doorbell chimed twelve minutes later. She pulled the door open to an ashen Lincoln, who charged forward to wrap his arms around her. "Are you okay? What's wrong? Are you sick? Please don't tell me you got sick from my favorite mac and cheese, I'm not sure who I'd choose."

She laughed against his chest. He came for her. Just because she'd asked. And he was worried. She wasn't quite sure how to unpack the emotion swelling in her chest. "It was some pretty good mac and cheese I'll grant you. I can understand the difficulty with your decision."

"What happened?"

"Nothing... I just wasn't ready for our date to be over yet. I shouldn't have let you leave." She kept her head glued to his chest, afraid of what she'd find if she looked at his face.

His grip tightened around her waist and she buried her nose further into his chest, inhaling the scent of his leathers. "Okay, so here's the thing." He slipped a knuckle under her chin and ran his fingers into her hair.

"I don't care if it's that something happens and you need me, you miss me and want to see me, or you miss me and wanna fuck me senseless, I will always be there for you. Always. So please don't hesitate, don't second guess yourself, if you want to see me, just ask and I'll move heaven and earth to make it happen."

"Fuck. Me. Lincoln Scott who knew you were such a fucking romantic?" Molly's voice came from the kitchen. "I can't cope with the swooning. I am glad to hear you're doing right by her though. I just replenished my Duct Tape and sheet plastic supply, so keep it up!"

Lincoln's chest shook with a deep, rumbling chuckle against Cleo's cheek. "Evening, Miss Morrison. I'd love to stay and chat, but your roomie wants to cuddle."

"Yeah, cuddle your dick."

Fuck.

Molly had outed her. How would he react to knowing the real reason she summoned him back to her? Cleo snorted, stepping back from his chest and covering her face with her palm.

He grabbed her hip and tugged her back against him.

"Why, Miss Bennet... Is it possible you called me here for a... a..." He dropped his voice to a hushed stage whisper. "Booty call? Did you call my booty?"

Her thundering heart and aching desire shouted down her sensible brain, robbing her of rational thought. "Oh, God."

"I mean, I'm totally here for it. In fact I'm pretty fucking thrilled. But I can't deny that it's unexpected."

Cleo's face burned, and she couldn't make words come out around the wad of embarrassment crammed into her throat.

He stepped further into the apartment, kicking the door closed behind him. Plucking off his shoes, he tossed them next to the door before pulling his shirt over his head.

Was he stripping off in the shared living space? Did she care? She dragged her bottom lip between her teeth. She'd never get tired of the sight of his toned body. Cleo's eyes widened and she had only a split second to react before bent and hauled her up over his shoulder. "Lincoln!" Her screeching was anything but ladylike. "Put me down! Lincoln!"

She swept hair out of her eyes and lifted her head as he strode through the kitchen where Molly sat eating ramen noodles. She dropped her fork onto the floor and her mouth dropped open. "Fuck, Linc. Are you Photoshopped or some shit?"

"Lincoln!" Cleo spanked his ass. He laughed, but didn't stop. "I'm going to break your fucking spine!"

He burst into Cleo's bedroom and tossed her on the bed.

She bounced on the mattress with a yelp. "Are you crazy?"

He didn't answer. He shoved his jeans onto the floor and crawled up the bed, hovering over her and planting a kiss on her nose. "Please don't worry about me hurting myself, Cleo. Not to get too jock-y on you, but I'm an athlete. I train hard and often and I know my limits. You're not my limit."

Her jaw dropped open once again as her brain short-circuited, and he took the opportunity to kiss her. "Do you want me to get mathy? Will that set your mind at ease? I feel like you're not going to let this go and I have every intention of picking you up again – especially when you hit me up for a booty call. It's hot as hell, Lizzy." He kissed her neck. "But if you want math, I can math."

"Math." She sat up enough to pull her own shirt off and dropped back onto the mattress.

"Kinda looks like you're hot for math here, Cleo. I'll try not to let that go to my dick." He winked at her before dotting kisses down her neck, chest and stomach. Her disloyal libido didn't want to hear the details. She sucked in a breath as sparks of desire fizzed each time his lips met her skin. "I really don't want to talk math with you. Can't you just trust that I know my own body?" He tugged her yoga pants and underwear to her ankles and freed one foot before pushing her knees apart. Her clit throbbed with impatience. "Can't you trust that I know what I'm doing and won't drop you?"

She panted in anticipation. "You're not playing fair, Mr. Darcy. I'm just concerned that you'll get h—" His tongue swept over her clit and she gasped as ripples of pleasure stopped her higher brain function. "Fuck."

"No more talk. Let's get this booty call started!"

CHAPTER 21

Lincoln

"What the fuck are you doing?" Russ leaned over his shoulder. "Are you...? I don't understand what I'm seeing. I feel like Jude should be here for this arts and crafts sesh, Uncle Linc."

"I'm making a bouquet of stationery."

"Okay... but, why?"

He pressed the fake flower onto the end of a pen and held it, praying the hot glue wouldn't stick his finger to the flower, again. "It's hard to explain."

"Try me." He dragged the chair over to the bed, sat down, and kicked off his shoes. "I ain't got nothin' but time." He lifted his feet onto the corner of the mattress, and crossed his legs at the ankles, sliding his palms behind his head.

Linc dropped the flower-topped pen into the Mason jar before grabbing another flower and the hot glue gun. "She has a stationery... thing."

"Like, she collects it?"

"Okay she has two stationery things." He squeezed a blob of glue onto the underside of the flower and pressed it on top of a freshly sharpened number two pencil. "First thing is she collects it. She loves all-things-stationery. Notebooks, pens, pencils, stickers, journals, planners – legit any kind of stationery you can think of, this woman collects it. I say collects because even if she lived to be two hundred and fifty years old, there's literally no way she could use all of this stuff."

Russell held up a finger. "That's one thing. What's the other?"

"She's... uh... protective of it."

Russ pulled his legs off the bed and leaned forward, draping his elbows over his knees. "Protective?"

"Yeah. There is a 'loaner section' of her stash. Stuff mere mortals can touch, versus the stuff that people will die for touching."

Russ chuckled. "Fuck. You have it bad, man. So which is this? Muggle shit, or die-for-touching shit?"

"Both. So the stuff in the Mason jar is common usage and this..." He held up a fountain pen and a small bottle of ink labeled "Writer's Blood." "This one is for the 'touch and die' pile."

Accepting the small bottle, Russ leaned back in his seat and studied the label. "Is it her birthday?"

"Nope."

"Then why?"

"Felt like it?"

Russ reached over and ruffled Linc's hair. "Dude. You're so fucking gone, it's totes adorbs." He pinched his cheek. "Don't worry, I won't tell anyone."

"Honestly, man, I don't give a shit who knows."

"She feels the same?"

Did she feel the same? Had Russ seen something in her behavior to suggest she *didn't* feel the same? "I think so." How the hell did this woman manage to tie him up in knots? He slid another flower-topped pen into the jar with a clink. "I mean, she probably doesn't want her mama to know she's in a relationship with me. I guess the woman is pretty hardcore."

"Professor Martinez? She's Austin's history teacher, isn't she? We could ask him what she's like."

"Let's not. Cleo was a little more 'fast and loose' when we were texting. She keeps things closer to her chest these days, but from what I gather, her parents are quite strict. They have high expectations of her and they don't suffer foolishness or distractions from her goal of graduating valedictorian."

"Is that her goal or theirs?" Russ handed back the bottle of ink and folded his arms. "Sounds like she's under a lot of pressure."

Lincoln tied a ribbon around the neck of the jar and made a poor attempt at a bow.

"Fuck. Give that to me. Let me fix it." Russ made light work of tying a perfect bow.

Linc smirked.

"Don't mock my epic bow-skills, or I won't help you ever again. Is Cleo under a lot of pressure?"

Linc nodded. "Yeah. I try to keep things light and fun."

"Hence Dave and Busters."

"She loved that, man. Her face was like a kid's at Christmas."

"Where have you taken her since? I haven't seen much of you these last weeks. On the ice, in school and off with Cleo, that's your MO."

Linc paused, glue gun in mid-air and narrowed his eyes. Was his friend speaking in subtext? Had he really been gone that much?

"Nope." Russ held up his hand like a stop sign. "This isn't me giving you shit. I'm genuinely happy for you. I just want to catch up. I'm not used to this new in-a-committed-relationship, Lincoln Scott. I miss my wing man, that's all." He gave a small shrug that poked at Linc's heart.

"I'm sorry, man. I guess I have been a bit wrapped up in Cleo these last few weeks."

Russ shook his head. "I get it. It's all shiny and new. I'm not complaining, or being needy – I really am just curious about what you've been up to."

Guilt pooled in Linc's stomach as he continued gluing flowers onto the end of pencils and pens. "We did mini golf, thrift shopping for books, we hit up the art institute again..."

He tapped a fingertip on his chin. "Oh, we went out to Twin Spirits distillery and took a tour. We got her some M gin and some Mamma's Moonshine for you and me. I hid it though, can't have you drinking it all before we have a guys-only night. We went garage sale-ing last Sunday morning."

"How are you fitting it all in? You must be exhausted."

"Not really, it's fun. It's nice to be with someone who knows all my deep and dirty secrets."

"Did you tell her you applied for the art competition?"

"Okay. It's nice to be with someone who knows *almost* all my deep and dirty secrets."

Russ arched a brow and narrowed his gaze.

"Don't look at me like that, Russ. I don't want to get her hopes up, or have her feeling responsible for my disappoint-ment when I don't get picked. This is easier, I'll tell her if anything comes of it, and if not..."

He shrugged. "She doesn't need to know." He slipped the last pencil into the jar and straightened the bow one last time before setting it onto the bedside cabinet. "Done."

Russ opened his mouth, and Linc reached over to cover it with his hand. "Nope."

Russ shirked his palm. "You don't get to cover my mouth just 'cause you don't think you're gonna like what's about to come out of it. That's not how this works."

"I can feel your side-eye energy right now, man. I don't need the words."

"I think you're confusing me with Morrison's sister. No one has side-eye energy like her. It physically burns your skin. Look, I know you don't want to hear it... but for someone who claims to tell Cleo everything... Linc, you need to tell her this too."

Unease churned in his gut. "I don't want to disappoint her."

"But you won't. I get that this new and vulnerable Linc is scary and doesn't quite feel comfortable yet, but she isn't like everyone else and we both know it."

Linc clenched his jaw and stood up, picking the bouquet of stationery up from the table.

"Fleeing the conversation?"

Linc nodded. "Going to drop this off before she gets out of work."

"Linc?"

Lincoln paused, turning his chin to his shoulder.

"You gotta let someone all the way in eventually."

The idea sent a shiver rattling up Linc's spine. He walked toward the door.

"Wait, isn't that from a movie?"

"The bouquet of pens?"

"Yeah, I'm racking my brain but can't figure it out."

Linc waved the jar at his best friend. "You've Got Mail."

"I knew you were a helpless romantic under all those fuck-off-vibes."

> Cleo: Why, Mr. Darcy, Someone left a delightful gift on my bedside table. I'm kinda disappointed you didn't climb through my bedroom window though.

Lincoln had gone for a night run, scrubbed the bathroom, taken a long, hot shower and climbed into bed with his clandestine copy of *Pride and Prejudice*. He'd seen both the BBC and Keira Knightley versions of the movie, but Cleo had told him the book was better, so he was giving it a go.

Russ was right, he *was* a hopeless romantic. And Linc wasn't quite sure what to do with that information.

> Lincoln: Alas, Miss Bennet, I tried. However, the neighborhood dogs got upset, people threatened to call law enforcement officers if I didn't get down, and I was afraid I'd be left to die if I fell on my head...

> Lincoln: Also, Molly was home and suggested going through the front door would be, and I'm quoting: less fucking stupid.

> Cleo: LOL! Sounds like her alright. Thank you, Lincoln. It's so thoughtful and the ink is the perfect color. I love it.

> Cleo: I mostly love that you don't think I'm insane for my stationery obsession.

Linc rolled onto his side, his cheeks aching from grinning so hard.

> Lincoln: Oh, hey, no, wait. I didn't say you weren't insane. You're definitely insane. I just think it's cute. You're my kinda crazy, Lizzy.

Lincoln: Wanna come over to watch a
movie tomorrow after class?

Cleo: You haven't asked me over before.

Lincoln: I know. I thought I should change that. It's just Russ here though, sometimes Jude comes by. Occasionally some of the team. I can come to you if you'd rather.

Cleo: I'd love to.

"Marvel fan?" Cleo ran a finger along the spines of the pile of Blu-rays sitting on the shelf.

"That's Russ. He's obsessed. Jude's obsessed with superheroes too. It's kind of adorable. There are other movies in a box under the bed if you want to look through those."

Her brows pinched in confusion and a blush flooded her cheeks.

"What?"

"A box of movies under your bed?"

A snort of laughter lodged in his chest and made him cough. Eyes watering, he leaned forward, braced his hands on his knees, and chuckled through his near-death choking experience. "They're... not." He waved a hand before coughing into it.

She handed him a bottle of water as he straightened. "Porn?" Her whisper, despite the fact they were alone in his dorm room, was endearing.

He nodded, twisting the cap off the bottle. He took a sip. "Regular movies, Lizzy. Not X-rated." He took another sip and chuckled again. "I mean, if watching porn is your kink, we can totally watch something together. We don't kink shame in this safe space. But you'll be disappointed with what's in that box."

Cleo shoved his bicep, shaking her head. "Porn is not at all my kink, Mr. Darcy!"

The door opened at the moment she raised her voice. Russ was grinning as he entered, and Will cocked his head with a questioning frown as he walked into the room.

"It's always the quiet ones. Cleo Martinez you dirty, dirty woman. I'm going to have to stop my sister from hanging around with one so uncouth!" Will winked at a now tomato-red Cleo who covered her face and groaned.

"I hate everything right now."

"Cool your jets, Zelda. It's all a bit of good natured ribbing."

"Zelda?" The way Cleo twisted her lips when she didn't understand something, made Linc want to grab her lip between his teeth.

"You can't have forgotten Mo is a gamer, can you?" Russ slapped an open palm against Will's chest.

"Oh, I haven't. I still don't get the connection to Zelda though." Cleo's frown deepened as though she wasn't sure whether she was being mocked or not.

"Nothing bad, Cho-Cho. Zelda's love interest in the game is called Link."

Something twisted in Linc's stomach at Will's use of Molly's nickname for Cleo.

"Easy, Turbo." Russ's voice was low and quiet. "He's known her a long time, and he's not interested in her like that."

Will grunted. "Yeah, you can un-ball that jealous fist of yours, Linc. I'm not moving in on your girl. Though I should probably give you some big-brother ass-kicking spiel about hurting her."

Cleo giggled and stepped toward Linc, slipping her palm

into his. "Can we at least leave the display of macho bravado until I'm gone? I appreciate the protectiveness, *William*, but Molly has already got you covered."

"No shit." Linc rubbed the back of his neck. "She's threatened many forms of grievous bodily harm if I don't take good care of Cleo." He let go of her hand and slid his hand around her waist. "Everyone can stand down. I have no intention of hurting her."

Her cheeks flared pink again. He dropped a kiss on her temple.

"Well, now all this soppy shit's out of the way, Mo and I will be leaving. My folks have Jude for the night, and we're going to throw some darts."

"Isn't that for old guys?" The blush staining Cleo's cheeks hadn't receded.

Russell's dramatic gasp and clutch at his heart as though Cleo had shot an arrow into his chest made her giggle.

Did all women have such a consuming giggle? Had Linc just never noticed? It wrapped around him like a warm blanket on a Minnesota winter's night.

Will's hand clapped on his shoulder. "Well, just for funsies then. Hurt her, and I'll hurt you."

"Will!" Cleo buried her face against Linc's chest.

"Yes, sir." Linc threw a salute. "You boys have fun."

Russ offered him a fist-bump before they left.

"I felt like you guys were gonna whip them out and measure them, like, right in front of me."

Linc chuckled. "If I've learned anything, it's that I can't compete with Will. I'm an average dude with an average dick. He's captain on and off the ice."

Cleo's eyes widened and her mouth dropped open. "I did not need to know that about my best friend's big brother, Lincoln!" She thwapped his chest with her fingertips. "He's the closest thing to a brother I have. I don't need to know about his... his..."

"Say it."

She rolled her eyes, gave a small head shake and folded her arms. "His penis, Lincoln. I don't need to know anything about Will Morrison's penis!"

"Uh..." Finn had let himself into the room, the door was ajar behind him. "Did I come at a bad time?"

"Jesus fucking Christ, it's like Grand Central station in here!" Cleo flopped onto Linc's bed with a theatrical sigh. She peeked from under her arm to greet the new addition to the group. "Hi, Finn."

"Hi, Cleo. I feel like you're not having the romantic bow-chica-wow-wow time you probably had planned with Linc, so I'm gonna grab my wallet and leave."

"Why is your wallet in Russ and Lincoln's room?"

"Honey, ain't nobody got time for the why things happen with us lot. You just gotta go with the cray. How are you and Mo-Mo doing? I haven't seen you guys in a while." Finn's cheeks turned as red as his hair.

"We're good thanks. Molly was talking about setting up another interview with some of the team soon, maybe you'll see her there."

Finn nodded, waved his wallet, and made his way toward the door. "From the sound of it, you might wanna lock this behind me this time."

Linc did just that and turned to Cleo, who'd tucked her legs so she sat cross-legged on top of his bed. "Mo-Mo?"

"Molly Morrison – Mo-Mo." Cleo's explanation did little to answer why O'Brien had a pet name for his best friend's little sister.

"So she calls you Cho-Cho and you call her Mo-Mo?"

Cleo shook her head. "I call her Molly, or Mol. Finn calls us Cho-Cho and Mo-Mo though. Will gets called Mo, I guess he thought it was funny to call her Mo-Mo. He did try calling her Mini Mo once though, that did *not* go well."

"What happened?" He pulled his laptop out of his backpack and booted it up.

"She threw a puck at him and busted his nose."

"No shit!"

Cleo nodded and reached for the theater pack of hot tamales on the bedside table. "We gonna watch something?"

"Yeah, no DVDs from under the bed though. We'll stick with Netflix and chilling."

"I have my period." Her hand paused on the way to her mouth, a piece of candy pinched between finger and thumb.

He climbed onto the bed next to her, placing the laptop on his outstretched legs. "Okay. I meant Netflix and actually chilling, not fucking. But now I have questions. Does that mean you're uncomfortable doing stuff on your period? Or you think it's a deterrent to me wanting to do stuff on your period?"

"Uh..." She tensed.

He turned to find her looking everywhere but right at him. He gave her thigh a squeeze. "Hey, if you're uncomfortable talking about it, we don't have to. I guess having two sisters has kind of forced me to be at ease with talking about 'girl things.'" He used his fingers to make quotation marks.

"I think I might be in shock. I'm not used to guys being... considerate of these kinds of things. Most guys I know recoil in horror at the word 'period' so it's just... unexpected."

Linc chuckled. "You're hanging out with the wrong guys. Or maybe my friendship circle is weird. Either way, I have no issue with your monthly bodily functions."

"I don't think you can do 'monthly bodily' to the English language, Mr. Darcy."

"Wow. This really does make you uncomfortable." He put

his laptop on the mattress and slipped an arm around her shoulder, pulling her to his chest.

"I know you know I'm not going to make you do anything you're not comfortable with. But think about it, okay? It really doesn't bother me, and from the category of 'things I wish I didn't know' for three hundred... my big sister says sex on your period can help with cramps."

Cleo pulled her head back, her eyes wide. "What kind of weird-ass conversations do you have with your sisters?"

He laughed. "I overheard her talking with her friends one night before she moved out. I can tell you, I learned a lot about how to be a man by eavesdropping on a group of women ranting about how not to be a man."

Cleo smiled at last. "Sounds smart."

"Yeah." He nodded. "And some of the guys are... I dunno, educators."

Her eyebrows shot up her forehead once again.

"No." He held a hand up. "We don't kiss and tell, I don't mean that kind of education. One of the guys is a Dom, y'know, BDSM?" He reached over and plucked a hot tamale from her fingers and popped it into his mouth, an explosion of spicy cinnamon hitting his tongue as he chewed.

"I always thought Doms were just into hurting people. Man, were my eyes opened when I started talking to him about it. As it turns out, true Doms, *real*, what they call 'old guard' Doms, are pretty into education. He's like our very own Dear Abby... or Dr. Ruth... for all things sex. Like a sex ed teacher, but not the weird, creepy, abstinence only teaching type. He knows shit, and he's only too happy to help out."

"This is a very strange conversation." She swallowed and took another piece of candy into her mouth.

"Isn't it though? Anyway, my point is, if it's something you're curious about, I'm here for it."

Her mouth snapped open so fast her jaw clicked. "B-bdsm?"

"What? No! I mean, each to their own, but I mean doing stuff on your period!"

She went quiet for a moment, chewing the cinnamon candy before swallowing hard. "I feel like I need an emergency girl meeting. I'm becoming more and more aware of just how sheltered my upbringing was. We didn't talk about periods in front of my dad, and my mom barely acknowledged them other than to ask if I needed a restock of 'supplies' every month. In high school, guys did the 'ew, icky, that's disgusting' and 'must be that time' thing, so having a rational, serious conversation with a guy is just mind blowing. My mind is blown. Lincoln Scott, you are an enigma."

Suddenly grateful to his sisters, a sadness crept over him that Cleo's experience hadn't been the same, safe-space his parents had fostered for their family. He reached for the laptop and she snuggled against his chest.

"Oh!" She reached over the edge of the bed and grabbed her purse. She pulled out a pair of glasses, slipped them onto her face and resumed snuggling.

"You wear glasses? Gotta say, Lizzy, they're kinda hot as fuck."

She laughed. "Thanks. Yeah, I wear contacts during the day, but when my eyes get tired, or there's a high chance I'll fall asleep, I switch to my glasses."

He planted a kiss on her temple. "Like I said, it's hot. Totally here for it."

"So... which Pirate is the kinky one?" She eyed him from behind her hair.

"Sorry babe." He shook his head. "First rule of Pirate Club..."

"Ah, but you already talked about Pirate Club." She pointed an accusing finger.

"I did. But I'll never be the one to out him for his kinks."

"Well that just makes me l... ike you even more. You're a good man, Lincoln."

Warmth from her cheeks radiated through his shirt. His heart kicked up a beat. Was she about to say love? Not wanting to want to freak her out, he remained still. Did she love him? "Just don't tell anyone. Can't have everyone thinking I'm a good guy."

CHAPTER 22

Cleo

"I almost said it!" Cleo panic-cleaned the counter at the coffee shop, scrubbing at the same spot with the same frantic energy she'd been channeling all morning.

Molly grinned. "You almost told Linc you love him?"

"We've been through this, Mol."

"Actually, Cho-Cho, we haven't. You keep saying 'I almost told him' and 'I nearly said it,' but you haven't actually voiced what the 'it' is. I need to hear you say 'it,' Cleo."

Cleo's chest tightened. "I…" Her breath caught on jagged edges of something she couldn't identify in her throat. Fear? Uncertainty? Vulnerability? She squeezed her eyes shut and gripped the edge of the counter.

"What's stopping you from saying it?"

Cleo shook her head. "I don't know. I thought I'd… I think he's the first. Saying it out loud, gives it power or something."

"What do we say about love?"

When Cleo couldn't bring herself to answer, Molly sighed. "Love is giving someone the power to hurt you – like, real bad hurt – and trusting them not to. You can't tell me you don't trust Linc. If you didn't, you wouldn't have been the overshare queen with him before you knew who he really was, and he obviously trusts you, too."

"I dunno, Molly."

Molly dragged her fingertip through the foam of her cappuccino. "Will says the team have never seen Linc like this before, Cho-Cho." She spoke into her cup.

"Like what?"

Two customers stood from their table next to the window, chairs scraping along the terracotta tiles. One of them waved, and the other called a quick thank you before they left. Cleo grabbed a tray and rinsed out her dishcloth, ready to clean the vacated table.

Molly grabbed her arm. "Can you stop running? For like a second, please? Talk to me, what's going on in your head, Her-me-o-nee."

"Ugh. You know I hate it when you butcher her name."

"Well, start talking, and maybe I'll say it right."

Cleo tilted her chin in defiance. "Say it right, then I'll talk."

"Fiiiiine. Dang. Someone's choosing violence today. I like smoldery Cleo, she's kinda badass. Hermione. Happy now?"

Cleo nodded. "I really dunno what my deal is, Mol. I'm scared. What if he doesn't love me back? What if I love him more than he loves me? What if my parents find out? What if my grades drop? What if—?"

"Slow. Your. Roll. Girlfriend." Molly leaned across the counter and flicked Cleo's forehead, right between her eyes. "This is some seriously high school angst going on here."

She waved her palm in front of Cleo's face. "First of all, you're a grown-ass woman. You can't 'what if my parents...' forever. At some point you're going to have to grab your life by the balls and make that shit your bitch. Take your parents out of the equation altogether. Say, for the sake of argument, it's none of their damn business who you let come to play in your lady garden. *You* get to decide who to spend your time with and who you fall in love with."

"I didn't really *choose* to fall for Linc, Molly. He's not my type."

Molly snorted. "Sure, sure. Okay, we can totally pretend he's not your type. But sometimes that's just how the dice land, girlie." She sipped her drink, licking the foam from her top lip before placing the cup onto the saucer with a light clink. "You *have* fallen for him, and you owe it to yourself to be happy. Really happy, in all things. Not just top-of-your-class happy."

Cleo went walked to the vacated table, picked up the empty cups and sugar packets, and gave its surface a wipe. "You don't think we're just incompatible?" She could almost hear Molly's eye roll behind her.

"Those noises you make when he's fucking you all the way to the Promised Land and back sure sound compatible. Stop talking shit. You're afraid, and that's fine, but you're absolutely compatible. And if you don't trust your clit or your heart, ask your brain. I'm pretty sure they're all on the same page with this one."

Cleo loaded the dirty dishes into the dishwasher as the café door opened and a group of six students walked in, followed by Lincoln.

"Yeah. Your face is doing that shit-eating grin thing again, Cho-Cho. Incompatible my ass." Molly flashed Lincoln a grin as he approached the counter. "Linc! Pull up a chair."

Cleo worked her way through the six students' orders, keeping an ear on Molly's chat with Lincoln to make sure she didn't embarrass the hell out of her.

"What can I get you, Hockey Boy? Shouldn't you be heading to the rink? Don't you have a game tonight?"

He leaned over the counter and planted a soft kiss on her lips. "I love that you're invested in my hockey schedule. I appreciate it, even though you hate the sport. Okay, *all* sport. And yes, I have a game, but I wanted to drop in and say hi first. I also brought you a little something."

"For me?"

"Well it sure as hell isn't for me." Molly drained the last of her coffee and slid the cup and saucer toward Cleo. "Refill please, brew-bitch."

"I'll sort the people in front of you first, wench. Wait your turn. Anything I can get you, Linc?"

"No ma'am. Thanks, though."

Cleo leaned forward but he pressed whatever was in his hand against the front of the counter so she couldn't see it. He jerked his chin at the coffee machine. "Serve your customers, Lizzy. This can wait."

Her stomach flip-flopped as she pulled her bottom lip between her teeth and narrowed her eyes in suspicion. She'd never dated someone who gave her 'just because' gifts before. She found herself enjoying the gestures and thought behind them even more than she enjoyed his gifts. Nodding, she pulled six mugs onto the counter, and started making the drinks.

"Still calling her Lizzy, eh? I think that's cute as hell."

"Know what I think is cute as hell?"

Molly's eyes danced with a hint of challenge. "What's that?"

"O'Brien having a pet name for you. Totes adorbs... as Russ would say."

Perhaps her best friend had finally met her match with Lincoln. He was giving her a dose of her own medicine and Cleo was here for it.

Molly's face paled and for a moment something flickered across her face before she slid her "don't give a shit" mask on. "We've known each other for a long time, *Lincoln*." Her voice was as cool as her pointed stare. "It's perfectly normal for friends to have nicknames for each other."

"Cool. Friends. Just checking. We don't need to be replacing a left winger 'cause your brother smashed his best friend's brains in because he's banging his lil sis, know what I'm saying?"

Molly's jaw dropped open and her nostrils flared. "That's not... we're... not... I don't..."

Cleo handed the last of the drinks across the counter and turned back to her friend and boyfriend. She'd never seen Molly rendered speechless before. Giving Linc a surreptitious sharp shake of her head to get him to stop, she pulled her brows low.

He nodded and placed a gift bag on the counter.

"What's this for?"

"I figured you could do with a little pick me up." His nonchalant shrug didn't distract from the slight blush staining his cheeks.

"Should I open it now?"

He shook his head. Picking up her hand, he tugged her toward him over the counter. He kissed her forehead. "Call you after my game?"

"Mmhmm. And thanks for whatever this is." She nudged the bag on the countertop while he backed away a few paces.

He blew her a kiss, and her heart squeezed as he left.

"I never thought I'd see the day when that jock found someone who made him smile like that, Cleo Martinez." Molly was still watching the door, but her voice was thick with raw emotion. "I've watched these guys since we started college. I know..."

She held up a hand as she turned to Cleo. "That sounds

creepy AF. But I have. I've watched them on and off the ice." She shrugged.

"Waiting for one of them to fuck up, or for a salacious story to fall in my lap for the paper. But he's been the golden boy. Top player, grades never drop below what he needs to stay in school, and while he's dated, he's never had a reputation for sleeping around or leaving a trail of broken hearts in his wake. He's just been... aloof? When he's with you, he's warmer. That lopsided, panty-melting grin of his could light up the national grid. And I'm not even his friend, just an observer."

What Molly was saying made sense, but a tiny voice at the back of Cleo's head reminded her that the night they met he was having a one night stand with the woman who left her bra in his dorm room. Cleo shook her head and cleaned the counter, again.

"Shake your head and deny it all you want, girlfriend. But you're different too. You're more at ease, more comfortable in your own skin, and dare I say it, there's the slightest hint of confidence creeping into your everyday life and as your best friend... I. Am. Here. For. It."

Was she at long last becoming more confident?

"What's that look? Hm? The words you're searching for are: Molly, you're right, I'm head over heels in love with Lincoln Scott, and it's totally okay. Better than okay."

Cleo giggled. "I'm worried about you. What Linc said... did he see something? Did something happen with Finn? Have I been so caught up in Linc and... everything that I missed something?"

"No ma'am. This is not about me, and there is nothing happening with Finn. Didn't you hear? He was out on a date with some ballet dancer last week. Not for the first time, either. People are *shipping* them." She waved a dismissive hand. "Not that I'm bitter about it, obviously."

"Obviously."

"Anyway, this is a tequila conversation, not a coffee shop conversation. Let's see what Linc dropped off for you."

Cleo opened the bag, pushing the pale pink tissue paper aside and slid her hands around the neck of a glass bottle.

"Pink moscato. The boy can pick a wine." Molly plucked the bottle from her hands and admired the bottle. "For you at least. The rest of us have standards. Would it have killed him to grab a good Merlot?"

"Ew." Cleo wrinkled her nose in disgust. "He knows I'd never touch the stuff."

"Yes, but I feel like he needs to work harder to win over your best friend."

Cleo pulled a raspberry lemonade scented bath bomb from the bag, followed by a pink clay face mask, a multi-pack of Russell Stover mallows, a box of hot tamales, a share-size bag of dill pickle Lays, and a box of ibuprofen. At the bottom of the bag was his blue Snow Pirates hoody she secretly lusted over and a copy of the latest Lucy Score novel she hadn't yet picked up from the bookstore.

"Daaaamn. Anyone would think you're on your period or something. This is a top-notch, self-care care-package if ever I saw one."

Cleo smiled and tidied the gifts back into the bag. "I do have my period."

"What? Wait. You're telling me Lincoln Scott, jock extraordinaire, Mr. Never settling down. Mr. my life is all hockey, all the time... Brought you a period package... to work... on a game day, on his way to the rink?" Molly fanned her face.

"I think I need a lie down. I'm swooning so hard right now. If I had a dick, it would definitely be at least al dente for the guy. Who knew he wasn't a douche goblin? So... hockey players might not have all their own teeth, but some of them have kind hearts? Why did no one tell me? I feel like my world is unraveling at the seams right now. Can you call 9-1-1? I think I'm having a heart attack. Wait. Does this mean my brother's not a dick? I have so many questions."

Two groups of four came into the café as the group of six left. Cleo threw her cleaning cloth at Molly. "Shut up."

"Accept it, Cleo. You're dating a hottie with a huge heart. In all my years of menstruating, I've never had a brother, or a boyfriend, bring me a period care package like that. I asked an ex to grab me tampons once. He laughed in my face and told me to get them myself."

"So what did you do?"

"I laughed in his face and told him to give himself a blow job."

"Sounds about right." Cleo took orders and made drinks while Molly flicked through the Lucy Score novel.

"What is it about these romance books you like so much? There's no blood, mayhem or death, there's no action or fighting, it's all just... love and feels."

"There's a guaranteed happy ever after, Mol." Cleo popped her head over the top of the coffee machine in time to catch another Olympic standard eye roll from her friend. "There's a comfort in that. Knowing that no matter what happens, they'll get their happy ending."

One of the customers dreamy-sighed as Cleo handed her an oversized mug of hot chocolate. The cream and marshmallows bobbed and swayed as she accepted the mug and handed over her punch card with a crumpled five dollar bill. "She's right. It's the dreamiest thing. Couple meets, couple falls in love, something disastrous pulls the couple apart, but they overcome it and find their way to their forever. It's darling!"

Molly pointed her index finger toward the back of her open mouth. "Gag. Puke. Vomit. Real life doesn't work like that."

Cleo opened her mouth to reply, but the customer got there first.

"But it *could*. It gives you hope."

"Hope that a ripped, God-like man with a delicious V leading into his grey sweatpants and a cock as big as my forearm will appear in your life? You mean it'll give you fantasy fodder? Or hope that you'll have some charming meet-cute, never fight over who does the dishes, or the fact he never picks up his mother-fucking socks and puts them *in* the laundry basket. There'll never be that 'what do you feel like?' 'I dunno, what do you feel like?' discussion because they both magically speak each other's language and never fight over the take out menu or what to watch on TV. It all sounds so delightfully dull."

The customer grinned. "It's not *dull*."

"It's predictable." Molly pointed an accusatory finger at the stranger before picking the book up and flicking from cover to cover and tossing it back on the counter. "Where's the excitement in getting to know each other? Where's the exciting plot-twist? The whodunit? Where's the regular, every day, non-model-like heroine falling for the dad bod dude?"

Cleo laughed. "You'll have to excuse my cynical friend here. She's having a bit of a personal crisis."

The stranger nodded knowingly and pointed at the book. "Read the book. It might surprise you, and if it doesn't, it might re-light that tiny flame of hope in your dark and twisty heart." She winked, picked up her mug of cocoa, and joined her friends at a table in the far corner of the café.

"I like her." Molly's smirk wasn't unkind. She could always read people from the shortest of conversations. She'd often come home declaring she'd met a new friend in the parking lot, or in the grocery store, or the bathroom of a bar. She had a way with people. "But not everyone gets their happy ever after." Her sigh was heavy, weighted with unspoken pain.

Cleo's heart ached for her. Was there something going on that Cleo had missed? Molly gave her a small smile which she returned before ducking behind the coffee machine out of sight. Was she over thinking everything? She couldn't figure out if she needed to step back and keep her head in the game or to relax and let life unfold. Did everyone else have these crises of faith? Was hanging out with Linc proving detrimental to their friendship?

CHAPTER 23

Lincoln

"Cleo, this is my younger sister, Amelia. Amelia, this is my girlfriend, Cleo."

Mia vibrated with excitement, her face stretched with a wide grin. She had chosen their favorite Greek restaurant, Christos, for dinner. They'd ordered drinks and a dip sampler and pita as an appetizer before sitting down to check out the menus.

Anxiety rested in a tight knot on his diaphragm, making every breath dense and difficult. His sweaty hands fiddled with the napkin on his lap. Sister meet girlfriend. Girlfriend meet sister.

It was no big deal.

People did this all the time. All. The. Time.

"Winky, you didn't tell me she was so beautiful."

Despite the urge to grimace at the old nickname, his heart swelled at his sister's compliment.

A faint blush crept into Cleo's cheeks as she shook Mia's hand. "Winky?" She pursed her lips and frowned.

Linc cringed, arching an eyebrow in her direction.

"Oh God." Mia covered her face with a groan. "I really

didn't think through using that nickname at a table with a woman who sees your actual winky, did I?"

Cleo laughed, her blush deepening. "If it helps, the subject of your brother's penis can go right over here." She slid an imaginary object to the edge of the table. "This can be the 'fuck no' pile."

Mia nodded. "Sounds good to me. For reference though, I couldn't say my L's for the longest time as a kid. So Linc became Wink and at some point I added a 'y'... Before I knew it was slang for dick, obviously, and it kinda stuck." She dragged a piece of warm pita bread through the hummus dip and took a bite. "This should be illegal, it's so good."

It was the next step, and a natural progression in their relationship. But he didn't do this all the time. He'd done this once, maybe twice before, and each time, it sent a pang of fear through his entire body. Amelia had hated his previous girlfriend, for no reason other than, "her vibe was off."

He'd lasted six months with her before things petered out. He hadn't cared much back then, but his relationship with Cleo was different. His stomach churned. What if Mia disliked Cleo too?

"Linc tells me you write books, Cleo. What genre?"

Cleo's brows raised and her eyes widened. "He did?"

The server came to take their entrée order and clear the appetizer plates. Linc ordered a gyro, Cleo the lamb shank, and Amelia the souvlaki.

"He did." Mia sipped her iced tea. "Was he not supposed to?" She gasped as her hand flew to her mouth. "Are they...?" She checked over each shoulder twice before continuing. "Do you write... *erotica*?"

Cleo half-laughed, half-snorted into her glass of iced water with lemon. "What? No!" She lowered her voice when she spoke again. "They're just contemporary romance short stories. I mean… there's steam, but they're not smutty. Not that I don't like smut."

Amelia was beaming. "Then can I read some of your stories?"

"What? Why? No!"

Mia laughed. "Girl, what the hell is in these stories making you all prickly? Okay, we'll let whatever impostor syndrome that's working on you linger for a while, and when it takes a nap, then you can show me your stories, deal?"

"They're really not that good."

"Isn't that for the reader to decide?"

Cleo opened her mouth, closed it, and opened it again, but before she could speak, the server placed her lamb shank on the table in front of her.

Linc fought a smile. Amelia one, Cleo zero. Mia was nothing if not persistent. Perhaps hearing someone who wasn't Linc smack down her fears might help Cleo realize her potential.

"Don't terrify my girlfriend, Amelia." Linc hoped his tone conveyed caution. While Cleo could hold her own, Amelia could be overbearing and unrelenting until she got her own way. He gave Cleo's knee a squeeze under the table and was rewarded with a small smile.

"It's okay." Cleo sliced off a piece of lamb and speared it with her fork. "I didn't think you talked about me to your family is all. It's… new for me. Truthfully, it's kind of nice that you're both interested in my hobby. My mom… well, she's not the biggest fan of it to be honest. I just find it hard to believe someone wants to see my words." She gave a shrug.

As Amelia cut up her pork, she shook her head. "That must be so hard. I forget how easy we have it with our folks sometimes. They're super supportive. Right Linc?"

His mouth dried up at her question. "Mhmm." He

nodded, slowing his chewing so he had an excuse not to say anything in reply.

"Sissy played the flute for years." Amelia gestured with her fork between bites. "They thought she was going to go to college for music to be a performer, or a teacher. None of us could believe it when she picked medicine. She traded her flute in for a scalpel, and they were totally cool about it. They don't care that I'm not going to college, do they, Linc?"

He finished chewing another mouthful of gyro and swallowed hard. She was right, they didn't care she wasn't going to college. They didn't care that his older sister almost dropped out after her first year because she'd partied so hard she missed so much class and her grades sucked. But with him... with him they cared.

"Do you think they'd be supportive of your art, Linc?" Cleo wasn't looking at him when she said it. He'd told her his parents didn't know about his art, but he hadn't mentioned his sisters, had he? Tendrils of cold dread curled around his stomach, threatening to bring up the gyro he was forcing himself to eat.

"What art?"

Cleo's head snapped up, the color from her face draining away as her eyes darted between Amelia and Lincoln. "I..." Her eyes widened.

While he wasn't angry at her for her slip of the tongue, his stomach churned. What would she say?

"Linc?"

He lifted his gaze to meet Mia's. Tilting her head, her brows knotted together in a questioning frown, and her lips were pursed. "It's nothing."

"From the looks of your girlfriend's 'I fucked up' face, it's most definitely something. Have you taken up photography or something?"

"Lincoln..." Cleo's voice was a whisper. Her jaw trembled,

and her hazel eyes were red rimmed as though tears threatened. "I'm so sorry."

He took her hand and slipped his palm against hers. He gave what he hoped was a reassuring squeeze, running his thumb along her knuckles. "Shh. It's okay. It's no big deal."

He turned to Amelia again. "I draw, Mia. Paint, pastels, sketching with charcoal and yeah, sometimes I take photos too." He swallowed as she processed.

"That's all? Christ, Cleo, from your reaction I was starting to think he was a mass murderer, or had gotten a really ugly tattoo of something... or... I dunno, had taken up something dull, like golf." She wrinkled her nose with a giggle. "Ugh. Can you imagine? My hockey playing big brother taking up something mind-numbingly boring."

"You're so judgmental, Mia."

"Bitch with a smile, that's me. I'm mean, but people think I'm joking."

Cleo cracked a smile, though her eyes were still watery.

"This is your deepest, darkest secret, brother dearest? This is as 'bad' as it gets? I'm kinda jealous. Surely there's more? How long have you been hiding this? Years? Dude. What did you think would happen if I found out?"

"Not you... Dad."

"Ah, yes, well... time away from hockey is no good thing." She puffed her chest out and lowered her voice, tilting her head in the same way their father tended to do.

"I won't tell him though, you should know me better by now." Pointing her index finger at him, she took a drink with her free hand. "I get it though. I didn't want to tell them when I got my piercings."

"Yeah, that's totally the same thing." Linc rolled his eyes at how blasé his sister's attitude was. It was different for her. Their parents didn't expect the same things from her as they did from him.

"Can you keep it under wraps please, Mimi?" He used his childhood nickname for her in the hopes it would help his case.

"Oh, Winky." She sighed. "You know I've got you, boo. Now... Miss Cleo." She leaned forward onto her elbows, cradling her face in her palms. "Tell me what other dark and dirty skeletons there are lurking in my brother's closet."

"Your sister seems nice."

"She's a force of nature. I thought I adequately prepared you for the inquisition, but I'm not convinced you can prepare for... well... *that*."

Linc had taken Cleo back to her apartment on his bike after dinner, and they were cuddled up on her bed.

"I really didn't mean to tell her."

He tipped her head back, fingers tangled in her long, dark waves. "I know, Lizzy. I wish you hadn't, but I'm not mad that you did."

She pulled her lip between her teeth, and he freed it with the pad of his thumb.

"Try not to worry too much about it. Whether or not she tells my dad is on her, not on you. She'd better not though."

She giggled. "Sounds to me like you have your own dirt on her you could share with your folks."

"I do. I'm not one for playing dirty, but I can hold my own." He winked at her and kissed the tip of her nose.

She tilted her head back so her lips met his. Her fingers clawed at his shirt as their tongues collided in a hungry dance. "Lincoln..."

Had his name ever sounded sexier? Had any woman ever made him so hard with nothing but one word and a kiss? He wrapped his arms around her, shifting her into his lap. She pressed herself against the erection straining in his pants and leaned her head back.

Dragging his tongue from her collarbone to below her ear, a low hum of approval rumbled in his chest. "Naked."

She burst into giggles, unbuttoning her shirt. "I gotta say, Lincoln, I kinda like this caveman version of you." She kissed him, nipping and biting at his lips as she wriggled out of the blouse. It slipped from her shoulders, revealing a red, lacy bra.

He dotted kisses down her chest while reaching to unhook the catch, pinching the skin of her breast between his lips in frustration as he struggled to open her underwear.

"Damnit! One of these days I'll get this fucking thing off first try." His pained groan would have made him laugh if he wasn't excruciatingly hard and desperate to get inside his girl.

As she took over and undid her bra, he pulled his shirt over his head and unbuttoned his jeans. Maybe it would at least ease the pressure building in his pants.

She trailed her bra off in slow motion, rocking her hips against his.

"Who knew Miss Bennet was such a tease?"

As soon as they were free from fabric, he cupped her full, creamy tits with both hands, lifting her already-hard nipples to his mouth.

Running his teeth over her peaks, he smiled as her breath hitched. "Doing okay there, Cleo?"

She nodded, dropped her head to his shoulder and dug her nails into his chest. "Linc?"

"Yeah, baby?" He nuzzled his stubbly chin in the gap between her ear and shoulder.

"Will you take me from behind?" Her voice was muffled against his skin, her breath tickling him as she spoke.

"Are you kidding me? Look." He pointed to the growing wet patch on his boxers peeking out from his open fly. "My dick is weeping tears of pre-cum joy at that question."

"Who said romance is dead?"

"My dick only weeps tears of pre-cum joy for you, Miss Bennet."

Her giggle stoked the fire in his stomach. Wrapping her wild hair around his hand, he pulled her back from his chest with a tug. He pushed her back onto the bed so he could unzip her jeans, hook his fingers into the band and pull them, and her panties, down her legs.

He licked his lips. Her hair splayed out on the blankets, her pink cheeks and swollen lips, the hunger in her eyes and beautifully naked body drove him to the edge of self-control.

He raked his palms along the outside of her legs, up to her waist, across her pelvis until his thumbs met, just beneath her belly button.

Lowering his hands until he reached her opening, he circled her clit with the thumb of his left hand while he slipped two fingers inside. "You're so wet, Lizzy."

Her body twitched and writhed as he curled his fingers, seeking out her g-spot. "Lincoln... I..."

He couldn't wait. He moved his hand from her clit, grabbed one of her hands which had traveled to play with her breasts and put it between her thighs. She didn't question him, but played with herself with little huffs and gasps while he peeled his jeans off and dumped them on the floor. "Don't stop touching yourself for me, Lizzy, okay?"

"O...kay..." Her breathless pants made his cock ache. Climbing up onto his knees, he hooked his hands behind her legs, flipped her onto her stomach, and tugged her down the bed toward him.

"Linc!" Her voice rose in a giggle as he pulled her hips off the bed. Her hand had come away from her pussy as he turned her, but she slid her fingers back where they needed to be. He pulled a condom from her bedside drawer, tore it open, and rolled it onto his throbbing dick.

"Have I ever told you what a delicious ass you have, Miss Bennet?" He grabbed her cheeks with both hands and squeezed before rubbing his palms over the soft flesh.

Gripping the shaft of his dick, he dragged the head through her slick folds. "Christ, I love how fucking wet you are for me."

He gritted his teeth and willed himself to calm down. What was it about this woman that turned him into a teenage boy?

He was constantly ready to blow his load in his boxers from the second she took her clothes off. Lining the crown up to her entrance, he eased inside her on a long hiss, her walls tightening around him.

"Deeper, Lincoln. Don't tease."

He grinned at her outspokenness. There was nothing sexier than a woman who knew what she wanted in bed and asked for it, and he couldn't help but oblige.

Her fingers worked her clit while he pulled all the way out, hesitated and drove every inch of his length back inside her. A ripple passed through her legs as her muscles tightened around him with each thrust.

"Linc... please..."

"What do you need, Lizzy? Anything."

Her face was buried in the quilt so she turned her head to speak. "Put your finger in... please?"

Not wanting to beat his girl to the edge, he slowed his pace. "Have you ever had anything in your ass before, Lizzy?"

She shook her head against the sheets.

Sweat trickled down his face and his balls ached for release. "And you want me to put a finger there?"

She nodded.

"Do you have lube?"

"I don't need lube."

"For your first time, I'm using lube." He ground his teeth together and clenched his jaw.

"Top drawer, at the back."

Leaning over the edge of the bed, he pulled the still open drawer out, finding the small bottle of lube with ease. Her whine and a sharp blast of cold air told him he'd slipped out. Cleo hadn't stopped playing with her clit, so her muscles twitched and clenched when he slid back in.

The contracting and flexing of her walls around him made it almost impossible to concentrate on anything other than coming. With a quivering hand, he popped the lid of the bottle and dripped some on her puckered hole.

"I'm going to need you to talk to me, okay? If it hurts, tell me and I'll stop right away."

She nodded.

"Cleo, I need you to use your words for this. It's important."

"Okay." How one word sounded so full of restraint and the ache to come he'd never know. Her fingers had slowed, circling the tight bundle of nerves at the apex of her thighs with languid strokes.

She met his lazy thrusts, pressing her hips back toward his. "Lincoln, please put your Goddamn finger in my ass. I can't last much longer."

He grunted, scooped some lube with the tip of his pinky and circled a few times before sliding it in up to his first knuckle.

Her hips wiggled in response. "More."

He eased his finger in further, up to his second knuckle. She clenched around his dick, her fingers gathering speed over her clit. "Lincoln!" She ground out his name, frustration coating the word, her voice, raspy and low.

Chuckling and shaking his head he pulled his pinky out and slid his index finger in.

"Yes..." Her moan was almost enough to send him over the edge.

"Come for me, Lizzy. I need you to come first."

"Another... finger..." She panted as his hips met hers. Haphazard, frantic slaps of skin on skin rang out around the room as he slipped a second finger into her tight hole. "Yes, Lincoln! Yes!"

Her hot, twitching muscles gripped his cock like a vise as she came apart on a cry, fingers of her free hand curled into the blanket as though she was holding on for dear life.

"Don't... stop..." Her demand and unrelenting pressure around him pushed him over the edge with a grunt.

This confirmed it: The woman was going to be the death of him.

CHAPTER 24

Cleo

Molly leaned over the coffee table and clinked her glass against Cleo's. "I need all the details. All of them. Don't spare a single one."

Nicola was tutoring for the evening, and Kasia was out with her boyfriend, leaving Cleo and Molly home alone to demolish a bottle of wine and a pizza.

Cleo groaned into her hands.

"Honest to God, Cho-Cho, I can't picture this ball of embarrassment in front of me asking Lincoln Scott for directions, never mind asking him to shove his finger in her ass. At least tell me... did you like it?"

Cheeks hot and face still covered with both hands, she nodded.

"Atta girl. Did you keep it to just fingers for your first time? Or did you try other things?"

"Like what? I wasn't asking him for his cock in there on the first go! I might be fifty shades of vanilla, but I know that shit woulda hurt like hell."

"Ohhhhh Cho-Cho. I'm not sure you're ready for leveling

up from fingers to… other things. But suffice it to say, there are a great many things you can stick in your ass to bring pleasure."

"I'm not drunk enough for this conversation, Mol."

"That's what I just said!" Molly grabbed the bottle of wine and topped up both their glasses. "We must fix that and drink."

"We must." Cleo agreed. Her phone flashed and vibrated on the table. Her mom was calling.

"Gonna answer that?"

"Nope." She popped the 'p.' When her mom had finished calling, she opened their group chat.

> Cleo: Hi Mom, can't talk right now, doing some work in the library for my group project. I'll check in with you guys tomorrow. Love you xx

"Cleo, you've changed. Ignoring Mamá Martinez's calls, what's next? Grand larceny?"

Cleo chuckled. While she'd lied about the 'why,' it felt good to make the decision that she didn't want to talk to her mom. Obligation and pressure had weighed on her every time her phone rang, or chimed with a message.

It was stifling.

Ignoring the call had been like popping the top button on a tight collar around her neck. Molly was right, Cleo was an adult, and it was time to start laying some boundaries so she could learn to breathe and live in her own space – even if the idea alone was terrifying.

❄

Cleo slid the lock of the restroom stall into place and pulled her pants down when the door to the bathroom smacked against the wall and footsteps rang out around the tiled room. If nothing else, the noise drowned out the sound of her peeing.

"Can you believe Linc is still with her?" Melissa had made eye contact as Cleo walked past to make her way into the bathroom. She'd turned her head to track Cleo's movements and smiled as she'd pulled the bathroom door open. She knew Cleo was inside, which would explain why she wasn't even attempting to speak quietly.

If the wind was blowing the right direction, people living in the next zip code would hear her shrill voice, echoing off the tiles.

Cleo's heart hammered in her chest and a wave of dizziness crashed into her. She braced her palms on the walls to steady herself.

"That bland fucking marshmallow, Martinez! I gave him her number as a joke after we hooked up. I thought it would be hilarious to fuck with them. Getting him talking to her and watch him grow tired of her... her blah-ness. But here we are. For some reason, he's still entertaining her. Probably out of pity."

Cleo leaned forward on the toilet, scrunching an eye closed and straining to line her open eye with the gap around the door of the stall. Melissa stood, hand on popped hip, examining her nails. One of her friends was leaning over the sink, washing her hands, and the other was bent toward the mirror, rubbing the tip of her finger around the edges of her freshly glossed lips.

"Linc's never been a player though." Lip Gloss smacked her lips, tucking a loose strand of hair behind her ear. "Or if he is, he's been discrete. He doesn't have a rep like some of the other jocks."

Hand-Washer nodded and turned off the faucet. "He's squeaky clean, Mel. Not the kind to be cruel or drop-drawers for a one night stand. At least, not that I've heard."

Melissa's eyes moved to Cleo's stall door in the mirror, and Cleo recoiled, shoving a hand over her mouth to stifle the gasp rattling in her throat. Did Melissa see her? She must've known Cleo was listening.

"He dropped them for me, didn't he?"

Cleo's pulse thundered in her ears.

"Just that once though... right?" Hand-washer finished drying her hands.

Melissa's answer was to arch an eyebrow and tip her head with a smirk.

"Melissa! How many times? Why didn't you say anything?"

"Wow. Were you... like, *dating*? Why's he with her if he was with you? Did he dump you? I have questions, Mel."

Cleo's hands trembled, tears pricked behind her closed eyelids, and she shook her head.

"Lincoln Scott did *not* dump me." She gave a triumphant grin before licking her lips. "*I* got tired of *him*, and I gave him Hermione's number for fun. She's not his type at all, and he'd never go for a girl like her."

"Except he did." Lip Gloss pointed a finger at Mel, who was dragging a finger along the curve of her perfectly sculpted eyebrows.

"Not for long. A girl like her..." She subtly tipped her chin over her shoulder. "Doesn't belong with a guy like him. The cosmos will right its cluster fuck of a mistake in short order." Melissa turned on her heel. "And when he's ready to fuck someone he doesn't need a crane to lift, I'll be waiting for him." She blew a kiss at Cleo's stall and strode out of the bath-room, cronies hot on her heels.

White spots dotted the edges of Cleo's vision. Hot tears poured down her cheeks as she leaned forward on her elbows, raking her fingers through her hair and willing her body to suck in oxygen before she passed out.

A sob escaped her as auto-pilot kicked in. She wiped, stood, and pulled up her pants. Melissa had been his one night stand. Ugly hearted, soulless, fake, mean girl, Melissa. She opened the door and stepped toward the sink. Tall, blonde, and beautiful, Melissa.

Cleo couldn't even meet her own eyes in the mirror as she washed her hands. Perfect, popular, experienced, Melissa.

Why had Lincoln continued texting her after she'd told him she wasn't Melissa?

Cleo leaned over the sink, letting her heavy tears plop into the porcelain bowl. Girls like her didn't date guys like him. Girls like Melissa dated guys like him.

It didn't matter that she was an unpleasant person, or that Lincoln had told Cleo how beautiful he thought she was. It didn't matter that he seemed happy with her...

Why would he want someone fat and boring like Cleo when he could have someone vibrant and pretty like Melissa?

She shook her head and ground the heels of her hands into her eyes in a bid to stop the tears. There was no hiding the fact she'd been crying.

Her best option was to haul ass home and claim sick for the rest of the day. She only had one class left. One of the girls at the coffee shop owed her a favor and wanted any extra hours, and her housemates weren't expected to be home for hours.

Get home. That's all she had to do.

She pulled the door open and a group of freshman girls

giggled as they stumbled into the bathroom past her. Were they laughing at her? Had they heard Melissa talking? She forced her shoulders away from her ears and rolled them back and down.

Fake it till you make it.

Clenching her jaw, she stepped into the corridor.

"Cleo?"

Russell and Will stood six feet away, chatting to a girl she didn't know.

A pretty girl.

She offered a smile, which probably came off as a cross between a grimace and constipated face. The furrowed brows of both men suggested they weren't buying it. She held up a hand. "Not feeling well. I'll be fine."

Russ nodded, but Will tipped his head to the side and pulled out his phone.

"Oh hey, you have something on your chin." Johnny stood an arm's length away, pointing at her face.

She wiped her chin with the side of her index finger.

"No, not that one. Third one down."

When she didn't reply, he kept speaking.

"Your pants say yoga, but your ass says McDonalds." He stepped toward her and slung an arm around her shoulder.

What was this guy's deal? Didn't he get the message the last time the guys spoke up for her? Usually people like him said shit to get in with their buddies and make them laugh, but he knew his teammates weren't taking it well. What was his motivation?

"Awww what's the matter, Martinez? What's with the sour face? Is it leak week? Do we have a code red?"

She swallowed hard, rage and shame brewing in her stomach. Swinging her elbow, it collided with his stomach at the same moment Russ grabbed him by the back of his collar and threw him into the wall.

"I thought we talked about this, Johnny."

"Russ! I d-didn't see you there."

Russ wound his arm back, and Johnny put both hands up to protect his face.

"Y-you can't hit me. T-too many witnesses. You'd lose your position on the team for fighting. Think it through, Stewart."

Cleo didn't wait around to see how things played out. She turned her back to the commotion, head bowed, silent tears sliding down her face, and slipped away through the crowd.

"Cho-Cho? Where you at? Are you home?" Cleo rolled over in bed and pulled the quilt over her head. Maybe if she stayed very still Molly wouldn't find her. A sob caught in her throat. She buried her face in the pillow as another round of body-shaking tears hit her.

"Cleo? Cleo? What's wrong?"

The door opened, and seconds later, Molly yanked the blanket off her. A warm hand rubbed her back. "Cleo, did he hurt you? Who do I have to kill?"

Sniffing, Cleo rolled onto her side and wiped her eyes and nose with the back of her hand.

"Oh Cho-Cho." Molly's sad eyes were almost too much to bear. She held her arms out wide, and Cleo leaned into her, resuming her sobbing before her head hit her friend's shoulder. "What happened?"

She couldn't bring herself to speak, words tripped over the grief and self-loathing lodged deep in her chest. She shook her head.

"Okay. It's all going to be okay. Whatever it is, I'm here and I've got you." Molly's warm and reassuring arms tightened around Cleo. "I brought your phone from the kitchen. It's going crazy with notifications. Do you want it?"

She shook her head again.

"No probs."

For a while, she cried into Molly's shirt. When she finally came up for air, Molly tucked her hair behind her ear. "Feel better?"

Cleo shook her head. "I don't think I have any tears left." She sniffed.

"Will told me what happened while you were crying." Molly waved her phone, which buzzed in her hand, and she ignored it, tucking it into her pocket. "He texted when you left school to say I should come find you, but I wasn't sure why. He said you already looked upset before Johnny was a prick in the hallway. What happened?"

"Melissa."

Molly pushed Cleo back by her shoulders. "Stop that fucking train right now. You've been crying for over an hour because of that bitch? Girl. No. Whatever the hell she said, she does not deserve your tears."

"I feel like I'm in high school again, Mol. Fat girl being bullied. What happened to love yourself? What happened to body positivity? What happened to "it's who you are on the inside that counts?" I can't... I..."

Cleo smoothed her hair out of her face. "She said things in the bathroom. I always assumed Melissa gave Lincoln my number by accident, y'know, like a typo or something? Maybe our numbers were the same except for one digit? But she did it on purpose. To fuck with me. Who does that to another person?"

Her voice was laced with an edge of hysteria, and tears threatened to fall again. "There was no guarantee he'd text, so I guess she deliberately left her bra there so he'd make contact? I dunno what the hell she was thinking, but she thought it would be a riot if Linc had to message me. She said the same thing out loud that I've been saying since I found out who he is."

"Don't say it. It's not true, Cho-Cho. It is not true."

"Girls like me, don't date guys like him, Mol. It *is* true."

"It's not true. Cleo, he's mad about you. It's clear for anyone to see."

Cleo pinched her lips between her teeth and shook her head. "And as soon as I composed myself enough to leave the bathroom, Johnny was there being his piece of shit asshole self."

"We both know Johnny is a proven dickwad who doesn't deserve to take up space in your brain, your heart, your life, or most of this planet. There's a special place in hell for dicks like him."

Molly's phone buzzed again. "Girl, people are worried about you. Can one of us at least reply and tell everyone you're alive?"

Cleo scooted back from Molly and picked up her phone from the bedside table. Linc had tried to call her four times and had sent six texts.

Lincoln: I just saw Russ. Where are you?

Lincoln: Cleo?

Lincoln: Lizzy, I need you to tell me where you are. Or at least that you're okay.

Lincoln: Please?

Lincoln: I'm coming over.

Lincoln: I'm outside. Let me know when you're ready.

She sniffed and pinched the bridge of her nose. "He's outside."

"Good."

"Good?"

"Yes, Cleo. It's good. If he'd heard about what happened, and hadn't tried to call you or find you, I'd have barbecued his testicles. He cares about you. Of course he was going to try to find you."

Cleo climbed around Molly and went to the window. When she pulled back the blinds, Linc was leaning against his bike, arms folded, legs crossed at his ankles.

To an untrained observer, he might've looked as though he was waiting for someone, but Cleo knew better. His nostrils flared and his jaw was rigid. His every muscle radiated anger and tension.

Her heart squeezed. As though feeling her gaze on him, his head lifted, he met her eyes, and his features softened. She nodded, and he pushed off the bike and strode toward the house.

"Good choice. I'll go let him in."

Cleo gnawed on the inside of her cheek and paced her room. This wasn't high school. These people were supposed to be grown adults. *She* was supposed to be a grown adult, and yet, she was crying in her room over some fat shaming assholes. Why did she give them so much power over her?

"Hey."

She couldn't look at him. "Hey."

"I don't know what you need right now, but I'm here. I just couldn't stay away."

She nodded, freeing another wave of tears to course down her cheeks. "I feel so stupid." She wrapped her arms around herself as though it could offer protection from the hurricane of emotions raging through her.

In her periphery, he took two steps closer, hesitated, then a third. Warm fingers wrapped around her elbow. She shook her head. "I can't. I'll break down again. I can't, Lincoln.

He pulled her arm again, and led her to him. "I'm not here just for the fun times, Cleo." He snaked his arms around her, folding her into his chest. "Break down if you need to break down. I'll be right here to help you pick yourself up."

CHAPTER 25

Lincoln

Cleo cried on his shoulder for an hour before falling asleep. He lay with her until dinnertime when Molly insisted they have grilled cheese and soup before Cleo went back to bed. Her puffy, sad eyes, disheveled hair, and curled shoulders screamed defeat. His heart ached.

He'd spent the morning training at the rink, and now his legs were burning and heavy. His shoulders knotted and exhaustion rippled through him as he rode the elevator up to his dorm room.

Russ was already away for the weekend with Jude. Linc had planned on spending the weekend holed up with Cleo, but she'd declined when he'd asked, citing a stack of untouched work she needed to catch up on.

Every cell in his body wanted to hunt down Johnny and break his face, but it wouldn't help Cleo. She didn't want more attention on her. She wanted to disappear into the background. She was already pulling away from him. Her texts were one word answers, and the fire in her vibrant, hazel eyes was dimming.

Rage sloshed in his stomach and he thumped the back of

the door as he closed it. Fucking Johnny. What damage did he have that drove him to be such a low life piece of shit and make everyone else's lives miserable?

Linc's phone vibrated against his thigh. He dropped his kit bag at his feet, pulled his shirt over his head and took his phone out of his pocket before taking his sweatpants off.

Dad calling.

He dropped face first onto his bed with a groan before shuffling onto his side and hitting the green button.

"Hi Dad."

"Is there something you need to tell us, son?"

All business, all the time. His dad's no-nonsense tone made Linc all the more keen to be a jerk in reply, but he pressed down the urge to wisecrack.

"Hi, Lincoln. How are you, honey?"

"Hi, Mom, I'm good, thanks. How are you guys?"

"I asked you a question, Linc."

Linc rubbed his eyes and sighed. He'd never heard his father talk to the girls the way he spoke to him. "You'll have to be more specific, Dad." He spat his words out with a bite. Rising to his father's bait was never his smartest idea, but he was primed for an argument and, from his dad's tone, it wouldn't take much to get one.

"You got a letter here, from an art gallery."

Linc's pulse boomed in his ears, his chest tightened, and his already clammy body broke out in new prickles of sweat. He bolted to his feet, dragging his free hand through his hair while he clutched the phone against his ear. *What the fuck?*

"Oh yeah?"

"It says…" A page rustled against the speaker. "Congratulations on making it through the first two rounds. You have made it to the quarter finals."

His dad's voice droned in the background, while Linc's brain scrambled to catch up. He had gotten through the first rounds. His heart attempted to soar but was rebutted all the way to his stomach by anxiety over the impending lecture.

"I'll ask again. Do you have anything you'd like to tell us, Lincoln?"

Don't be a dick. Don't be a dick. Don't be a dick.

"I entered some of my art into a competition. No big deal."

Don't be a dick. Don't be a dick. Don't be a dick.

Hands clapped on the other end of the line. "No big deal?" His mom's excitement eased his anxiety. "Lincoln this is wonderful news, congratulations! I had no idea you were into art! The letter says something about an exhibition if you win—"

"I'm not going to win, Mom. I don't even know why I put myself forward. I'm not good enough for an exhibition. I just—"

"I can tell you *exactly* why you put yourself forward."

Linc winced at his dad's tone.

"It's that girl, isn't it? Cleo… whatever her name is. Amelia told us you had a new girlfriend. She's clearly filling your head with all this flowery bullshit."

Every clipped word from his father's mouth stoked the anger deep in the pit of Linc's stomach.

His mother gasped. "That's enough, Martin."

"You're damn right it's enough. Lincoln, do we need to have yet another talk about what you're at the U for? Do I need to remind you about keeping your head in the game and not screwing up your chances of making something of yourself?"

"No, Dad, you don't. I know *exactly* what you want from my time here." Could you dislocate your eyeballs from rolling them too hard? Linc was close to finding out. That, or his teeth would turn to dust from all the clenching and grinding.

"Stop fucking around, and keep your head in the game."

Fuck it. The growing inferno of anger clawed up his chest and burst from his mouth, unchecked. "Maybe I don't want to keep my head in the game. Have you ever considered that, Dad? Have you, for one moment, ever stopped to think about what *I* might want from my time here? Or from my life for that matter?"

"Lincoln..." His cold voice carried a warning.

Lincoln's head said stop, but his heart raged on. He'd had it with the double standard in the Scott house. It was time to make his stand, draw his line in the sand. He was on a full ride to school. It wasn't like his father could pull financial support and upend Linc's life. He needed to let the words out that he'd been keeping inside for so long.

"No, Dad. I'm not you. I'm not NHL material; we both know that. I never have been. I'm good, but I'm not *great.*"

His dad grunted, and a small gasp escaped his mom on the other end of the phone.

Linc sucked in a breath and steeled his spine. "And maybe I don't *want* to be great. I'm quite happy to live in the shadow of former-NHL superstar Martin Lincoln Scott. But what about what I want, huh? Maybe I want to be an accountant like Mom, or a free spirit like Amelia, or maybe I want to go to med school like your perfect first born."

Dad might not have been the cause of his anger, but he'd stoked it, and Lincoln wasn't in the mood to rein it in. "My point is, it's *my* life, not yours. I'm here on a scholarship, and as long as I keep my nose clean, my grades up and don't fuck up on the ice, I'm happy and school's happy. Why can't you be happy?"

He paused. He should stop. But if he stopped, he might never again get the chance – or find the balls – to confront his dad.

"I don't need to impress scouts or make a name for myself, and I don't mind the whispers or sneers about how I'm nowhere near as good as my NHL star father. I have no idea what I want to do after college, but playing pro-hockey is not it. Now if you guys don't mind, I need to have a shower and get an assignment finished up before I turn in for the night. Keeping up appearances is exhausting work."

He didn't wait for a 'goodbye' before he hung up and fell back onto the bed. The phone rang again. Dad.

With a growl, Linc flung the phone across the room before turning his head into the pillow and letting out a roar. Dad was probably mad, big mad, and Linc didn't want to deal with another lecture.

He'd said his piece, it was time for his father to stew for a change, instead of vice versa.

Linc's shoulders were lighter for having said the words that got mangled in his throat any time he'd previously tried to speak them. But a headache brewed behind his eyes and his muscles remained taut. He pulled off his boxers, adding them to the pile of clothes on the floor on his way to the shower.

He'd simmer with his thoughts under a stream of cold water in hopes he could wash away his bad mood. Then all he had to do was figure out how to convince his girlfriend she was perfect just the way she was.

Shoulders lighter, Linc strode down the corridor. Ahead Cleo stood talking to Molly outside their English class on Monday morning. Her yoga pants clung to her in all the right places and her oversized, off-the-shoulder sweater showed just enough skin to drive him crazy. Molly acknowledged his approach with a barely noticeable twitch of her eyebrow.

He slid his hands around Cleo's waist and squeezed as he buried his lips into her hair. He tensed for a beat, unsure whether she would shirk him off or accept the embrace. She softened in his arms, and relief washed over him.

Thank fuck.

"Hola, *preciosa.*"

Her low moan of appreciation for the Spanish he mumbled against her neck warmed him.

"¿Cómo estás?"

She tipped her head against his shoulder. "Are you learning Spanish, Mr. Darcy?"

"I might have downloaded Duo Lingo. I'm pretty sure the app laughed at my pronunciation yesterday, but it's there when I need an ego check." He pecked her cheek.

Giggling, she turned to face him. "Who knew you were such a romantic?"

He nuzzled the side of his jaw against the side of hers. "Don't tell everyone. I need my soulless, jerk on the ice rep to remain intact. It can be our little secret."

"Linc!" Russ made his way across the hall to stand next to Molly. "Did you break your phone?"

Cleo's brows pinched into a frown, and Linc shook his head.

"Your sister hit me up. Sounds like you're avoiding the parentals and I need to know the party line... y'know, so I can toe it?"

Linc chuckled. "Bumped heads with my dad. No biggie. Just need to cool off before I get back into it with him."

Russ's eyes flitted between Cleo and Molly before landing on Linc. He tipped his head, unspoken questions written across his face, then nodded. "As long as you're okay, you know I've got your back, man."

"Thanks, Russ. 'Preciate it."

Casting a final lingering "WTF is going on with you" look, Russ jerked his chin. "Later?"

"Later."

"Wanna talk about it?" Cleo's eyes swam with concern, as Russ walked away.

"Clearly not with his BFF. Or in the hallway. Read the room, Cho-Cho." Molly elbowed Cleo, who gave an embarrassed smile.

She cupped his jaw with her warm palm. "Are you okay?"

He shrugged in response. "I just told my dad some hard truths. Didn't go so well. It'll blow over."

"Maybe you should try talking to him again – it might help. I know they're not always great at showing their love, but they really do just want what's best for us."

"I know you're trying to help, Lizzy, but you don't know my dad." He ground out each word between gritted teeth. Squeezing down the torrent of "mind your business" bubbling up in his throat, he swallowed against the current.

"I just mean—"

He almost missed Molly's subtle movement. She wrapped a hand around Cleo's elbow and gave a small shake of her head.

"I really don't want to talk about it, Cleo. Please?" He beseeched her with his eyes, hoping his thick with effort tone was enough to dissuade her from the conversation.

"But they're your parents, Linc. You can't just cut them off."

Molly groaned.

Flames of anger lapped along his spine. He clenched and unclenched his hands and took a step back from her. "I feel like you missed the 'I don't want to have this discussion here' memo. But one thing's for damn sure, family can't treat you whatever the hell way they want just 'cause they're family. They don't get a hall pass to make me feel like shit just 'cause they're my family."

She opened her mouth to respond, but he shook his head and turned on his heel.

"Linc, what about class?"

Class. Schoolwork. Grades. They were the only things that mattered to Cleo.

He stepped away from her, forcing air into his lungs to calm himself. She didn't know he'd applied for the art competition. She didn't know he'd let someone outside of her see inside his soul. She had no idea his worlds were colliding.

Even if she did know, wouldn't school still be a priority for her? Would she understand the tug of war in his chest?

She'd somehow managed to get under his skin, to convince him it wasn't only okay for him to stop hiding who he truly was, but to own it.

A battle raged inside of him. For the moment he was Bruce Banner, but the Hulk was dangerously close to bursting out of his clothes and smashing everything in his path.

Let your freak flag fly, wasn't that the MO of the Marvel-verse?

So what if his freak flag was a love of art? People liked all kinds of things. Nowhere did it say you could only like one thing. He could be artistic and athletic at the same time, right?

Striding towards the double doors leading outside, he paused. One thing was for sure, he had reached a point in his life where he could no longer hide his freak flag, and he was mad about that too.

As he swung a leg over his bike, he made a mental note to stop watching Marvel movies on repeat with Russell, though it wouldn't put an end to the identity crisis consuming his every thought.

He'd applied to the art competition. He'd confronted his parents about living in his father's shadow, and he'd let Cleo see his innermost self. The toothpaste was out of the tube and there was no putting it back.

But even if he could, would he want to?

CHAPTER 26

Lincoln

The one-goal advantage was the most dangerous lead in a hockey game. Considering how fast a goal could be surrendered, it was never a smart move to get too comfortable when you were ahead. Linc would have given anything to be facing a one goal lead. The Pirates were three to nothing down, and Alabama was verging on getting themselves a shutout.

Shutout. Shutout. Shutout.

Superstition said you couldn't say the 'S' word, *shutout*, on a game night before the final buzzer, for fear of jinxing the goaltender. But the Pirates needed all the help they could get. If mentally whispering the 'S' word could bag them a comeback, he'd whisper it all the way to the third period.

If Jeremy Lewis came down with a terrible case of the shits during the period break, Linc wouldn't be mad about it. Alabama's hot-shot winger had scored two of the three goals on the board and assisted on the third. It was as though he had a turbo booster in his skates.

Linc growled as he stomped into the locker room for the second intermission. He shook off his gloves, leaned forward, elbows on his thighs, and cradled his head, hoping the fuck off vibes were rolling off him in waves, and no one would bother him.

No one except Johnny. Was the guy really that stupid? Or did he just have a death wish? His eye was still a dark shade of purple and his lip was held together by a single paper stitch.

Linc had his suspicions who'd graced Johnny's face with their fist, but everyone was keeping tight-lipped about the whole thing.

Linc stood as Johnny approached. Sweat dripped from under his helmet, and the wound on his lip tugged on his smirk.

"What?"

"Just checking in, Scottie Boy."

Linc narrowed his eyes. There was always a sting in this guy's tail. He wasn't there for funsies. Did the guy *want* to have the shit beaten out of him? All he ever seemed to do was push people's buttons. Linc couldn't figure him out, but things didn't add up.

"I had a question."

Linc gestured for him to continue.

"I'm wondering if all those paint fumes are going to your head, 'cause you're playing like shit on a stick tonight."

Linc's fist connected with Johnny's already bruised jaw before he even had time to take another breath, let alone utter another word. Swinging again, Linc's knuckles connected with Johnny's eye, clipping the edge of his helmet.

As Linc wound up up for a third strike, strong hands wrapped around his arm. Johnny flinched, ducking his face behind his forearms.

Blood trickled down his chin from his lip and nose. Linc strained against whoever had stopped him from taking another swing.

"That's enough! Go home, Lincoln."

"But Coach—"

"I don't wanna hear it." Coach crossed the locker room and waved a dismissive hand. "Go home."

Johnny snickered, blood staining his teeth as his lips curled into a snarl.

"You too, Johnny."

Johnny's jaw dropped open.

Linc yanked his arm out of the clutches of his teammate.

"I want both of you in my office tomorrow morning."

No one moved. Linc's chest heaved from restraint. His eyes locked in silent battle with Johnny, who glowered in return.

"Move!"

Johnny stalked across the dressing room and tossed his helmet onto a bench.

"As for the rest of you, get your heads out of your asses and get back out on the ice." Coach turned, yanked the door open, and stomped out of the locker room.

"You gonna be okay?" Russ fastened his helmet and popped his mouth guard in.

Flexing his jaw, Linc nodded.

"Go see your girl." His best friend smacked his shoulder, grabbed his stick, and joined the line of players ready to trudge back out onto the ice.

For once, Linc didn't want to see his girl. He didn't want to see his teammates and he didn't want to talk to his family.

He needed to find a way to vent his excess rage before he destroyed every relationship he had.

"I'll take another." Linc held his empty tumbler toward the bartender.

"Same again?"

It was one of the few bars in town that didn't ask too many questions when it came to ID, and the staff either didn't notice a fake ID, or didn't care.

He shouldn't, but what the hell? Linc nodded.

"I feel like you might wanna reconsider, Linc."

Jeremy Lewis leaned on the bar, cradling a bottle of beer and sporting a shit-eating grin. "Man, if I had a buck for every time I felt like bailing on a game and hitting the bar, I'd be rich. Didn't have you pinned for someone who'd *actually* do it though."

"Shouldn't you be on a bus back to BFE Alabama, Lewis?"

"We're staying the night." He tipped his empty bottle to the bartender who placed two fingers of scotch in front of Linc. "I'll take another please. Where are your teammates, Lincoln?"

"Where are yours, Jeremy?"

"Is this really where we're at? 'Cause I gotta tell you, man, if we're at elementary school level of "I know you are, but what am I?" I will win. I am the master of being a childish douche nozzle."

"This isn't the usual post-game bar."

"I know. It's why I'm here." Jeremy slid onto the stool beside him and accepted the bottle from the bartender. "Guessing it's why you're here too. Wanna talk about it?"

"Nope." Linc swirled his glass, and the golden liquid rolled over the two ice cubes. Maybe if he stayed focused on the drink in his glass, nothing else would matter.

"This have anything to do with Johnny White's face looking like a kaleidoscope of color?"

Nope. This prick isn't gonna let it drop.

Apparently the growl Linc intended to keep inside was audible, because Jeremy chuckled.

"Thought as much." He took a long pull of his beer. "Not that there's any love lost between him and me. I mean, he's a grade-A douche canoe. We have our own issues. But maybe I wanna throw a few cheap shots at him for funsies for whatever he's done to piss you off. Bros before a-holes and all that jazz…"

"I'm not talking to you about my private life, Lewis. We're not friends."

"We're not. Colleagues at best. Kinda sorta, since we're on opposing teams. But it looks like you're going to break that glass into a million pieces any second now from how tightly you're clenching it."

Lincoln loosened his fingers around the tumbler.

"I'm going out on a limb that you might need to talk, and correct me if I'm wrong, but I'm the only poor fucker here. So I guess that falls to me."

The bar was empty save for a couple of old guys shooting pool in the corner. It was a rundown dive bar on the edge of town, away from everyone he knew, which was kind of the point.

"I'm fine." He gulped down half his drink. The bartender appeared with an ice pack wrapped in a cloth. "I'm fine." Linc wasn't sure if he was repeating himself for the barman, or to convince himself, but he took the ice pack and put it on his swelling knuckles.

The bartender arched an eyebrow, gave a half shrug, and moved along the bar to wipe down the counter.

"Do you do anything outside of hockey?"

Jeremy tipped his head and looked up at the ceiling, pursing his lips. "*Is* there anything outside of hockey?"

Linc snorted. "Yeah. We're not talking about this."

"I wanna play pro, Linc. That's the dream. But it's *my* dream." He picked at the label on his beer with his thumbnail.

"Some people get into college on a full ride and they have no intention of playing pro. They want free schooling and are good enough to make it happen. No shame in that game." He picked up his bottle and swirled his beer around before taking a drink. "You not wanna play anymore?"

"It's not that. I love the game. We both know it's in my blood."

Jeremy nodded, one eye squinting as though deep in thought. "Must be some serious pressure being the son of an NHL All-Star."

"You have no idea." Linc finished the rest of his drink and slammed the glass onto the counter more forcefully than he intended. Sliding the glass toward the bartender, he winced. "Sorry."

"You're right, I might not have first-hand experience. But I know enough of the game to know a little about a little. Pressure from your dad to be great, just like him, right?"

Linc sighed. "It's like he's retired from the game, but at the same time, he's not. I'm not good enough to go pro. I'm not as good as he was – hell, I'm not even as good as you are. But he seems to think if I train just a bit harder, go to one more training camp, and play in front of just the right scouts, things would happen for me. Sometimes you just gotta know your limits, and I know mine."

"But you don't *want* to play pro, even if you were good enough."

A jolt of surprise shot through Linc. If he were talented enough to play NHL level hockey, would he? Would he push forward to play on a national scale? Would he *want* to do it or would he just feel obligated to make his father's dream come true?

A frustrated sigh escaped him as he scrubbed a hand across

his jaw. "I don't know the answer to that, Lupes. Maybe if I was better at the game I wouldn't feel like such a fake and failure."

Jeremy snorted, then took a sip of his beer. "That's the spirit, warming up to me nicely, Linc, nickname and all. I guess that's the trouble with feeling like a fraudster, Linc. Once you're prone to feelings of inadequacy, it doesn't matter how good you are, that voice will always shout louder. Even if you went pro, you'd still find a way to feel like you've hoodwinked people into thinking you're good."

"You think so?"

"I know so."

"How do you deal with it?"

Jeremy chuckled. "I pat myself on the back for being an epic trickster god and convincing people I'm actually good enough at something that they believe me."

It was Lincoln's turn to laugh. "That works?"

"Sometimes more than others." Jeremy shrugged. "What would you do if you didn't play hockey? What's your major?"

"Communication studies... and a minor in art history." Lincoln flexed his fingers under the melting ice pack, ready to spring into action if Jeremy said a single negative word about the fact he was studying art history.

"Huh."

"Huh what?"

"At ease, angry man. Yeah, I see you flexing those digits. This face is way too pretty to be broken by your damn fist. You're not the only one who knows their limits. I'd have no chance against you. I don't have backup in this place and no one knows I'm here, so they'd never find the body." He winked and indicated to the almost empty bar.

"I dunno why you're so defensive about the fact you're doing an art history minor. I wouldn't give a shit if you were doing an art history major, for fuck's sake. My opinion on your life choices doesn't matter a fuck, Linc. Are you happy? Is it something you can see yourself doing as a career? And in the words of our great leader, Ms. Marie Kondo, does it spark joy?"

Linc laughed, his muscles relaxing, and he flagged the bartender down for a glass of water and two beers.

"What can I say?" Jeremy shrugged again. "I like reality TV shows. Anyway, does art history set your heart on fire? Does it take you closer to what you wanna be when you grow up?" He wrinkled his nose at his last question, as though growing up was something that tasted awful to say.

"Do whatever the fuck lights you up inside. Do it shamelessly and unapologetically. Life is too short to live in the shadow of where you really want to be. It's too short for regrets."

His glassy eyes met Linc's. Unshed tears reflected in the dim light of the bar. He swallowed hard. "We don't get enough time to spend a chunk of it doing something someone else wants us to do." His voice broke on the last sentence.

Linc's chest tightened. Jeremy's parents had been brutally murdered in a mass shooting. "I'm sorry, Jer. I didn't mean to—"

"Ah." He held up his hand. "It's fine. I don't mind talking about them, especially if it serves to help someone realize they need to do all the things they want to do, because time isn't our friend." He took another drink.

Linc nodded. The shooting had made the national news, and hockey circles being what they were, it was impossible to keep it under wraps. If anyone knew about not having enough time, it was him. "Have you changed how you're living since they… uh… since you lost them?"

Jeremy shrugged. "Bought a boat. My mom would be so pissed." He shook his head with a sad smile. "This isn't a pity party, though. This is about you."

He tilted his bottle toward Linc. "Whatever is tugging at your heart, you should probably give in and let it. If you want to run off and join the circus, go do it. If you wanna be a professional ballerina, I dunno man, that ship has probably sailed but if anyone could become a geriatric ballet dancer my money's on you."

He leaned forward and pushed Linc's shoulder. "You do you, boo. So your dad's pissed at you for not doing pro hockey, he'll get over it. Ultimately he'll realize that you're not him and your dreams aren't his dreams. Maybe he'll get on board the Linc-train, maybe he won't, but either way, you'll have stayed true to yourself and done something worthy of your time."

Linc took a sip of the beer the barman set in front of him and slid the other bottle across to Jeremy.

"I was supposed to come out for one drink." He picked up the fresh beer, reached it toward Linc who clinked the neck of his bottle against Jeremy's.

"It's never just one drink. Gotta admit, when Coach sent me home from the game tonight, the last thing I could have predicted was ending up here with you."

Jeremy nudged him playfully. "You're living every woman's fantasy right now, man." He winked and sipped his beer. "Okay, maybe not every woman. But there's... like... at least one."

Linc rolled his shoulders. Talking to Jeremy had lightened his load. Finding an unbiased opinion had cemented his decision to step out from his father's shadow and live the life he wanted to, even if it was the harder path.

"Now, wanna tell Uncle Jeremy why you're using Johnny White's face as a piñata?"

CHAPTER 27

Cleo

"If you're gonna keep ignoring your boyfriend could you at least turn the vibration off? It's distracting. And annoying AF."

Cleo's phone vibrated across the counter of the coffee shop. Was she avoiding Linc? Possibly. Did she feel bad about it? Absolutely. She sighed and picked up her phone, three missed calls and a handful of texts. "He knows I'm working." She put it back on the counter.

"Yeah, on a Wednesday night, Cho-Cho. He also knows it's quiet." Molly gestured around the almost-empty café and pointed at the open book in front of Cleo. "So quiet that you're doing homework and chatting to yours truly. Answer the man, for crying out loud. He'll send a freakin' SEAL team to hunt you down if you don't."

Cleo giggled. "He wouldn't. But I take your point." She unlocked her phone and checked for messages.

Lincoln: Wanna watch a movie after work?

Lincoln: You okay? Busy night?

> Lincoln: I can't help but feel like you're avoiding me, Miss Bennet.

> Lincoln: I'm sorry for snapping at you and taking off the other day. I have a lot on my mind. I know, no excuse for being dickish.

> Lincoln: Spoke to Coach this morning. He told me I need to buck up or I'm out.

> Lincoln: I'll be here when you're ready to talk.

"Wow. That poor, desperate boy. Put him out of his misery, Cleo. Do it now, or I'll wrestle that damn phone from your hands and do it for you." Molly pointed a condemning finger at her. "And be nice."

Cleo shook her head. "I'm always nice."

"Mmhmm. Be extra nice. 'Kay? I get the impression he needs nice right now."

"And you're more concerned with what he needs than what I need?"

"Nuh uh. Whatever this is..." She waved her palm in front of Cleo's face. "Not here for it. It's not me you're pissed at. Hell, it's not even Lincoln you're pissed at. So don't come at me with your bad mood, Cho." She fell silent for a moment before adding. "You shouldn't *at* him either. Don't *at* us girlfriend."

Unease sputtered in Cleo's stomach. Who was she truly mad at? Melissa? Johnny? Herself? Why couldn't she shake the agitation and move forward? Linc's outburst was minimal, but her reaction was... more. Invisible bands tightened across her chest.

The door opened and one of the Pirates walked in. *Dallas? Houston? What the hell is this guy's name?*

"Austin, what are you doing here?"

Austin. I knew it was something Texas-y.

"Felt like a hot cocoa on my way home. How are you ladies doing?"

"Good, thanks. Shitty game last night." Molly was always after a story.

Austin shrugged. "It happens."

Cleo grabbed a to-go cup. "Cream and marshmallows, Austin?"

"Please." He pulled out his wallet, bruised knuckles catching the light as he plucked a crisp bill from the billfold.

The bands around her chest tightened. "Rough game last night?" She took the money and rubbed at the knot building behind her sternum.

He kneaded the back of his injured hand. "This is from a few days ago." He met her eyes with a pointed stare, his dark gaze saying everything his words weren't. He was the one who'd punched Johnny. "It's on the mend. Linc's look worse."

Her eyes widened before darting to Molly, who shifted in her seat.

"What happened to Linc's knuckles?"

Austin's eyes narrowed. "Got thrown out of the game for fighting." He glanced at Molly before raising his eyebrows. "I figured you'd know already."

Cleo pulled her lip between her teeth and gnawed on it before shaking her head. "Who?"

He flexed his hand. "Johnny."

A hand fluttered to her open mouth. "So when you say thrown out, you mean..."

"Coach sent him home for laying into one of his own, yeah. Asshole deserved it though." Whatever Austin saw pass over her face made him hurry to follow up. "He didn't say anything about you this time. Took a shot at Linc about his art or some shit." He chuckled. "Seems Johnny was the last to know about Linc's skills."

"You knew?"

"A bunch of us did. Kinda hard to keep a secret when you're part of a team as close-knit as ours. Linc seemed bent out of shape about it though, so we played dumb, let him think he was Hermione Grangering the shit out of his year with that time turner thing they gave her. At least we did, until Johnny opened his damn mouth. Dude has a death wish – sooner he's out of here the better."

Cleo let his words seep into her brain for a moment.

"Are the rumors true then?" Molly's eyes twitched with anticipation. She sucked at hiding her excitement when she got wind of a story.

"Seems that way. He's on the move, 50:50 says whether it's 'Bama or Chi-town. Either way, we'll be glad to see the back of him. He's wet rot. And no..." He pointed a finger at her. "You can't quote me on that."

"Is Linc okay?" Cleo handed him the drink.

Austin shrugged. "Doubt it." He turned toward the door.

"Austin?"

He paused, glancing over his shoulder.

"Why'd you do it?" She gestured at his hand.

"I fight. It's what I do."

Cleo laughed despite the apprehension stirring in her stomach. "You don't just go around punching randos, Austin."

He pursed his lips and took a sip from the to-go cup. "It's a family thing."

She wanted to press him further, but the door opened and he made a swift exit. A woman walked in holding a superhero gift bag.

"Hey, if it isn't romance novel girl!" Molly's eyes brightened with recognition.

"Ah! The romance cynic. I'm Sabrina."

"Molly, and that's Cleo." She jerked her chin over her shoulder.

Sabrina laughed, a belly laugh that shook her whole body. "I know who you both are – ha! That sounds kinda stalker-creepy, doesn't it? I don't mean it like that. I met Cleo at the blackout party."

Cleo scrunched her face up, trying to place the woman. "Spin the bottle?"

Sabrina nodded. "Yeah. What is it about college parties that turns fully grown adults into kids again?" She snorted. "Spin the bottle. I didn't even play it as a child, but gimme a few red solo cups full of liquor of questionable origin and I'm buzzing with the thrill of having to mack on a complete stranger."

Molly raised her coffee in salute. "We don't judge here."

"Except romance books." Sabrina winked at Cleo and pointed a finger-pistol at Molly.

The corners of Molly's mouth tugged into a pursed-lipped smile. "Except that."

"Can I get you something, Sabrina?"

Her flawless skin darkened with a blush at the question. She rolled her lips between her teeth and shook her head. "No, thanks. I was hoping you could play mailwoman for me? I know you're with Linc, and he rooms with Russell Stewart, right?"

Cleo nodded slowly, struggling to figure out where the woman in front of her was leading them with her strange answer.

"This is weird. I know it's weird. I've talked myself in and out of doing this no less than thirty-five million times today."

Molly leaned forward. "Doing... what, exactly?"

Sabrina held out the gift bag to Cleo. "Could you give this to Linc, to give to Russ, to give to Jude, please?"

Adorable. Utterly adorable. She'd gone to the trouble of picking up a gift for Russell's daughter, and delivered it to Cleo to pass along.

"You're giving a gift to Russell's daughter, through three degrees of separation? Well this just gets curiouser and curiouser."

Sabrina's cheeks darkened. She swept her hair from her face before knotting her hands together. "I... uh."

"Have a raging lady boner for Russ and wanna use his kid to get to him?"

Cleo groaned inwardly at Molly's bluntness.

"What? No!" Sabrina's eyes widened and her brows rose. "It's not like that at all. Is that what he's going to think, too? Shit. Fuck. I knew I shouldn't have come." She stepped forward, reaching for the bag, but Molly snatched from Cleo's hands.

"Hmmm. Okay, so you want Russ to take a stroll in your lady garden, but you're not a cold, calculated, wench. We can work with that."

"Molly!" Cleo covered her eyes and groaned.

"What?" Molly rolled her eyes.

"I'm sorry about her." Cleo flapped an elbow in Molly's direction. Leaning over the counter she tugged the bag from her grasp and set it on the counter. "This is a very sweet gesture – I'll be sure Russell gets it."

"Why don't you just give it to him yourself?"

"I didn't want things to be weird. Jude has the same birthday as me, and when I saw this at the store, I couldn't walk by. I don't even really know them. I mean, I just met them... It's too weird, isn't it? It's definitely weird. Fuck."

"It's adorable." Cleo hoped her insistence would calm Sabrina down. Beads of sweat prickles across her forehead and her chest rose and fell much too fast. "Take a breath. He's going to appreciate it. It's not too weird – it's sweet."

Molly jerked a thumb over her shoulder. "She's just saying that so she doesn't have to fill out an incident report form when your ass crumples onto the tiles."

Sabrina snorted a laugh. "Why is this so complicated?"

"Men?" Cleo tucked the bag under the till.

Sabrina nodded.

"Romance novels." Molly raised her mug again and took another slurp. "That shit gives people all kinds of dumbass ideas."

"Like what?" Cleo leaned on the counter.

"Well, for starters, they make them think we wear lacy thongs and bras all the time. No one talks about period pants in books. Or the pH-panties."

"PH panties? What the fuck are you talking about?" Cleo's eyes met Sabrina's, who was seemingly every bit as confused as she was.

"Y'know, that section of your underwear drawer with stained panties from your goo-goo from your foo-foo?"

Cleo's face sizzled as she covered it with her palm. She groaned. "Oh God. You really don't filter anything you say, do you?"

"Why should I? It's perfectly natural. Acidic discharge interacting with the dye on our undies and staining those expensive suckers right up." She waved a finger between Sabrina and Cleo. "You can't tell me it doesn't happen to you. But I *can* tell *you* that you never read about the real-life shit like that in books. It's always the perfect love story. No farts, period pants, or pH panties."

Cleo reached over the counter and shoved her friend's shoulder. "Ignore her. You're right, she's a cynic. I get why you wanted to go the indirect route. But seriously, Russ is a great guy, you could have taken it to him yourself."

Sabrina scrunched her eyes closed and shook her head. "He was... eh... a bit pissy with me when we met. This... this is better. Anyway, I gotta jet. Feel free to pretend you found that gift and keep me out of it altogether. Thanks for being the mail carrier though." She didn't hesitate before fleeing the café, leaving the door to slam closed.

"There's definitely a story there. What a weird night." Molly slid her empty cup to Cleo. "You gonna talk to Linc?"

Cleo already had her phone in hand and Linc's message string on the screen.

> Cleo: Are you okay? I heard about the game last night.

> Cleo: I close up soon, can I come over? I have something to give to Russell too. Two birds, one gift bag.

> Lincoln: You could, but it would be a wasted journey since I'm parked outside.

> Cleo: Of course you are.

A shimmer of anticipation flashed in her stomach and she couldn't fight the smile that broke out across her face.

> Cleo: Coffee?

> Lincoln: Thanks, but that smile was the serotonin hit I needed today.

> Cleo: Can you see me blushing through your stalkery binoculars?

> Lincoln: Yup. It's like a beacon of adorableness. Can I give you a ride home?

> Cleo: I'd love that.

The door opened, and there stood Linc, wearing his signature blue jeans and a black polo shirt. Dark circles underlined his eyes, and while he smiled, it wasn't his usual light-up-Broadway, panty-dropping smile. One knuckle had a Band-

Aid over it – the rest were bruised, and his disheveled hair fell into his eyes.

She hurried out from behind the counter and launched herself into his waiting arms. She couldn't help it. Breathing in his clean, fresh scent, she planted a kiss on his cheek, hesitating for a beat, hoping he'd turn to capture her lips in a full kiss. Her heart slammed against her chest.

"Not yet, Lizzy. If I kiss you here at work, you'll get fired and they'll need to clean this place with bleach."

Warmth spread throughout her body, and she smiled before tracing the line of his jaw with her fingertips. "I hear you had a rough night last night."

His eyes flew to Molly who gave a half shrug. "Nope. Not it. Will didn't tell her either."

Cleo jabbed a finger toward Molly. "Don't think I've forgotten about the fact you didn't tell me, Miss Morrison. Freakin' hockey reporter best friend who didn't bother to tell me you got into a fight."

Molly tutted. "Look, it wasn't my story to tell."

"But you're telling the whole school via newspaper, right?"

"Well, duh." She flipped her hair over her shoulder. "Drama sells. People love that shit. They love when Linc gets involved. It so seldom happens that people will absolutely eat it up."

Linc shook his head. "It was nothing."

"Nothing got you and that asshole JW sent home. I looked for you in the bar post-game..."

Cleo raised a questioning eyebrow.

"To make sure you were okay, obviously." Molly gestured at Linc.

"And to get a quote." Linc gestured back at Molly.

She didn't deny his accusation. "But I couldn't find you. Where'd you go?"

"Had a drink with a friend across town."

"What friend?" Molly narrowed her eyes and crossed her arms.

Cleo fought the smile tugging at her lips. Molly's interrogations were CIA level effective. People generally crumbled like a house of cards under her glower and probing questions. Linc, on the other hand, smirked, his lips and eyebrow twitching.

"No one you know, Molly. And in case you're accusing me of infidelity, he had way too much dick for my tastes."

Cleo barked out a laugh. Unhooking her arm from his waist she walked back to the counter. "Want a drink while I finish cleaning up?"

Molly pretended to write on an invisible notepad. "Sorry guys, Lincoln Scott confirms he's just not into you." She winked. "Anything else you'd like to go on the record about?"

Linc pulled a chair out from a neighboring table. He slipped onto it, chest against the back of the seat. "So, Miss Bennet, busy night? Or ignoring me?"

Was her face on fire? Did the air evaporate from the coffee shop? Out of the corner of her eye, Molly smirked and mouthed "told you so."

He chuckled, blue eyes piercing hers. "I see."

"B-but I didn't answer."

"Your eyes did all the talking."

"And that's my cue to leave." Molly smacked the table. "Actually, my cue to leave was when he arrived, but we all know I'm a nosy bitch and have a tendency to outstay my welcome. For the record though, this place got pretty Central Perk in here. Not your typical Wednesday night lull."

"It's adorable and only mildly terrifying when you defend your best friend."

"Only mildly? I'll have to try harder next time. Later,

bitches!" Molly grabbed her bag, flipped them off with a grin, and left.

"You wanna tell me why you're ignoring my messages?" He stood, closed the distance between them, and slid a warm finger under her chin as he tipped her head.

Hurt. His eyes swam with hurt. Pain so visible and raw it squeezed her heart like a vise. She took his hand from her face and kissed along each of his swollen knuckles. "You wanna tell me why you're breaking your hands on people's faces?"

They were at the edge of a precipice. Both swirling in white water rapids of emotions, hurtling toward the waterfall's edge, to plummet into the jagged rocks below.

She didn't want to fight. She didn't want to add to his pain, and she didn't want to confess her darkest, most deep-seated fears.

She wanted to kiss him, to forget everything going on around them and just exist in his arms.

"Linc..." Dragging her palm along the stubble dotted on his jaw, she giggled at the tickling sensation. Wrapping her fingers in his hair, she pulled him closer for a kiss.

"Wait." His strained rasp between kisses made heat rush to her core. He crossed the coffee shop. Flicking the lock on the back of the door, he flipped the sign to 'closed.' Intensity and desire burned in his eyes when he turned to her.

She'd always wondered what the woman was staring at in the gif where she dumps a bottle of water over her head and now she understood. Cleo was seconds from pulling a bottle of water from the fridge and doing just that.

Linc smoldered as he approached. Dragging his thumb across his bottom lip, he eyed her like a starving person eyed a triple decker club with extra meat.

Her pulse quickened as he made his way behind the counter. She untied her apron, slipping it over her head and throwing it on the counter in a ball.

"I'm not usually one to avoid my problems by..." He licked his lips. "Avoiding my problems."

"But?" Her voice was airy and breathless. Her core throbbed in time to her racing pulse. Need. Pure, unadulterated need clutched at her insides.

"But I'm making an exception right now, Lizzy." He dropped to his knees, picked up her foot, and popped off her flat. He dragged one leg of her yoga pants down and off before draping her leg over his shoulder and pressing her body back against the counter with splayed palms on her stomach.

"W-what i-if someone sees?"

"They can only see your back from the door." He ran his finger over the fabric of her panties, and along her slick folds. "I can always stop if you'd prefer."

His lips curled in a knowing smile, and the mirth flashing in his eyes vanished when she shook her head. He licked his lips again. "Hold onto the counter, Miss Bennet." Shouldering her legs apart he peeled her panties to the side to gain access.

"Not gonna work." His growl sent a ripple of desire through her. He yanked her panty leg down, threading her foot through before discarding the fabric and settling back between her thighs. As his tongue met her aching and desperate clit, her head rolled back.

They needed to talk – about so many things. And they would, right after she stopped fighting the already building climax cascading through her body and gave the man on his knees before her what he wanted.

CHAPTER 28

Lincoln

Spoiler alert: They didn't talk.

Linc ate her out against the counter in the coffee shop, gave her two screaming orgasms, and took her home.

"Want me to come in?"

Her cheeks were still flushed after their antics in the café and the ride back to her apartment. She shook her head, handing over his helmet, guilt flashing in her eyes. "I have an early start."

He could have said he'd leave early. He could have said he wouldn't stay the night. He certainly should have suggested they at least talk about the increasing pile of *stuff* weighing heavily between them.

But he didn't, and they didn't.

He drew her to him, kissed her as though it would be the last time his lips would taste hers and waited as she sashayed into her apartment.

When he got home, he presented the Avengers gift bag to Russell, who'd just stepped out of the shower and was leaving a trail of soapy droplets through their room as he towel-dried his hair.

"Is this your way of telling me you won't be at Jude's party this weekend?"

Linc shook his head. "Not from me. Some chick brought it into the coffee shop for Cleo to give to me, to give to you, to give to Jude."

"What a long-winded game of telephone." He opened the bag and tipped it. The present inside was also wrapped. "Who wraps a present inside a gift bag? Isn't that the whole purpose of a gift bag? Y'know, to *be* the wrapping paper?" He plucked the card from the gift and opened the envelope.

"Avengers gift bag and card? I feel like whoever this chick is, has Jude down to a T." Linc pulled off his shirt and jeans, slumped onto his bed and propped himself up on his elbow.

"'To Jude, saw this and thought of you. Dream big, and keep eating cereal straight from the box. Use this to break those glass ceilings you're hurtling toward.'" A wry smile twisted Russ's face as he read.

"Doesn't say who it's from?"

Russ smirked. "Nope. We're not talking about this." He pointed the card at Linc. "Spill. How'd the talk go with Zelda?"

Linc chuckled. That nickname wasn't going away among his friends. "Uh... okay, I guess?"

"Fucked her, didn't you?"

"Nooooo. Not quite."

"But you didn't talk?"

Linc shook his head.

Russell flung his wet towel at Linc's head but it fell to the floor next to the bed. "Dude! You need to talk to her. This shit weighing between you both isn't good for either of you."

"Since when are you a relationship counsellor?"

"Since my best friend finally found a woman to fall head

over heels with and I don't want to see it implode because of some dumbass bullshit."

Damn that was a good answer. "I haven't…"

"Said the L word yet? I figured. Doesn't make it any less true though. It's clear as day. It oozes out of you both when you're together. Kinda gross really. To be honest you should probably see a doctor about it."

Linc laughed. While he was sure of his feelings for her, he wasn't sure she felt the same. She was fond of him, sure, but love? Did she love him? Was he willing to lay his vulnerability out for her and find out?

"Stop thinking about telling her, and tell her."

The next morning, an email came through about their group project grades while Linc was eating breakfast with Russ in the Sugar Bean.

"What's with the face?" Russell gestured his spoon at Linc's phone.

Huh. No freakin' way. "Got our grades."

"Aaaand you flunked out? I'm not sure what your face is saying right now."

"Can't be right."

"You're having a one sided conversation right now, you know that, right?" Russ leaned over the table and stabbed his fork into Linc's scrambled eggs. "You snooze, you lose." He scooped them into his mouth, chewed, and swallowed. "Come on, man. Spill. It can't be *that* bad, can it?"

"That's just it, it's not. I got an eighty nine on my individual score."

"Then what's the problem?"

"Cleo got an eighty five."

Russell hissed. "Eesh. That's gonna sting. She's all about dem grades, right?"

Linc nodded.

"It's only a few marks, maybe it won't be such a big deal."

Linc closed his email and fired off a text to Cleo.

> Lincoln: Buenos días, preciosa, have you seen the results of our English assignment? Go team, Clinc!

> Cleo: So, we're gonna put a pin in the 'Clinc' thing.

> Cleo: And yeah, I saw it.

> Lincoln: I wonder if she mixed the results up and loaded yours to my page by accident.

> Cleo: I already checked. She said they're right.

> Lincoln: You... already checked?

The three dots indicating she was replying started moving, stopped, started, and stopped again. What the hell was she trying to say?

> Lincoln: Because a dumb jock like me couldn't possibly outperform you in an English assignment, right?

> Cleo: I didn't say that.

He clenched his jaw, closed his eyes, and counted to ten. He didn't want to fight with her, but her meaning was clear.

> Lincoln: You didn't have to.

Cleo: That's not what I meant.

Lincoln: Enlighten me.

Cleo: It just looks like my mom was right, having a life outside of school work seems to be adversely affecting my grades.

Lincoln: And by life outside school you mean me.

Cleo: And work.

Lincoln: But mostly me.

Russ cleared his throat. "It's a big deal, isn't it?"

Linc raked a hand through his hair. "Yeah. It's a big deal."

"Knock, knock. You wanted to see me, Cap?" Despite saying the words out loud, Linc knocked on the wooden doorframe of Will's dorm room. He left his door open during the day as an invitation for the team to drop in if and when they needed him.

"Yeah, Linc. Come in. Pull up a seat." Will gestured to the end of his bed and rotated his chair to face him.

Closing the door behind him, Linc dropped onto the edge of the mattress. "Sup?"

"We both know I'm not the flowery, softly, softly, type. But I'm worried about you, man. You're distracted, on and off the ice. It was none of my business until you smashed JW's face with your fist, and now you made it my problem. What can the team do to help? What can I do?"

Linc hissed out a low breath and rubbed the back of his neck with his palm. "Damn, Will. It's not like that."

"You laid into one of your own during a period break, Linc. What *is* it like, then?" He held up his hands. "Look, you know I love Cleo. Girl's like my own sister and I wanted to rearrange Johnny's face for what he said about her too, but you snapped, and we can't afford to have a loose cannon on the bench, man."

"It wasn't just—"

"I know. He gets under your skin. Hell, he gets under *everyone's* skin, dude's an asshole and he has his own consequences to face, but you can't just go around hitting people. You gotta find a way to swallow it down and, y'know, not assault your teammates."

Linc nodded, covering his face with his palms.

"I know there's other stuff going on. I dunno what, but I know there is. You've been off for a while now. I'm not prying – I'm here if you need to talk about it – but the team needs you to get your shit together. At least for practices and games. Can you do that?"

Could he? He had no real choice. Whatever rage monster had been let out needed wrangling back into the cage in his chest. He could do that, right? He nodded at an expectant Will.

"Cool. Is there anything else you wanna talk about?"

Linc shook his head. "Thanks, but I need to work through this myself."

Will frowned. "Molly mentioned—"

Linc groaned.

"I know, I know, but she means well. Anyway she mentioned you had some kind of – and I'm quoting here – 'incident' with your parents. I don't know what it was, and I don't need to unless you say otherwise, but try as they might, and with all the best intentions, our parents aren't always right about everything."

His eyes widened and he tipped his head to the side.

"I know, they mean well too, and they think they know you better than everyone. But truth is, they don't. No one knows you the way you do. One thing I *do* know though? They love you, and while they might be pissed at first, I believe they'll come around."

Linc's voice was a ragged whisper when he spoke. "And if they don't?"

"If they don't, we've got you."

L inc left Will's dorm room, stopped at his own to get changed into sweats and sneakers, and made his way back out into the frigid air. He was going through his pre-run stretches when Melissa crossed the street toward him.

"Linc!" She waved and flashed her million dollar smile. "Linc! It's been a while. How are you?" She twirled a strand of hair around her finger, giggled for no reason, and threw her head back as she touched his chest.

He stepped back. "I'm good thanks, Mel. How are you?"

"Oh, y'know. Same old, same old. Hey, I was wondering if you wanted to come to a party at Beta Kappa Pi, tonight." Her tongue snaked out to wet her lips.

"Melissa, I'm with Cleo." He folded his arms. "And even if I wasn't, my answer is still no."

Been there, done that, and have no intention of doing it again.

"Oh." Her face fell for a moment, before the fake-smile was back in place. "But I heard you two were past-tense." She curled a slender hand around his forearm.

"No, Melissa. We are present and future tense."

She shrugged, and a strangled, tense giggle erupted from her chest. "Can't blame a girl for trying."

He peeled off her hand and dropped it. "Actually, I can. It's pretty shitty to be asking out another woman's boyfriend."

Her jaw dropped open.

Mission accomplished. She turned to leave, paused, and stepped closer to him so she could speak in his ear. "I'll be waiting when it all turns to shit." She cocked an eyebrow and licked her lips.

"Don't hold your breath."

As she strode away, movement in his periphery made him turn. "Cleo." Her name was a choked plea.

Her face was pale, her eyes sad, and her lips downturned. She turned and bolted. He stepped onto the road but a car honked, jolting him back onto the sidewalk.

He didn't have to wait long before his phone vibrated in the bicep pocket of his sleeve.

Cleo: I can't do this anymore.

Lincoln: Nothing happened with Melissa.

Cleo: Maybe it should have.

Lincoln: Excuse me?

Cleo: You should be with someone like her.

Lincoln: Someone ugly hearted and mean?
Wow. Thanks.

Lincoln: "Angry people are not always
wise," Lizzy.

Cleo: I'm not angry. And quoting P&P at me
won't work either.

Lincoln: "You expect me to account for
opinions which you choose to call mine, but
which I have never acknowledged."

Cleo: Lincoln... stop.

Lincoln: "My affections and wishes have not changed, but one word from you shall silence me forever."

Cleo: I'm sorry Lincoln. It's over.

CHAPTER 29

Cleo

"You did... *what*?"

Cleo hung her head in her hands and groaned. "I know. I had to. I don't have time for boys, Mol. He's in my head and my grades are sliding."

"One grade, Cho-Cho. *One*. Don't blow your stack or anything, but I think this is a gross overreaction. He's going to come over, you know that, right? Please tell me you know he's going to come over."

"It's raining." Cleo pointed out the window as though that would somehow stop Lincoln from turning up at her door.

She was doing the right thing, wasn't she? She needed space. Space to get her head on straight, space to get her grades back up, and most of all space to breathe without the infernal thumping of desperate need between her thighs...

He might not like it, but he'd respect it.

She knew that much. All she'd done lately is *feel*, and she needed space to *think*. Thinking was her happy place, her comfort zone, she'd been cruising in the unknown for long enough to need a shot of familiarity.

"Honey, a funnel cloud could form over this building and it wouldn't stop that boy from getting to you."

"I feel like you're exaggerating a little bit."

"Oh really?" Molly pulled the blinds back far enough for Cleo to get a clear view of the street below.

Sheets of rain pelted the concrete as Lincoln pulled up to the sidewalk and parked his bike. Kicking out the stand, he swung his leg over and tugged off his helmet. She should have known he wouldn't have accepted a break up via text. Her stomach sloshed. She was better than a break up text, *he* was better than a break up text, he deserved more.

But she wasn't strong enough to break up with those imploring blue eyes in person.

She swallowed and grabbed the counter, her knuckles turning white. She was going to have to face him. She hadn't thought beyond the text. What else could she do? Avoid him around campus every day? It wasn't a feasible solution. She had class with him. She couldn't avoid him.

Shit.

She couldn't avoid him.

Someone knocked on the door. Molly tilted her head and her lips pursed. "I love you Cho-Cho, but if you're breaking up with this boy for real, you've gotta do the actual breaking up." She held her hands up in surrender and backed away.

Another knock sounded on the door.

"Fuck." Steeling herself, she sucked in a few steadying breaths, and made her way to the door.

She could do this. She could look into those pools of swirling emotion and tell the man she'd unwittingly fallen for they were over.

She unlocked the door and pulled it open, unprepared for what was waiting for her on the other side. Lincoln leaned his right elbow on the doorframe, his head bowed, and water streamed off his leather jacket onto the carpet underfoot. Rain water trickled from his hair, onto his face.

His sad, red eyes said he'd been crying, but they were filled with an intensity she hadn't seen before. "That was a chicken shit move, Lizzy."

She held the door part-way open, body shielded by the wood, hoping it would protect them both from her emotions. She couldn't let him in, if she did, she'd fall into his arms and forget the whole idea of space.

He pushed off from the wooden frame and stood upright, his imposing frame sucking the air from her lungs. Droplets of water sprayed everywhere as he ran a hand through his hair.

She couldn't speak. Her heart wanted to grab a fistful of his shirt, back him against the door across the hall, and kiss him until he forgot she'd ever texted him. Her head, on the other hand, had her heart in a cage and was calling the shots.

"Are you letting me come in?"

She shook her head.

He took a step back, but the air between them remained thick and heavy.

"I need to hear you say it out loud."

Swallowing hard, she shook her head. "Why? It'll just hurt more."

"What could hurt more than the woman I love telling me she's done with me, Cleo? In a fucking text, no less. I'm already broken. There is no deeper level of hurt."

The woman he loved? Her stomach lurched, heart pounding in her chest and ears.

"You can't love me." She shook her head but couldn't stop his words sliding into the cracks of her heart, wrapping their warmth around her. He couldn't love her.

He shrugged. "Miss Bennet you must allow me to tell you how ardently I admire and love you."

Her hand smacked over her wide-open mouth. "You c-can't love me, Lincoln."

He waved his hands, palms up, clipping the doorframe with his fingertips, but barely flinched at the impact. "You think that just because you don't love yourself, no one else can love you? Well here's evidence to the contrary, Cleo. *I* love you."

He thumped his chest twice. "I love all of you. The confident air you wear in public and the vulnerabilities you don't let anyone see. I don't care what your grades in school are, I don't care what shape your body is, and I don't care if you're tone deaf and love singing crappy pop songs at the top of your lungs in the shower." He scrubbed a hand over his jaw.

"And I'm sure as hell not ashamed of it. I don't care who the hell knows. I'll head over to the history department and tell your momma right now." He spun on his heel, primed to move.

His words crashed over her as though he'd thrown cold water at her. The coiled dread in her stomach released, sending jolts of panic through her limbs. She grabbed his elbow, her hand slipping off the wet sleeve. "You can't."

He loved her. Did that change anything? Did she love him? She had feelings, sure, but had it reached L-word feelings? Molly said it had, but did she even know what love felt like? She closed her eyes. He loved her.

"Cleo..." His voice was pleading. "Have you ever seen Dirty Dancing?"

She bit the inside of her cheek and nodded.

"Right now I feel like Patrick Swayze when Baby wouldn't tell her dad he was her guy. That's where I'm at right now. Am I not good enough for you? Are you ashamed of me?"

When she stayed silent, he struck the doorframe with the side of his clenched fist. "Answer me, Cleo! Tell me why? Don't I at least deserve that?"

A door further up the hall opened and a head poked out. "Everything okay down there, Cleo? You need help?" Cory curled one hand into an open palm, cracking some of his knuckles.

Cleo forced her lips into a sickly attempt at a smile at her neighbor's obvious display of bravado.

Lincoln took two steps back and ran both hands through his hair before holding them palm-up to her neighbor and nodding.

"Thanks, Cy. We're fine here." Cleo tried again for a more reassuring smile.

Cory nodded but didn't move. "Raise a hand to her and you'll have me to answer to, we clear?"

Cleo's heart squeezed at the look of dismay that flickered across Linc's face before he gave a sharp nod. Cory retreated into his apartment but left his door open an inch.

"How can you tell me to be brave? You tell me to own my true self, wear it on my sleeve, to show the world who I really am... and all the while you're... you're a goddamn hypocrite, Cleo."

She recoiled at his words, the door between them doing little to fend off the splinters of painful truth he spat at her.

"You encouraged me to do what my heart told me to, and you live in this box of fear, patrolled by your bulldog mother. You tell me to follow my passion, but you can't stand up to your controlling parents. Academia isn't the only route for you, Cleo, and you're suffocating under the fear of failing and disappointing people whose opinions shouldn't matter as much as they seem to."

She folded her arms, if the door couldn't protect her from his words, maybe her limbs could.

"You work in the coffee shop 'cause your mom said you should. You're working toward graduating top of your class... 'cause your mom said you should. What about what you want? Hm? You know this... what you're doing... it isn't a normal college experience, right?"

She couldn't meet his gaze. "Maybe I don't want normal."

"What did you say?" His knuckle cradling her chin sent sparks of warmth through her, but his words of judgement boomed in her ears.

"I said maybe I don't want 'normal,' Lincoln." Her chest heaved, rising and falling with a behemoth effort. She wanted to scream. Bile crept up into her throat and she forced herself to swallow. Her jaw trembled, and her eyes burned, but she wouldn't cry in front of him. She wouldn't let him see he'd hit the mark with every word.

"I want to succeed and none of this stupid shit..." She waved a dismissive hand. "... Is going to help me get to where I need to be."

"This stupid shit... you mean this..." He waved a hand between them. "Us. We're stupid shit?"

Deny it. Tell him no. She hesitated for a beat, a beat longer than she should have. Lincoln's face fell. It was as though his chest cracked open before her very eyes.

"Linc..." She jerked the door open and stepped toward him.

He raised a hand to stop her. Gave her one last dejected look and walked away. When he was finally out of sight, hot tears spilled down her cheeks in waves as her body shook with hiccuping gasps.

"Wow. That was... public." Molly hooked a hand through Cleo's elbow and closed the door with a soft thud.

"How long have I been here?"

"I gave you fifteen."

Cleo sniffed and nodded, wiping her wet cheeks with the back of her hand.

"Wanna talk it out?"

Cleo shook her head.

"Dinner?"

Another shake.

Worry pulled Molly's brows into a deep frown, and her eyes wrinkled at the corners. Cleo was grateful she was holding back whatever judgement and lectures lay behind her twisted shut lips.

Giving Molly's arm a gentle squeeze, Cleo released herself from Molly's grip and made her way to her room.

He loved her.

A new wave of tears trickled down her cheeks. She stripped off, fighting the lethargy working its way through her muscles, and found a clean pair of pjs to change into. She fell into her unmade bed, her pillow huffing out a puff of air as she landed.

Nothing he'd said to her was untrue, but it twisted like a poisoned dagger in her stomach. Maybe she could sleep away his words, her actions, and she'd wake up to everything being okay again. Maybe she'd wake up and his love for her would be enough for her to start to love herself.

His chair was empty in English class the next morning, and their shared classes for two days after. She couldn't concentrate on anything the professors in her classes said because the pain in her chest was oozing through every fiber of her being.

She hadn't taken a full, deep breath since he'd left her apartment. Every one got caught around the stubborn ball of anguish lodged in her throat.

She missed him.

Her phone mocked her with an empty notifications page, and every time she caught a glimpse of her beloved *Pride and Prejudice* on her bookshelf, tears threatened.

Everything was ruined, she couldn't concentrate, she couldn't sleep, and she couldn't stop worrying about where Lincoln was and if he was okay.

"You could text him, you know." Molly accepted her foamy coffee with grabby hands.

Cleo shook her head. The door to the Sugar Bean opened and three of the Pirates walked in. Will, Austin, and Russell. Her blood froze in her veins and her mouth dried up.

"Keep breathing." Molly's whisper did little to reassure her, but Cleo appreciated the suggestion all the same.

"W-what..." She cleared her throat and swallowed. "What can I get you guys?" Still sounding croaky, she cleared her throat again.

Will leaned on the counter, rolling his eyes and bobbing his head as though he was having an internal conversation. He bit his lip.

"W-Will? Are you okay?"

Pushing back from the counter on a sigh, he turned to face Molly.

"Don't look at me." She shrugged and took a sip of her drink. "I got nothin'."

"Will?"

He turned back to Cleo and opened his mouth but snapped it shut. "Know what? It's none of our business."

Cleo folded her arms. Maybe they'd ward off whatever onslaught she was about to receive. "But?"

Will shook his head. Russ shuffled forward two steps and kicked Will's shin.

"The fuck?"

Russ widened his eyes and made a very deliberate head gesture in Cleo's direction.

"Christ, and they say men can't be subtle." Molly muttered something about growing a pair into the porcelain of her mug as she took another sip. "Look... Would one of you spit out whatever the fuck you came to say before my best friend has an aneurism from all the tension consuming her right now? For those of you unsure what you're looking at, her shoulders are practically a scarf for her ears. She's strung so tight she's gonna snap, guys. Get to it."

Will threw a helpless glance at Austin who planted his feet, glowered, and leaned back against a table. His dark eyes seemed almost black under the orange tinted hue of the coffee house lights.

"Do any of you actually want a drink?"

Three heads shook.

"Snacks?"

More head shaking.

"We can't get Linc out of bed."

Cleo clamped her lips between her teeth. The sob rattling through her ended up a short squeak in her throat. *Oh, Lincoln.*

"We have a big game this weekend, and we really need him fighting fit."

"Or at least upright." Austin's grunt didn't give Cleo any more clue as to whether he was angry at her, or simply unhappy that he'd been dragged into a mess that wasn't his. Whatever the male-version of resting bitch face was, this man had perfected it.

"Guys..." She turned to the sink. Picking up a cloth, she turned to scrub at the counter she'd already cleaned twice that evening. "I'm not sure what you want me to do..."

"We're not really sure either." Russ's words were soaked in desperation, and his face was pale. "I know we are out of line for even being here, but he's still dodging his family's calls. His sister showed up at our dorm room and sat next to his bed for two hours, but she couldn't get more than a snort from him. I've known him for years, Cleo, and I've never seen him like this. I don't know what to do. I'm worried."

Molly remained suspiciously quiet throughout the entire exchange, her eyes trained on her now-empty coffee mug. She twisted a lock of hair around her finger. She only ever did that when she was anxious.

"What if I make things worse by talking to him?"

A look passed between Will and Russell.

Cleo pointed a finger between them. "What? What was that look?"

Russell rolled his neck.

Will avoided her questioning stare.

Austin's glower intensified.

Molly sighed and slapped her thigh. "They're trying to tell you that you can't make things any worse."

Cleo's mouth formed an 'O' shape, but she wasn't sure any noise came out.

Will cleared his throat. "Anyway, uh, we wouldn't be here if we weren't desperate. And now our meddling asses are going to get the fuck out of here."

The three men stalked out of the coffee shop in silence. As soon as the door snapped shut behind them, her phone burned a hole through her apron against her thigh.

Her fingers itched to type out a message or call him. Her heart rattled against the bars of its prison, while her brain screamed not to be an idiot.

"I gotta get going. See you at home, 'kay?" Molly squeezed her hand, grabbed her bag and bolted out the door in a flash of unreadable looks and unspoken words.

The last thirty minutes of her shift were painful. Each second counting down to closing time got louder, goading her into sending Lincoln a message.

As she trudged through the door to her apartment, she

expected the regular evening bustle, her housemates drinking cheap wine and arguing over what to watch on TV, but she was met with an unsettling quiet. The lights were off, the TV silent and there wasn't a roommate in sight.

Where had everyone gone? She dropped her bag on the chair next to the dining table and pulled out her phone.

Cleo: You home?

Molly's phone chimed somewhere in the belly of the apartment, so Cleo followed the sound. She found her friend cross-legged on the bed, reading the Lucy Score novel Lincoln had given to Cleo as a gift.

"Thought you didn't believe in all that love shit." Cleo folded her arms and leaned on the doorframe. When Molly didn't reply, she crossed the room and flopped onto the bed in front of her. "What is it, Mol? Why'd you run out on me earlier?"

"You know you're my ride-or-die, girl, but I can't keep quiet on this. I'm sorry. Usually I'm one hundred percent in your corner, no matter who you're facing but with this... with Linc..."

Cleo plucked at some non-existent lint on Molly's comforter. "With Linc... what?" Her voice was raspy, coated with guilt, and her shoulders, heavy.

Molly sighed. She set the book over her thigh, saving her page. "I can't stand quietly by and watch you make the biggest mistake of your life."

"You think breaking up with Linc is the biggest mistake of my life?"

"No, that's the second biggest mistake of your life."

"I'm confused, Mol. What's the first?"

Molly lifted her head to meet Cleo's eyes. "He's right, Cho-Cho. You're killing yourself in school, working every hour of the damn day, spending more time in the library than in your own home, and for what? Your mom? I love your mom, girl, you know I do, but these are her dreams, and fears, not yours. On one hand, you're telling Linc he needs to let the world see his art. You told him he shouldn't care so much about what his father thinks, be your best self, rah, rah and all that other don't hide under a bushel shit. And on the other you're doing the exact thing you're telling him he shouldn't. You're living your life based on what your mom wants for you. Firstly, that's kinda hypocritical."

WTF? I'm not a hypocrite. Cleo opened her mouth to defend herself, but Molly didn't stop.

"Secondly, you need to live a little and have fun, figure out what the hell you want from life for yourself. If you end up busting your ass so much with school and working at the coffee house that you keel over and die before graduation, what's it all for anyway?"

She shifted her weight on the bed. "I don't want you to get so far down a path in something you convince yourself you love, that when you realize you're miserable living up to someone else's expectations, it's too late to change."

Emotion swirled in her stomach as she blinked back tears. How could her best friend be saying all these things to her?

Molly reached over and plucked Cleo's hand off the bed and squeezed it between her palms. "I know this is a lot, and I know you probably feel betrayed, or ganged up on, or, I dunno, something else. I've had your back from day one, Cleo. I said nothing last year. I'd hoped when you met Linc this year, you'd watch him transform into his artistic, butterfly self and you'd realize this pressure you carry over you like a cartoon anvil wasn't your own."

Too many words jammed in Cleo's throat, but none broke free of the plug of emotion lodged there. Her eyes dropped to the bed again and she shifted her position again, bunching up the blankets underneath. "What else?"

"What makes you think there's more?"

"I know you, too, Molly Morrison. What else? Spit it out."

"I found your stories."

Cleo arched an eyebrow. Her spine tingled like a blast of frigid air through an open door in a winter storm swept up her back. "You... did?" She folded her arms. "What were you doing under my bed?"

"I was borrowing your hockey sweater."

Cleo snorted. "Under my bed?"

"Fine. I was looking for batteries. My favorite USB vibrator broke, my back up needed charging, and my back up back up needed new batteries. I happened upon your shoebox full of stories and got distracted reading them. I think you should have them edited and published."

The laugh that burst from Cleo sounded something close to the bray of a donkey. "You're shitting me, right? There's no way they're good enough. My mom said—"

Molly cut her off with a shake of her head and a widened palm over her face. "Shh. This isn't about your mom. So you don't write literary enough shit for her, who cares? There are plenty of self-published authors out there who write damn good fiction and make a shit ton of money from doing something they love."

Cleo's heart fluttered and her stomach clenched. Could she really publish her stories? Did she want to? She hadn't given them much thought other than getting them out onto the notebooks she'd expertly hidden under her bed. Did she want to do more with them?

A rush of excitement spread through her, as though she'd stepped outside into a summer day. Heat prickled over her skin. When an idea for a story came to her, she couldn't sleep until she'd given it a voice and written it down. It was as though her entire life's purpose was to say what the characters needed to say.

Was there a chance she could make a living at doing something that came as naturally to her as breathing?

Cleo narrowed her gaze. "How do you know what self-published authors do?"

Molly shrugged. "I knew you'd have some kind of self-deprecating argument as to why you couldn't publish your stories. So I did some research."

"This is a lot. I need to process."

"I figured you would, but I couldn't stay silent any longer."

Cleo raked her hands through her hair and shook her head. "I wouldn't even know where to start."

"I had a feeling you'd say that, too." Molly leaned over the edge of her bed and grabbed her laptop. "You already have the stories written, believe it or not, that's most of the battle."

She opened her laptop and hit the power button. "I mean, it's hard AF work from here on out, but so many people don't ever finish writing. You have enough short stories under your bed for at least two whole books."

"Should I be freaked out by the amount of time you seemingly spent under my bed, Mol?"

"I mean, you could do with using a fucking vacuum sometimes..."

Cleo giggled.

"This is where you start." Her friend spun the laptop to face her. The browser was open to a Facebook group.

"20Booksto50k?"

"It's a 'what you do now you've done the writing part' kind of group. It has everything you need to know about publishing and marketing your book."

Cleo's jaw dropped open. Her heart warmed at the

amount of work Molly had put into this before bringing it to her. "Is there anything else?"

"As a matter of fact, there is." Molly snapped her laptop shut and leaned forward far enough to flick Cleo's forehead. "Stop being a fucking idiot about Lincoln fucking Scott."

CHAPTER 30

Lincoln

"Go away!"

The knocking on Lincoln's door was persistent.

Bang, bang, bang.

Make that persistent.

One thing was for sure, Russell wasn't going away. Linc groaned, shoved the quilt off his face, and rolled over. His muscles ached and his bones clicked and popped. How long had he been lying in bed? He sat up and stretched on a yawn. The knocking continued.

"Russell, man, I swear to fuck, unless someone is dying, you're about to get your ass kicked." He jerked the door open. "D-dad?" A ball of icy dread settled heavy in his gut.

His father wedged a foot against the door and smacked an open palm onto the wood. "Took you long enough. Get showered and dressed – we're having food."

And probably a lecture.

"Yes, we're going to talk, Lincoln. That's what grown-ups do. They don't avoid their parents' phone calls and lie in a pit of their own filth for three days pretending the world isn't still spinning outside. You stink. Wash."

L inc lingered under the jets of hot water for longer than he should have, but there was something almost biblical about having a hot shower after three days without one. When he stepped back into his room, a towel wrapped around his waist and water dripping from his hair. His bed linens had been changed, and his father sat against the headboard cradling a cup of coffee.

"Seems you're having quite the time of it." He blew over the rim of his mug and took a tentative sip of the black liquid. Black, just like his soul. Linc wasn't sure exactly what profound, holier than thou bullshit was about to spew forth from his father's mouth, but he didn't want to hear any of it. It wasn't new – he'd given the same variation of the "it's your job to carry the torch" spiel countless times over the years.

"Can we wait until I've at least got a plate of food in front of me before we start the Linc lecturing?"

His father's eye twitched, but he fell silent and sipped his coffee while Linc got changed.

"Did Russ call you?"

"I thought we weren't talking before food." He paused for a beat before throwing a Molly Morrison level eye roll and tutting. "Russell called Mia, who came to visit you, then came home in a panicked mess. You really are dramatic sometimes – you know that, son?"

"Guess it runs in the family." Linc's grumble was loud enough to be heard as he turned to open his bedroom door. "Are we eating here?"

"There's a hash brown casserole already in the oven."

Linc bit down the urge to say something about how Mom

had trained him well. He'd changed the bed, made a pot of coffee, and had a breakfast casserole cooking – how very domesticated.

He pulled out the coffee pot and topped up his dad's mug before filling one for himself. Unlike his father, he liked it with milk and sugar. His eyes fell to the mug Cleo used for her tea when she visited. A pang of sadness struck him in the chest.

"Christ, you're like a kicked puppy, making sad eyes at a friggin' mug."

"Don't." He shook his head to emphasize the warning. "You don't get to have an opinion on my love life."

"Sounds like I don't get to have an opinion on any part of your life. Except that's not quite true is it?" He sighed, twisting his wedding ring around his finger a few times. "You're right about one thing though."

Linc cocked his head. Had he ever heard his dad admit Linc was right about anything? "What's that?"

"*My* opinion on *your* life? That's none of *your* business. It doesn't matter, or shouldn't matter anyway." Eyes trained on the steaming mug in front of him, he kept fidgeting with his ring. "I'm sorry you felt pressured into doing things I wanted you to do, like you had no other option, no room to express your own... well, anything, I guess."

Dad was apologizing. To him. Had Linc fallen back to sleep? Or somehow hit his head? "You're... sorry?"

His dad's lips tugged into a smile under another eye roll. "Yes, Lincoln, I'm sorry. I make mistakes too sometimes, you know? And while I'm not always man enough to admit I'm wrong and apologize... well, let's just say your mom was pretty clear about my need to vocalize my fuck-up this time."

He rubbed his neck as a flush crept into his cheeks. "The guest room bed is not the most comfortable of places to sleep. From now on, we're gonna refer to it as The Thinking Room. While your mom was smoldering in her anger at me, I had time to do a lot of thinking. And you're right."

He sipped his coffee before rising from his stool and checking the casserole. If they didn't eat fast, every hungry college kid on the floor would get a whiff of the potatoey goodness and want in on the molten cheese deliciousness.

Dad scooped casserole onto three plates, leaving one to the side. "I told Russell I'd protect his portion with my life."

Linc laughed. "Sounds about right."

They returned to their seats, barely able to contain themselves from shoveling piping hot casserole in their mouths.

"You were saying I was right." Linc gestured at his dad with a forkful of food. "Continue."

It was his dad's turn to laugh. "You *are* right. I have no business trying to steer your life in any one direction. I guess I saw how good you were on the ice and assumed you'd follow in my footsteps. I didn't think to check. I just pressed forward thinking I knew best."

He scooped up a mouthful of casserole, but paused before putting it in his mouth. "I had no idea how talented you were outside the rink, and I'm sorry about that. I was so blinded by what I wanted for you out of life that I didn't see you."

Linc shoved down the ball of emotion in his throat with a heaped forkful of casserole. He swallowed hard. The conversation was not at all going how he'd expected. Maybe his dad had been kidnapped by aliens.

"Anyway, I didn't come here to fight. I wanted to tell you to follow whatever your dream is, and since I'm so damn clueless, maybe talk about what that dream might be – because I'm interested. Not because I wanna change your mind."

"Man, Mom must've come down hard on you."

His dad nodded, mouth full, and swallowed. "She was right to, though – I was being an ass. Some parents would give anything to have a smart boy in college with his head on his shoulders. Your grades are good, you're playing well, and you're not doing drugs..." His eyes flashed wide. "You're not doing drugs, are you?"

"Not unless Cleo counts as an addictive substance."

Dad chuckled. "I was so blinded by the bright lights of the NHL rink at the end of the tunnel that I lost sight of the fact it's not my rink anymore. And in all my thinking, I realized something. I'm proud of you. I don't think I've said that to you before, and that's kinda shitty of me too."

Linc fought the urge to reach his hand out to check his father's temperature. He'd never been so open. Sure, Mom probably coached him on what he needed to say, but he was eating humble pie and saying it out loud.

"I don't know what to say, Dad. I appreciate it. Really." His mind whirred. He'd been so afraid of losing his father after his confession of not sharing his dream to go pro. Now he had his dad's permission not to pursue it.

Everything was different.

Would he truly be supportive of his art? Only time would tell, but this was huge. The weight he'd been shouldering had lifted, but his heart sank because he couldn't share the moment with Cleo.

He stifled a sob by cramming a forkful of cheese and potato into his mouth.

"Whenever you're ready, I'd like to see your art. It's not my thing, and I'll probably say all the wrong things, but I want to try to support you, Lincoln."

Lincoln nodded. Was he ready for his father to see inside his life? He'd sketched some pictures of his dad on the ice after he'd retired from playing professionally. Maybe he'd get one framed as a gift for his birthday and see how things went.

Dad wiped the corner of his mouth with his thumb. "So, tell me about this girl of yours."

Linc had apologized to Will and their coach. He'd gone for an eight mile run and bossed the hell out of their morning practice. He'd eaten his pre-game meal of chicken and pasta, and he was ready to face the back-to-back games against Alabama and Michigan. If only mending a broken heart was so easy.

"You ready?" Russ elbowed him as they stepped off the ice after warm up.

He nodded. "Sorry, man. I know I've been all-the-way fucked in the head this week."

Russell's glove hit him across the side of the head before he could blink. "Shut up, it's what we're here for. I'm just glad your dad was able to get your stinky ass out of that cesspit before we had to call animal control."

He winked. "You know I normally wouldn't have pushed, but we need to win these games. We're so close to making the playoffs, I can almost feel that itchy-as-fuck playoff beard."

Linc chuckled. "Then let's make the playoffs." He offered his glove, which Russ fist bumped with his own.

"Damn straight."

The Zambonis were done with the ice, the anthem had been sung and the crowd was boisterous. The atmosphere around the rink crackled with excitement... and hope. Playoffs meant more work, more practice, and muscle aches in places he didn't realize muscles existed, but it was his favorite kind of hockey, and he'd be damned if they were going to lose these games.

Somehow being free of his father's expectations made him want it just a little more.

"Saw your girl in the stands, Scottie. I can see why you got all bent out of shape. She's hot." Jeremy Lewis stopped beside him, primed for the opening puck drop.

His girl? Cleo was here?

Austin won the faceoff and passed it to Finn, who cradled it up the wing. Linc scanned the crowd. Foam fingers and pennants waved in all directions, but the blur of faces wasn't easy to pick through. Someone nudged him.

"Looking for her now, aren't ya?"

Linc shook his head. "Not letting you fuck with me, Jer. You're just trying to get under my skin."

The whistle blew for icing. Jeremy popped his mouth guard out and chewed it around a smug grin. He shrugged, confident, nonchalant, and irritating as hell. "If you say so."

Linc shook his head, attempting to clear the Cleo-thoughts from his mind. He was there to play, not be manipulated into losing a shot at the playoffs by Jeremy-smug-fuck-Lewis who had resorted to distractions 'cause he knew the Pirates was the stronger team.

Some people would do anything for the win, and Linc wasn't letting them have it easily.

Two periods down, the game was tied. Linc had missed a backdoor goal that would have put the Pirates ahead. Anger fizzled through his bones as he pursued every single puck of the shift. 'Bama's goalie was tired – he was moving further out of his crease than he needed to and his passes had grown sloppy.

Lincoln was going to get the damn goal back. Jeremy's best friend, AJ, had been stuck to Linc's heels like stink on shit. Every time Linc moved, there he was, relentlessly chipping at him, goading him into a penalty. But Linc wanted that goal back.

Every time his ass hit the bench, he scanned the crowd, but no matter how many times he looked, he couldn't see Cleo. Jeremy had to be fucking with him, which only served to make Linc madder.

Sometimes in hockey, everything aligned – fluke, luck, talent, Mercury not being in retrograde. Whatever puzzle pieces fell into place made something almost magic happen. He needed one of those moments.

Excitement thrummed in his veins as he skated up the ice toward Alabama's goal. There was less than ninety seconds on the clock, not a lot of time to make a difference. Despite the weariness seeping its way into Linc's thighs and arms, he wasn't going to give up until the last buzzer sounded.

Russ had the puck back at the blue line, the defensive yin to Linc's offensive yang. He shot it to Finn, who shouldered past a white shirted Charger toward the net. The goalie moved out to meet him, leaving the backdoor wide open once again. Linc smacked his stick on the ice, calling for the puck. He met Finn's eyes, noting the subtle nod from his teammate.

Linc picked up the pace – where AJ was bigger, Linc was faster. He pulled away from the burly defensive man. Stopping at the edge of the crease, he smacked his stick again. Finn sailed the puck across the slot. Linc caught it, lined up, and shot.

The scrambling net minder managed to get a toe to the puck, stopping it before it crossed the line, but he couldn't get back into position fast enough to stop Linc chipping the rebound into the net.

The lamp lit and the crowd thundered. Finn threw himself at Linc, grabbing him in a bear hug. The fans counted down from ten, and the final buzzer sounded.

"Hey, Linc?" Jeremy slowed to a stop a few feet away, shouting to be heard over the roars of the crowd. "She's at your two o'clock, about a dozen rows up, with that chick who writes for your school paper."

Both Finn and Linc turned. Molly faced the ice, arms wrapped around someone in gleeful celebration. The woman she hugged wore a Pirates shirt with the number thirteen on the back and Lincoln's surname, Scott, across her shoulders.

She turned, brushing her dark waves from her smiling face.

"Don't fuck it up." Jeremy slapped him on the shoulder. "And good game." He winked and skated off toward his own team.

He had never before understood when people said they were so happy they could burst, but his entire body vibrated with pure joy.

Cleo.

Their eyes met. He cocked an eyebrow, and with a casual shrug, she twirled in place for him, stopping for a beat with her back facing him and throwing a half smile over her shoulder before turning to face him.

His girl was in the stands, wearing his shirt, and his Pirates were one game from making the play offs. Maybe dreams really did come true.

CHAPTER 31

Cleo

Cleo held her breath, pausing before she turned to him. The jersey had cost a small fortune, and the merch stand only had one left – a triple XL, which came to her knees. If he rejected her after this, she'd be torn between wanting to burn the damn thing in a backyard bonfire and getting her money back.

The smile that split his face was enough to unwrap the wad of anxiety resting on her chest. She could breathe again. She'd have to apologize for being the top class jerk she'd been, but he was smiling, not flipping her off. She'd take her wins where she could get them.

Five long minutes later, Molly tugged her out of the row of seats. "Text him and tell him we'll meet him in the bar."

With trembling hands, Cleo pulled out her phone, but there was already a message from Lincoln waiting for her.

Lincoln: Miss Bennet if this is some
torturous joke, my heart can't take it.

Cleo: No joke, Mr. Darcy.

Lincoln: You wanna be my girl?

CLEO'S FACE HURT FROM SMILING.

Cleo: I don't think I ever really stopped. The last week has been hell on earth.

Lincoln: It's only been a week? Fuck. Let's never do that again.

Cleo: You're really going to give me another chance?

Lincoln: Fear makes us do all kinds of dumb shit, Lizzy. I had no intention of letting you go, I just hadn't figured out how to convince you to stick around yet.

Cleo: Molly's dragging me to the bar, can we talk when you're changed?

Lincoln: Just talk?

Heat seared her cheeks. She bumped into someone as she walked.

Molly apologized for her. "Don't text and walk." She threaded her arm through Cleo's and guided her through the bodies leaving the rink. "Ugh. Your face is doing that gooey, loved-up thing again. It's disgusting."

Cleo laughed. "Isn't this what you wanted?"

"Gooey, loved up, Cleo, far outranks depressed, ragey, Cleo. I just want you happy. If that's with Linc, cool, he's a good guy. If it's by yourself, that's cool too."

They crossed the street and walked the two blocks to the bar. Nerves twisted in her stomach and her palms were sweating. She wiped them on her thighs as she ordered a diet coke. "You going to interview someone tonight?"

Molly swirled her straw around her glass of gin and Sprite. The lime segments jingled against the ice cubes. She took a sip, a smirk tugging at her lips. "Yeah, your freakin' boyfriend. I can't *not* interview Linc after that shit he pulled on the ice tonight. Then you can go bump uglies with him."

She raised her glass and clinked it against Cleo's soda. "I'm glad you came to your senses. For the shortest not-a-real-break-up in history, that nearly-a-week was the longest week of our damn lives. You were a rotten person to be around, Cho-Cho. I'm glad you didn't wake up and choose violence again today." She winked.

Russ approached, his tie loose and his top button open. He radiated don't-talk-to-me vibes, and the building crowd parted to let him through. He nodded at Cleo. "He's on his way."

Molly swiveled on her stool to talk to someone Cleo didn't recognize.

"Hey, Russell?"

He peeled his eyes away from the bartender to meet her gaze.

"Molly said your mom is an editor."

"She is indeed." He flagged down the bartender and ordered a beer. "You need an editor?"

Cleo shrugged. "I think so?"

Russ laughed. "Are you asking me?"

"No... I... I'm not sure what I have is worth... editing."

"Mom will know. She used to edit for a publishing house, but she got laid off in a recent merger. She freelances now and most of her clients are indies. If there's something there, she'll know."

Cleo chewed on her straw. She'd asked, and he hadn't laughed at her, not that he would, but the idea of doing something with the silly stories she had under her bed made her cringe.

"Did you tell him about the other night?"

He shook his head. "Nah. I thought he might want to hear it from you."

"Tell me what?"

Her heart stuttered, tripping over its own beat. "Lincoln." His name was a whisper. Gooseflesh spread on her arms and neck as he stepped closer, his proximity radiating heat even through the thick layers of her clothes.

His hands rested on her hips as he lowered his head to talk close to her ear. "Do you know how fucking hot it is seeing you in my number, Lizzy? It's making it very... hard... to concentrate."

He pressed his erection against her ass, and she forgot whatever thoughts had been rattling around her brain. He brushed his lips against her cheek. "Did Russ tell me what, Lizzy?"

She sighed against his chest. "I came over the other night." Talking to him with her back to him was easier.

Russ picked up his beer from the bar and tipped it at Cleo and Linc. "Catch you later."

Linc nodded against her neck, and she sucked in a sharp breath. "You came over?"

"Yeah." Her voice was breathy, and the only thing she could think about was his skin touching hers. She leaned forward and tapped Molly on the shoulder. Sliding her hand into Linc's, she stepped toward Molly. "We're going to talk."

Molly's lips twitched. "I wanna make a joke right now, but I know you do need to *actually* talk so I'll swallow it down. Needless to say, it was hilarious and pithy."

"Noted. Let me know when you get where you're going for the night?"

Molly grinned and nodded. "Yes, Mom. Go fix things with Mr. Darcy."

Cleo gnawed on the inside of her cheek, stomach flipping. She wasn't used to having to apologize, and the need pooling in her panties wasn't doing much to help her foggy brain. His grip tightened around her hand as he led her outside the bar. He paused when they got to the street.

The streetlights shone a hazy orange glow over him. The way he filled out his suit jacket, with his humble smile and sparkling eyes, almost undid her where she stood. A not-so-small part of her wanted to drag him down the alley next and have her way with him. What was it about game-night-Lincoln that made her lose her mind?

"You're drooling." He reached a knuckle under her chin to close her gaping mouth.

"It's been a while."

"Felt like a lifetime. Where are we going?"

"We could walk to my place? Or yours? Talk on the way?"

The warmth of his palm against hers spread into her chest as they walked in silence.

"I've missed you." She slowed to a stop, tugging on his arm so he'd look at her. "More than I realized was possible to miss someone."

His sad smile encouraged her to keep going, without saying a word.

"I don't know where to start." She walked toward him, faltered, and stepped back. If she touched him, it would be game over, there'd be no words, and she needed to use her words. "The guys came to the coffee shop the other night."

He groaned and covered his face with his free hand.

"Don't be mad at them. They weren't trying to make me feel bad – they were worried. I guess they figured if anyone could get you out of bed, it would be me. Kind of ironic really since usually I'm the one dragging you into bed." She snorted and twisted the hem of her shirt. Fuck, this was hard. "Anyway, I came over, but you were talking to your dad. Russ offered to let me stay, but I didn't want to intrude, so I just dropped off the casserole and left."

"You made the casserole?"

She nodded.

"I thought my dad made it, and he didn't correct me. In fairness, if I'd known you were in the vicinity of the dorms I'd have run after you."

"I'd venture your dad knew that. Did you work stuff out with him?"

Linc nodded. A car drove past, the sidewalk almost vibrating with the bass pumping from the under lit vehicle.

"Lincoln, I'm sorry. I freaked out. I got overwhelmed and I lost my damn mind. I know they're all excuses, and none of them make up for me being shitty to you, and pushing you away, but I'm sorry. As soon as you walked away from my door, I..." Tears welled in her eyes, and she blinked them back, shaking her head.

"I know I had no right to be upset. I said the words. I threw on the brakes, but..." She swallowed. "I hated every minute of the last week. I'm tired of being apart."

Reaching out a steady hand, he brushed tears from her cheek with the pad of his thumb. She turned into his open palm, enjoying the sparks dancing along her skin from the contact. Sighing, she closed her eyes. "I wasn't sure this would ever happen again."

"You think I'd just give up that easily?"

"You were pretty hurt that I was pushing you away, Lincoln. I wouldn't have blamed you."

"It troubles me how you think I could just walk away... from you... from us. This isn't a fling to me, Cleo."

She squeezed her eyes shut, willing the tears to stop.

"And I wasn't lying when I said I was in love with you. I *do* love you, Lizzy."

Pinching her lip between her teeth, she shook her head. "I don't know why." Her words burst out on a hiccupping sob.

She'd spent so many years hating herself, that being faced

with the idea that someone like Lincoln could love her sucked the breath from her lungs.

She detested herself for how she looked, for never being enough, for always needing to stay in line, always chasing one more A to be worthy... worthy of her parents' love... of her own. So much self-loathing and self-doubt shrouded any compliments she'd ever received, or positive thoughts she'd had.

"I don't think people ever really need to know why someone loves them, but you do have to work on accepting the fact I do." He slipped the hand cupping her face behind her head and drew her to him, wrapping his arms around her in a tight embrace. "I'll tell you every day for the rest of your freakin' life until you hear me, Cleo. You're beautiful, inside and out, and I love you."

This man had seen her naked, both physically and emotionally. He'd seen the parts of her she'd never been brave enough to show anyone else, and he hadn't run. In fact, he'd run toward her, unrelenting, and was always encouraging her to stop running away from herself. Her eyes fluttered open, and she swallowed hard. "I love you, too, Lincoln."

He stepped back, but leaned his forehead against hers, their noses brushing against each other. "I'm so glad." His breath tickled her face. "It woulda been super awkward if you didn't love me back." Holding her gaze, he slipped his hands onto her hips, then up her ribcage and around to her shoulder blades.

He brushed his nose across hers, once, twice, and before he could do it a third time, she rolled onto her toes, pushing herself up to close the space between them, and kissed him.

What started apologetic and soft, turned hungry, fast. He kissed her as though she was the air he needed to survive, as though he hadn't taken a single breath in the week they'd been apart.

She melted into his unyielding hands, holding her against him. She stepped back, cold metal meeting her spine. Snaking her arms around his neck, she pulled him closer.

Even body to body, he was too far away. She fisted his shirt, and their kiss swallowed his moan of approval.

Whoops and hollers, applause and cheering jolted them from their voracious kiss and their heads collided as she startled.

"Take that beautiful woman home and show her a good time!"

She turned to hide her sizzling face in Linc's shirt with a giggle. "Oh my God, Lincoln!"

His arm tightened around her waist. "I don't want to wait." His low growl sent chills up her spine. She clenched her thighs.

"I'm not exactly wearing accessible clothing, Lincoln."

He couldn't mean what it sounded like he meant. Threading his fingers through hers, he led her a few feet along the sidewalk. "Don't care. The park's up ahead. If I don't get inside you soon, I'm going to ruin these pants, Cleo." He paused, searched her face with questioning eyes. She nodded once. He grinned.

The buzz of anticipation was almost deafening. She'd never thought about sex in a public place before, let alone followed through.

He came to an abrupt halt next to a waist-high wall which lined the park. A small building flanked the other side. He turned to face her, jaw rigid with tension, eyes somehow still shining even in the dull light. Cradling her face with both hands, he placed a chaste kiss on her forehead. "My beautiful Athena... when we get back to your apartment, I will worship you like the remarkable goddess you are. But for right now? I'm going to fuck you senseless."

Her face heated, the urgency lacing his words making her dizzy.

"Lizzy…" His voice was strained. "I'm not kidding. Pull those yoga pants down and bend the fuck over the wall." He'd already freed his dick from his pants and was tearing a condom wrapper with his teeth while he slid his hand along his length in languorous strokes.

Hooking her thumbs into the band of her pants, she wiggled them off her hips. Had anyone ever wanted her so desperately? Had she ever been so fucking wet?

As she bent to shove the fabric over her knees, she looked over her shoulder as she worked the pants down her legs.

Sliding the jersey up, a hiss escaped between his teeth. "Miss Bennet, that is one fine-as-fuck ass." He licked his bottom lip before rolling it between his teeth.

Whose life was she even living? She had the hottest guy in Minnesota eyeing her like he was a starving man and she was the last meal on earth.

His hand trailed up her inner thigh. "I'm telling you now, I'm not going to last long. I know I should be ashamed of myself but… fuck." His head lolled against her back as his fingers met her wetness, and she bit down an embarrassed moan. "So fucking hot."

She willed down the nervous discomfort of being so shamefully turned on and coaxed herself to get out of her own incessant mind.

He lined up with her entrance and she wiggled against him, urging him inside her.

"Glad to know I'm not the only hungry one in this relationship." He eased into her on a sigh, her walls stretching to accommodate him, and she bent farther forward, shuffling her feet apart.

"Hold on tight, Lizzy." He wrapped an arm around her,

bracing her stomach, pulling her against his chest. She gripped the wall and tensed around his cock.

She'd never felt so wanted, so wanton, so needy. Before Lincoln, her whole life had been spent hiding pieces of herself so no one would see, no one would judge, no one would crush her with their words.

His fingers found her clit and she shivered at the jolt of pleasure. He pulled out before sliding all the way back in, building a rhythm with his hips.

His free hand worked its way under her layers of clothing. Tearing the cup of her bra from her skin, he freed her breasts and sought out her tightly budded peaks. She cried out as he rolled her nipple between his thumb and forefinger, driving his impossibly hard cock deeper inside her with every thrust.

"Lincoln..." Her shallow pants were irregular, and her body, shuddering. "Not going to last..."

"Come for me, Lizzy." His demand spoke straight to her core. She was a passenger to the orgasm building. When her legs trembled, he gripped her harder. Her fingers curling around the edge of the wall were numb, as his lips nipped and kissed her neck. She felt him everywhere.

In the romance novels she'd read, when the hero demanded the heroine come for him, she all but came undone around his oversized cock in an instant. Cleo had always considered it pure fiction, until Lincoln was growling in her ear to come for him.

Her entire body surrendered to his will. Her muscles clenched. Her breath caught. Waves of undulating pleasure coursed through her as her orgasm burst from deep inside.

She tried to muffle her scream, turning her head into her shoulder, but when he pinched her nipple, she threw her head back against his chest and stopped caring who heard.

He came on a grunt, his teeth sinking into the fabric of her jersey. They stood in silence for a few moments, chests heaving, pulses racing, muscles tensing.

"Fuck. Pull your pants up, Lizzy. Let's get you home before I spread you out on that wall like a fucking buffet and eat you till dawn."

Cleo hadn't seen Lincoln since what Molly was fondly referring to as "The Wall Incident." Upon hearing her best friend had sex in a public place she'd dug out a thermometer to check she wasn't ill. She had also threatened to call the doctor to check her blood and finger prints to make sure she hadn't been consumed by a demon.

The Pirates played their last home game of the season and made it into the playoffs. Linc had requested the pleasure of her company for celebratory Sunday breakfast at a hole-in-the-wall café he'd found while poking around Trip Advisor.

She slid her oversized sunglasses onto her head and scrolled her Facebook feed while she waited for him to arrive. The glaring sun suggested sundress and flip-flop weather, but the subzero, winter temps and the two feet of fresh snow outside suggested otherwise.

The bell over the door tinkled as it opened. Her heart picked up its pace as Lincoln crossed the café. "Buenos días, Lizzy." He kissed her cheek before pulling out the chair across the table and dropping onto it with a smile. "You look beautiful."

"Buenos días, mi amor. No one looks beautiful dressed in fourteen layers with icicles dangling from their eyebrows and nose, but thank you."

He leaned across the table on his forearms, a smile playing on his lips. "I'm pretty sure I could get you down to zero layers and melt those icicles pretty darn quick, Miss Bennet. And I just so happen to love the permanent pink staining your cheeks in the winter time, not to mention that adorable cold nose."

She shifted in her chair, discomfort clawing at her gut.

"One of these days, I'm going to say nice things about you and that feeling won't clam you up tighter than a duck's butt, you know? I don't care how long it takes, we're gonna chisel the shit out of those walls of yours."

His sympathetic eyes and encouraging tone told her he meant every word, but she couldn't imagine a time when she'd just accept a compliment and it wouldn't feel so... icky.

"What are your plans after breakfast?"

She cocked her head to the side and narrowed her eyes to slits. "Why?"

He shrugged, but the mischief on his face and his leg bouncing under the table, suggested he was up to something. "I have something I'd like to show you, if you're game?"

CHAPTER 32

Lincoln

Lincoln's heart thundered in his chest. If he wasn't breathing quite so loud, he was sure she'd hear it. His palms were sticky with sweat and his gut churned with nervous energy.

"I don't think it's open. The shutters are down. The opening hours online say it doesn't open on Sundays except for special events and exhibits." She tilted the screen of her phone so he could see.

His only answer was a smirk.

"Lincoln! It's closed, we can come back another time."

The keys jingled as he freed them from his pocket. "It's cool – I know the owner."

"You sly dog." She pushed his shoulder. She hated surprises. Her life was organized and planned, and her calendar was written out every week with military precision.

While anxiety coursed through his veins, hers would undoubtedly be worse. He slipped an arm across her shoulders and gave her tense muscles a gentle squeeze. "Relax, Lizzy. We're allowed to be here, promise."

A twist of the key in the lock and a shove with his

shoulder opened the stiff door with a long creak. "Okay, fine, I admit it kinda sounds like something from a creepy horror movie, but I promise I'm not taking you somewhere to be murdered."

Reaching a hand around the doorframe, he groped at the wall until he found the switch. "Wait here."

The muscle above her eyebrow twitched. She checked over both shoulders and rocked onto her toes and heels a few times before rubbing her hands over her biceps.

He worked his way through the space until he found the right section. Tugging the tiny chains, he turned on the individual lights. Panic rose in his chest and self-doubt crept into his pores. It would be fine. She was going to love it.

He jogged back to the entryway. Cleo had made her way inside, and closed the door, but her back was to the open room. He tucked a hand into hers and gave a gentle tug. "Come on, Lizzy."

He walked slightly behind her and to the side so he could take in her every reaction.

She glanced over her shoulder and he gave a reassuring nod forward. "Keep going."

As they rounded the corner, her hand flew to her face and her eyebrows darted up her forehead. The moment she saw it, recognition was obvious. Her eyes widened and filled with an ocean of tears she couldn't have held back if she tried.

Emotions flickered across her face. It was like watching a slideshow of pictures, each lasting only a second before another took its place. Surprise, wonderment, curiosity, finally settling on pride.

The delight radiating from her beaming face warmed him in the cool room. Her head snapped to him and back to the wall.

"Lincoln... w-what... what is this?" She stepped forward

and reached out an inquisitive finger, pausing before she got too close, leaving her hand in mid-air.

He cleared his throat. "I entered that competition you found and tied for first. The exhibition starts tonight, for one week, but I asked if they'd let me sneak you in to show you around before, well, everyone else sees it."

She clutched a hand to her chest, taking in each of the pencil drawings. "Is this your dad?"

"Yeah." He nodded. "During his NHL prime, he played for the Blackhawks in Chicago. That's him in the United Center. I sketched it from a photo a reporter caught the night he won the Stanley Cup the first time."

She wiped her cheeks and turned to the next drawing. "That's Russell. Is that his daughter?"

"Jude, mhmm. That one I sketched in-the-flesh, she was much smaller, and less mobile, than she is now." He chuckled at the memory, warmth blooming in his chest.

"Amelia?"

He nodded, thrilled she was able to identify the subjects of his pictures.

"She looks so happy." Her breathless voice held an awe that squeezed his very soul. "Who are these people?"

"That's my mom's parents, and the baby in their lap is my mom. I always loved how she stared up at them with such adoration. It took me so long to capture her eyes. This one I tore up and started over four times before I was happy with it."

"Lincoln…" Fresh tears trickled down her cheeks and onto her coat as she stood staring at a drawing of herself. Her chest heaved, then her breath caught, and she didn't move to stop the tears coursing down the side of her nose. She skimmed her finger along the dark wood frame. "Lincoln, this is…"

He said "you" at the same moment she said "beautiful,"

and her breath hitched again. He squeezed words around the thick ball of emotion lodged in his throat. "You don't hate it?"

She turned to him, confusion swirling with her tears. "How could I possibly hate this, Lincoln? It's incredible."

"It was after our first night together. You fell asleep on your tummy, arms hugging the pillow, hair spread across your bare shoulders. I needed to capture the moment forever."

She stretched her hand out to his chest. "Can I keep this? When the show is over? Can I have this? Please, Linc?" She spoke faster and with more urgency the more she stared at the sketch on the wall.

He stepped behind her, snaking his arms around her waist and resting his chin on her shoulder. "Of course you can. You really like them? My parents are coming tonight. Mia and Russ too... I'm scared they won't like them."

"They won't like them." Her voice was so firm with assurance a chill rolled through him. "They'll love them, Linc."

He nodded against the side of her head. "I almost sent in pictures of inanimate objects. It would have been safer ground, less embarrassing... but these... these are my heart and soul on paper. Go big or go home, right?"

She giggled, sniffing before wiping the sleeve of her coat on her cheeks. "Thank you for sharing this with me. You're so very talented, Mr. Darcy, and so very brave."

Pulling out her phone she spun the two of them so their backs were to the sketches on the wall. She turned on the forward-facing camera.

Puckering her lips, she kissed his cheek. Eyes full of warmth and love. She snapped a picture. He folded her against his chest, wrapping an arm around her shoulder.

"A nice one this time. I know we'll get pictures tonight, but I want to capture this memory."

She squeezed him and smiled. "Such a romantic, Mr. Darcy."

He nuzzled against her ear. "Don't tell anyone. Oh! We better get a bunch of pictures of us tonight. Playoffs start in a week, and we're going the whole way."

Confusion pulled her brows into a deep V. "I don't know what that means."

"It means…" He kissed her forehead. "I'm gonna look like a Sasquatch in about a week, and you're gonna be complaining about being seen with someone who looks disheveled and unruly."

She pushed him away, giggling. "Then I guess we'd better get our glad rags on and celebrate in style."

The champagne glass trembled in his clenched fingers. He tucked his free hand into the pocket of his dress pants, and his thumb worked back and forth over the fabric as he paced.

"Christ, Linc, you look like you're gonna blow chunks!" Russ's warm palms flat against Linc's back and chest forced his torso upright. "You're fuckin' green, man. Chill out." He patted his chest with a steady hand.

"Easy for you to say."

Linc's parents had picked him up on their way to the gallery. It was a small celebration, close friends, family, and, surprisingly, a smattering of local art collectors, who had been invited to peruse the exhibits at their leisure.

Cleo and Molly were due to arrive any minute. The main doors hadn't opened yet, but his heart raced, nervous energy thrummed through his body, and he couldn't stop his foot from tapping against the tiled floor.

His parents stood next to Mia in front of his work. His older sister and her family couldn't make it but had instructed the others to take plenty of pictures. Everyone had made an effort. His dad and Russ wore suits, and his mom and Mia were dressed for a red-carpet affair. Mia had even been allowed to have one glass of champagne, which she gratefully accepted with an eye roll and a wink thrown at Linc. Jude looked like a princess running around in between everyone's legs, giggling, ringlets bouncing on her shoulders.

Cleo walked into the room wearing a scarlet dress, and time stopped. Was he dreaming? Linc's mouth dropped open and instantly dried up. He had to be the luckiest man on earth. He was gawking at the beautiful woman gliding toward him, and he didn't care. His older sister, Beth, had taught him the line curving above her cleavage was called a sweetheart neckline but Cleo looked anything but sweet.

The ruched fabric hugged her killer curves like it was made for her. Her heels, hidden under her floor-length gown clicking on the tiled floor.

Her dark waves were pinned to one side and fell over her creamy, bare shoulders. Her lips, the exact color of her dress, tugged into a knowing smile as she approached him.

"Fuck."

"Fuck!" Jude repeated at the top of her lungs.

"I'm going to fucking kill you if that sticks." Russ leaned close to Linc's ear to grit out his words and rescue the still trembling flute glass from his hand. "Also, you are one lucky fucking bastard."

Linc's face broke into a smile as he nodded, but he still couldn't otherwise move or take his eyes off the siren headed straight for him. His tongue snuck out to wet his lips, but his mind was blank. There was only his beautiful girl in a sexy as hell dress.

"You're drooling." She brushed an almost-kiss on his cheek.

"Shamelessly." His voice broke as he croaked out the word.

He opened his arms wide and shook his head. "You look...
Fuck, Lizzy, you're stunning."

Her cheeks darkened and she lowered her gaze to the floor,
but he caught her chin with his fingertips. "No way. I'm not
letting you evade this one, Cleo. You've literally stolen my
breath away. My brain has stopped functioning, and all my
blood has rushed straight to my dick. If I'm going to be stunned
by your beauty, you're going to have to take a compliment."

Molly nudged Linc with her elbow, carefully cradling her
glass of champagne. "And what a compliment it is. Nothing
says 'you're a fucking stunner' like a raging boner pitching a
tent in your boyfriend's dress pants. I wanted to hug you,
Linc, but now it's weird." She grinned and pulled him in an
awkward side-hug.

"Congratulations! I mean... I'm low-key salty my face isn't
on the wall, but people would have been so distracted by my
divine countenance, they wouldn't have been able to enjoy any
of the other pictures." She flicked her hair over her shoulder
and tapped the side of her nose with her finger. "I getcha."

Someone cleared their throat to his right. Molly bolted
toward a neighboring display of art when Linc's mother joined
the small circle. Linc shifted his weight, drawing his jacket
closed, hoping it would hide the erection wrestling against the
material of his pants.

Russ chuckled, coughed and grunted "timberrrr" behind
his fist. He smacked Linc on his bicep and leaned in. "That's
the sound of wood falling, my man. Cockblocked by your
own mama, eeeeessssshhhhh."

"Lincoln, aren't you going to introduce us to your
friend?" His dad was standing beside his mom, his lips
twitching against a smile. Linc made introductions.

"Uncle Linc!" Two little bodies flung themselves at his
legs.

"What? I thought you guys couldn't come!" He turned to face his sister, Beth, and her husband, Jared.

She leaned over and kissed him on the cheek. "Wouldn't miss this for the world, lil bro. Is this Cleo? Are you Cleo? Sweet baby Jesus, you're beautiful."

"She is!" Emily, all of six years old, nodded frantically. "You look like a princess!"

Cleo crouched down to her level and held out a hand for Emily to shake. "You must be Emily."

Emily untangled her arms from around Linc's leg, offered her tiny hand to Cleo, and nodded again.

"I'm Cleo, I'm a friend of your Uncle Lincoln's."

The little girl shook her head. "You're his girlfriend!" Her stage whisper left something to be desired, but she burst into giggles behind her hands. "Are you going to marry him?"

Without missing a beat, or looking at anyone other than Emily, Cleo pursed her lips and tilted her head. "Maybe someday. But not right away. We don't know each other well enough yet. What if he snores?"

The little girl giggled.

"What if he..." Cleo tapped her chin with her fingertip. "What if he can't cook? Or he doesn't put his stinky socks in the laundry?"

"He can't dance."

Linc facepalmed, his niece was ratting him out to his girl-friend. This kid!

Cleo gasped. "He can't?"

Emily's face turned solemn as she shook her head.

Cleo produced a fake notebook and made fake notes. "What else?"

The whole group was captivated by the exchange. Big blue eyes gazed up at him before turning to her mom, then back to Cleo. "Sometimes..." She glanced at her parents again. "Sometimes he sneaks me candy when my mom doesn't know."

"He *does*?" Cleo clutched a hand to her chest. She tutted up at Linc with a shake of her head and a smirk.

"He plays hockey real good." Jack's tiny face peeked out from between Linc's legs.

Cleo paused scribbling on her invisible notebook and craned her neck to look at his four-year-old nephew. "You must be Jack."

Jack ducked behind Linc's thigh.

"He is Jack, but he's shy." Emily's confirmation came with a stroke of Cleo's forearm. Cleo had made a friend.

"Well, Jack is right, your Uncle Lincoln is *very* good at playing hockey. I mean..." She smoothed out her dress on her thighs. "I don't know much about hockey, to be honest, but I know your uncle scores a lot and that's a good thing, right?"

Russell snorted from behind Linc, which was silenced when Linc's elbow collided with his soft tissue.

"But you know what else he's really good at?"

Emily's eyes widened, and she shook her head.

"Want me to show you?"

The little girl nodded.

Cleo eased herself upright with a bone-click. She offered her outstretched palm to Emily, who took it and tugged her forward.

"Be right back to finish documenting your sins, Mr. Darcy." The wink Cleo threw over her shoulder as his excited niece tugged her away was almost his undoing.

"Right." Beth clapped her hands together. "Who has a ring? He can't let that one get away. They need to marry, right this second, and have a million babies."

Amelia slipped a ring off her thumb and raised it in the air. "Totally here for the Clinc shipping."

Lincoln hadn't taken his eyes off his girlfriend's swaying ass as she chattered to Emily on their way to look at his exhibit. He rubbed the back of his neck before tugging on his collar.

Was she taking every molecule of oxygen from the room with her as she walked?

His mom sipped her champagne. "From the love hearts popping out of your head, son, your sisters aren't too far wrong."

Linc couldn't imagine spending another day of his life without Cleo. Seeing her with his family, and chatting to his sister's kids, made it easy to envisage their life together. She was it for him. Whatever it took to keep her by his side, he'd do it.

When he turned to his family, his sisters and mother were all staring at him dreamy eyed, with soft smiles on their faces.

Mom stroked his cheek. "She's good for you, Lincoln. You're different with her, more relaxed, less guarded... braver." She gestured toward his artwork, where Cleo had picked Emily up and was showing her each piece. "Your art..." She swallowed, dabbing a Kleenex to her glistening eyes. "I had no idea you were so good, Lincoln." Her chin quivered. "We..." She slipped her hand into his father's and raised both hands. "We are so very proud of you."

"And we need a sold sticker for that sketch of me on the ice, Lincoln. I want it to show it off to all the patients in my office."

Choked up with emotion, Linc nodded. "I have a bunch of them, Dad. You can take your pick."

"Uncle Linc?" Emily was back at his side, tugging at his hand.

"Yes, sweetheart?"

"Will you draw me on the wall too?"

Linc chuckled. "Of course I will."

"And can Auntie Cleo come trampolining with us next weekend?"

"What? No... I... I didn't ask her to call me that." Cleo's frantic whisper made him smile.

Beth waved her hand. "She gets attached pretty fast when

she likes someone. You're basically her new bestie. I'm surprised she didn't ask if we could take you home."

Cleo beamed. "When do your playoff thingies start? Will we have time to go trampolining next week?"

A groan from behind them had everyone turning to see who else had arrived. His teammates Will, Finn, Sébastien, Austin and Ryker stood in various states of formal dress.

Will had a hand spread over his face. "Cleo, you've been friends with Molly for how long now? And you're still *this* clueless about hockey?"

Finn swaggered toward the group, tapped Linc on the chest. "Gotta get your woman up to speed, Scott. She's the first of the WAGs, she's gotta know her shi—stuff." He worked his way around the group and made a beeline toward Linc's exhibit.

"We were in the neighborhood." Austin shrugged. "Door was open, and the sign said there was alcohol."

Linc smirked. "Sure, sure. Well, we mere mortals appreciate you gracing us with your presence."

His friends made their way toward Finn, who stood next to Molly, staring at the frames hanging on the wall.

A hand on Linc's arm jolted him back to the circle. "You need a minute?"

He looked down and Cleo was looking up at him, her eyes soft and her lips curved into a small smile. His heart threatened to explode in his chest. "Thanks, Lizzy. I think I'm okay though." He sucked in a deep breath. "Certainly not what I expected, a little terrified now that it's all just..." He waved toward his art. "Out there, for all of them to see."

"They've known for a while. They played dumb so you wouldn't feel weird about it."

"Zelda's spillin' all our secrets today." Russ shook his head with a smile as he wandered off toward the team.

Dad handed him champagne, taking the empty glass from his hand. "You have a good group of friends there, Linc."

"I do, Dad. We're gonna win the playoffs too."

"Damn straight we are!" Russell hollered, fist in the air. Molly hissed a shh at him and smacked him in the stomach with the back of her hand.

"I like her." Amelia's eyes lit up at having found a kindred spitfire.

"I have a question." Mom looked back and forth between Linc and Cleo. "Why do you call her Lizzy?"

CHAPTER 33

Lincoln

Sweat streamed down his neck, soaking the collar of his half unbuttoned dress shirt. His belt dug into his hips. His now unsheathed cock was flying at half-mast, and his shoes were still on. This woman was driving him insane.

Cleo lay on her bed, hair stuck to her clammy face. Her mascara and lipstick were both smudged. He'd freed her tits from their red satin prison, and her dress was bunched around her waist. She'd never looked more beautiful. That just-fucked look worked for her.

She stretched her arms over her head. "I think you broke my vagina, and you *definitely* ruined my dress." Her lazy smile sent jolts of warmth into his chest.

He unbuckled his belt and freed himself from his dress pants. "It's just a little rip." He shrugged. "I warned you. It's not my fault you didn't move fast enough."

She sat up and reached behind her with both hands. He grabbed her ankles and yanked her toward him. "Oh, hell no. That dress isn't coming off yet."

She flopped back onto the mattress. Her airy laugh breathed life into his veins. He dragged his tongue from her ankle up the inside of her leg. She sat up, pressed both palms against his chest and shook her head. He stepped back, confusion ringing in his ears. Was she rejecting him?

She slipped off the edge of the bed onto her knees, and his dick twitched in response to the promise her position made. She wrapped both hands around his length, and a groan rattled from his chest. "Cleo…"

Her hazel eyes met his as she pumped twice. She grinned and sucked her teeth, running her tongue along her scarlet-stained lips before licking the tiny pool of precum from the tip of his now-throbbing erection.

"Cleo…"

She giggled, mischief alight in her eyes. Was it possible to die from your girlfriend's tongue teasing your cock into oblivion? His eyes rolled back in his head as her tongue trailed the length of his shaft. She gave his balls a gentle squeeze before dragging her tongue back to the tip. His eyes snapped open as she eased him into her soft, warm mouth. She closed her ruby red lips around him, and sucked, without taking her eyes off his.

"Fuck, Cleo." He tangled his hands into her hair, fighting every urge to take over the pace and fuck the back of her throat. He tightened his grip around her head, and she giggled around him, the vibrations driving him closer to the edge. Her tongue worked his dick like it was her life's mission to make him come.

The door burst open, and when Cleo gasped, he slipped from her mouth.

"Just letting you know the guys are — fucking hell, Cleo."

Cleo crossed her arms over her bare chest, but it did little to hide her cleavage. "Molly!"

"Girl… Seeing you on your knees, lipstick smeared over your face, smoldering, fuck me eyes, and titties hanging out of your dress like that, I'm having all kinds of feelings right now. That is hot. As. Fuck."

"*Molly*!"

Linc chuckled at Cleo's growl, he didn't care if his girl-friend's best friend has burst in on them in such a state. He hadn't moved. His eyes were trained on Cleo's face. Her cheeks warmed, her pulse fluttered at the base of her neck, and her chest rose and fell with heavy breaths.

"I was just letting you know, Will, Finn, and Austin are here watching Sunday Night Hockey."

"Arrrrrrrrrrrrrrrrrrrrrrrgh." The frustrated noise that escaped Cleo had his dick hardening next to her cheek.

The soft click of the door closing was accompanied by her tongue lapping at his tip.

"If we don't go out there right away, they're gonna roast us."

"Let them." Her eyes sparkled as she eased him back into her mouth.

Cleo entered the room behind Linc wearing a low-riding pair of plaid pajama pants and her new "my heart belongs to a Snow Pirate" t-shirt that matched her hoody, at the same moment the guys erupted into chaos. Her eyes flickered to the TV in time to see a replay as she walked behind the couch. Linc smiled. Would she want to learn about the game?

"No way! Absolutely no fucking way." Finn's face was almost as red as his hair.

"I mean, I see it. The call was good." Will folded a slice of pizza and took a bite, nodding.

Cleo reached over the back of the couch and grabbed a slice of pizza from the open box resting on Linc's thigh. She took a bite and gestured the remainder of her slice at the TV. "I'm with Will. He was absolutely offside."

Linc's mouth hung open, slice of pizza mid-air. All eyes turned toward his now-beetroot girlfriend. She'd unpinned her hair, freeing it into unruly waves cascading over her shoulders, and while she'd taken off most of her makeup, her lips stayed a stubborn red.

"Holy fuck. Did you just weigh in on a hockey call?" Molly spoke despite having a mouthful of food.

"What?" Cleo took another bite, chewed and swallowed. "He was so clearly offside that even I could tell." Her face was the same color as the dress she'd taken off.

"Nope. Don't buy it. Have you been studying hockey?"

She shook her head, but no matter how hard Cleo was trying to stay cool and nonchalant, Linc knew better. His sweet, bookworm, goddess of knowledge had done her thing and read up on the rules of hockey.

She rounded the couch and dropped to the floor next to his feet, reaching around for another slice.

"Cleopatra Isabella Martinez!" Molly pointed her pizza crust at Cleo. "You can't lie to me, you've been learning the game. At fucking last. I'm a proud mama bear right now."

If looks could kill, Cleo's laser-glare would have struck Molly dead where she sat. Molly ignored the scowl and waved her crust again before dunking it into a small tub of ranch dip. "Does this mean I won't have to bribe you to come to games anymore? 'Cause I'm totally here for that."

Cleo groaned. "I read up on the basics. I figured if my boyfriend plays I should probably at least know which end of the stick he's supposed to be holding."

Finn swallowed a mouthful of food. "I mean, not to be pedantic or anything, but I'm pretty sure he prefers when you hold his stick."

Linc leaned over behind Will to smack a chuckling Finn

upside the head. Finn held up his hands. "Just sayin'… and you can't tell me I'm wrong, either."

Weaving his hands into Cleo's thick, shiny tresses, he rubbed her scalp. She leaned into him, tilting her head back. Bending over, careful not to tip the pizza box on his leg, he kissed her temple. "I can't put into words how grateful I am right now. Thank you."

She cast a glance over her shoulder, cheeks still red.

"Good for you, Zelda. Learning the game. That's a pretty big gesture." Russ burst open a share-sized bag of Lays and offered them around.

"I figured if he could read *Pride and Prejudice*, I could read the rules of the game he's loved since he was a kid."

"You know what this means, don't you?"

Everyone turned to face Molly.

"Hockey wedding!"

Cleo

"Are you sure about this?" The stranger moved the adjustable light over top of Cleo to get a better view.

She nodded, though her stomach was in knots. "I'm sure."

"Which size?"

She pointed to the middle one.

"And where do you want it?"

Running her finger along the space under her wrist, she frowned before nodding. "Here, please."

"Did you tell your mom you were doing this?" Linc tucked a stray lock of her hair behind her ear.

"This is my spreading-my-wings moment, Lincoln. Telling them about it first kinda defeats the purpose, don't you think?"

"Your girl's got a point, man." The tattoo artist plonked onto the stool next to Cleo's seat and placed the template over her skin. "Here?"

She moved his hand half an inch to the left. "Hmmm... no, here, off center."

He nodded and lowered the stencil to her skin. "You ready?"

Sucking in a smooth, deep breath, she flexed her fingers. "I'm ready."

The artist had designed a stack of four books with a steaming cup of tea on top. She'd opted not to get it big enough that you could see names on the spine, but both she and Linc knew if she had, *Pride and Prejudice* would be top of the book stack.

Much to her surprise, the artist had already started. The needle made barely any noise and was more irritating than painful. Getting a tattoo was something she'd always wanted, but never been brave enough to do.

Mamá would hate it.

Lincoln had been not only supportive of her idea, but encouraged it wholeheartedly. He'd sat with her for hours while she scrolled Pinterest boards, searching for the perfect bookish tattoo.

Forty-five minutes later, she was done and standing on the sidewalk, hand folded into Lincs, wondering what the fuss was about. She had to laugh at her past self for being so anxious. In a strange way, she felt liberated, as though this day was the first of her new life, her own life. A better life.

Lincoln brought their clasped hands to his mouth and kissed the back of hers. He pulled his phone from his pocket and stepped closer to the edge of the sidewalk. "Snap for the 'gram?"

"I feel like I shoulda made a TikTok or something, but sure."

They squeezed together, cramming both their faces, Cleo's newly tattooed arm, and the storefront behind them into the small space. Cleo beamed as he snapped multiple shots.

"Now for the next life-altering moment of the day." He slipped his hand back into hers and squeezed. This was the much scarier part.

The coffee shop was only a few blocks away, but he tucked her against his side as they walked through the cold.

"You sure you don't want me to come in with you?"

She chewed on her thumbnail. "No, it's okay. I need to do this myself."

He rubbed small circles at the base of her spine, her apprehension unknotting under his touch. "She's lovely." He kissed her cheek. "I'll just be down the street. Call me when you're done, okay?"

She nodded and took her book bag from him. Pushing open the door to the *Sugar Bean*, she took a deep breath. It smelled just like it had a few days ago when she left after her last shift. A woman sat alone clicking on a laptop with an empty mug beside her.

"Mrs. Stewart?"

The woman lifted her head, swept her glasses from her face and plopped them onto her laptop before standing and extending her hand. "Natalie, please. Russell has told me all about you. It's so nice to finally meet. Let's order some drinks, and we can start talking about your path to becoming a self-published author."

Epilogue

TWO YEARS LATER

Lincoln

"You ready?"

An unshakable, hundred-pound weight of ice-cold dread sat in his gut. "No, Russ. I'm not. At all."

"We can always come back another time. There's no rush. You're not asking her today, right?"

"Right."

In just about every romantic movie he'd ever been forced by his sisters to watch, the terrified guy, ready to propose to his forever girl, ambled into a jewelry store with his fluffer best friend. The sensible, "you can do this," "no, that's too expensive," best friend to help keep him from passing out. It had always seemed fictitious, until Russ reached back and grabbed Linc by the arm, dragging him into the store.

"Come on, big guy." Russ smacked an open palm on his shoulder. "We can't get her to say yes if you stand out on the street staring at the window for the rest of your life."

A strangled half-laugh erupted from Linc's chest. Yes. That was the only possible path in front of him. They were destined for each other. Their souls were tied together forever. There was nothing he was more certain of.

Then why was he so close to pissing his pants in public like a potty-training toddler?

He rubbed at his chest. Was he having a heart attack? His vision blurred at the edges.

"Fuck, man. Pull yourself together, Linc. I can't have you passing out. I'm a terrible liar, she'd never believe me if I told her you fainted for no reason. And unless you're going to propose to her from a hospital bed, we need you to stay upright."

Linc swallowed down his anxiety and nodded. "She'll say yes, right?"

"Dude, I have never seen two people better suited to each other. She adores you, of course, she'll say yes."

"You're my best friend – you're supposed to say that." Linc rubbed the bridge of his nose, sliding his thumb and fore-finger across his closed eyelids. Diamonds sparkled in every display case. From every angle, the light reflected off the precious jewels. "So... many... diamonds."

Russ nodded. "Do you at least know what kind of metal she'd like?"

Linc leaned over the cabinet, nodding. "Yeah, that one."

"That specific ring? Just like that? You stood outside shaking for fifteen minutes before you let me open the door. We've been in here three seconds, and before anyone has come near us to hit us with a sales pitch, you just... picked one?"

"That's the one." Linc tapped his finger on the glass at the ring.

"An excellent choice, sir." A woman in a white, button-down blouse with a navy jacket appeared from nowhere.

"Jeez, you should wear a bell!"

The woman smirked, but otherwise ignored Russ's rude remark.

"And I'm the jumpy one?" Linc rolled his eyes at Russell and turned his attention to the selection of rings the sales assistant pulled from the cabinet. She plucked the ring from its red cushion and handed it to him.

Other than the fact it was a silver-toned band and a teardrop-shaped diamond, it looked like every other ring in the case.

"What's the metal? White gold?"

"This one's platinum, but if you'd rather, we have a similar diamond in white gold available too."

"Platinum's perfect. I'd rather she didn't need to get it replated in the future."

Russ's jaw dropped. "You've researched these? Since when?"

"Since the night at the gallery when she met Emily, and I knew I was never letting her go for the rest of my life."

The sales clerk swooned. "That's so romantic." Her hand covered her chest. "I love my job." A nervous giggle rippled around the room as Linc inspected the ring pinched between the tip of his thumb and index finger.

"Good diamond? I mean, I'm not looking for a flawless diamond, but I kind of see it being an heirloom for our kids, so I'd rather it was something half decent."

"Yes, sir."

He turned the ring to see the price tag and Russ whistled.

"That's quite the price tag, Linc."

"Like I said, I've been working on this for the last two and a half years. I'm good. I'll take it. Will I need to bring her in to get it resized? She's an L."

"This ring must be destined to go home with you. It's an L too, that hardly ever happens." The woman behind the counter beamed as she took the ring to box it up. Linc pulled his credit card out of his wallet and slid it across the display case.

"You already asked her dad, right?"

Linc nodded.

"But not doing it today?"

Linc shook his head. "Know what we are doing today though?"

"What's that?"

"Chocolate cupcakes."

Half a dozen chocolate cupcakes in one hand, a bottle of her favorite crappy wine in the other, and an engagement ring burning a hole in the inner pocket of his blazer, he let himself into their new home. "Cleo?"

"In the kitchen!"

The smell of paint lingered in the air, and stacks of precariously balanced boxes crowded the space. The house wasn't huge, but it was theirs, and they'd both worked incredibly hard to be able to afford the down payment.

"Lemonade?"

He nodded, suddenly parched.

She turned to grab glasses from the top rack of the dishwasher. Everything they owned was being washed before being going into its forever home in their cupboards. While she wasn't looking, he slipped the ring out of its box and tucked it into the icing of one of the cupcakes. When she turned back, he slipped off his jacket and draped it over the back of the chair.

"Cupcakes?"

He nodded. "Figured we could power through the unpacking a bit easier if we were on a sugar high."

She laughed, handed him a glass of lemonade, and grabbed two small plates.

He put her cupcake on one plate and set it on the table in front of her empty seat. The frosting on the cupcake he'd pulled out for himself had shifted, getting on his finger. He licked the frosting. Bottles of cold water in hand, Cleo froze on her way to the table, cheeks flushed. Had she spied the ring already?

"What?"

She slipped onto the chair, placed the glass on the table and let out a giggle. "You... and chocolate cupcakes."

"What about it?" He looked at the box, then her face. Her eyes were fixed on his lips. "Do I have chocolate around my mouth?"

She bit her lip and shook her head.

"Then what?"

"Do you remember our first trip to the institute?"

"That's years ago, now, Lizzy."

She nodded. "It's okay that you don't remember. You're right, it was a long time ago."

After a beat of silence, he answered as though he hadn't planned the whole thing. "The woman behind the desk gave you a cupcake, and you shared it with me."

Cleo's face lit up. "A *chocolate* cupcake, and I thought my body was going to burst into flames as I watched you eat that thing."

"Wait. You... *watched* me eat the cupcake?"

"Mmhmm. Shamelessly. It was like watching porn in public. I had to keep my legs glued together so you couldn't hear my clit screaming at you to do what you were doing to that cupcake to it."

"Aaaah. That's what that noise was. It all makes sense now."

She snorted. Her hungry eyes lingered on his mouth. Not

yet. He needed to get through asking her so the weight on his chest would ease.

"Maybe you should return the favor, let me watch you lick the frosting." He slid her plate toward her, but her eyes didn't move from his face.

Damnit.

"Cleo!"

She tipped her head to the side, arching her eyebrow. "Yes, Mr. Darcy?"

Raking a hand through his hair, he shook his head. "You're not making this easy for me, Lizzy."

"Why, Mr. Darcy, I'm hoping things get rather... hard for you if I'm being quite honest." She winked at him and threw her head back with a laugh.

"Do me a favor?"

"What's that?"

"Look. At. Your. Cupcake."

When she turned her head, he dropped to one knee. Her eyes flicked back and forth between the ring and his face. "Lincoln..."

"I hadn't planned to do this right now, but it radiated like a damn beacon in my pocket the whole way home, and I couldn't hide it. I didn't want to. There's literally no reason to wait. I thought about keeping up the Darcy thing, but he fucked up his first proposal so badly... well, the asshole left me nothing to work with."

Cleo was still staring at the ring, then back at Linc, then back to the ring.

"Marry me, Cleo. Be the Elizabeth to my Darcy for the rest of our lives."

Her jaw trembled as he plucked the ring from the chocolate frosting and paused. "Didn't think this bit through." He licked the frosting off the ring and held it out to her. "What's it gonna be, Lizzy? You're killing me..."

"Oh, it wasn't a rhetorical question? You need an answer?" Linc groaned.

"Always so dramatic, Darcy." She winked. "Yes. A thousand times, yes!"

He slipped the ring onto her finger. "Wasn't that Jane, rather than Eliza Bennet?"

"Shhhhh... you can't argue *Pride and Prejudice* semantics with me when I'm being blinded by my new bling."

"What I'm hearing is, 'Lincoln, you're right about something in my favorite book, and it's so hot right now.'"

"That too." She dragged her eyes away from the sparkling gemstone and quirked an eyebrow. "Speaking of hot... do we make calls and then get naked... or—"

He didn't let her finish her sentence. Their new bed was due to arrive in a week, but he could do everything he wanted to do to his new fiancée on the mattress on the floor. He stood, draping her over his shoulder as he rose. Her giddy peals of laughter warmed his heart. He smacked her ass, and she wriggled against his grip.

"Lincoln Scott, put me down!"

"Never."

Coming together over another woman's bra wasn't likely to be anyone's idea of a romantic first encounter. It wouldn't go down in history as one of the greatest romances of all time, but it was the greatest love story of his life, and he couldn't wait to see what came next.

If you're interested in getting a glimpse of Cleo and Linc in the future, go here for their bonus scene.

CHAPTER 34

Sabrina

Since when did Target sell vibrators? It really was becoming a one-stop-shop. She was tempted to try the vibrating feather, but the vibrating arc looked like it would be more fun, so she grabbed the multicolored box and tossed it into the cart next to the pack of razor-blade refills.

Something special happened when you walked through the sliding doors of a Target store. It was as though you were transported to another world just by crossing the threshold. A world where everything you never knew you needed lay under one roof. To get to the magical world of all the things, you first had to pass by a gauntlet of a Starbucks counter, restrooms, and fresh hot popcorn.

Corporations knew you needed to empty your bladder before you embarked on an Olympic sport level shopping trip. Get them in the door, and don't let them leave.

Maybe the universe also knew you needed to keep your hands occupied with chocolate Frappuccinos and the most delicious snack known to humankind. If you walked around with both hands free, you'd end up selling your left kidney to pay for the $1,600 cart you'd inevitably end up with at the checkout.

Sabrina was doing a service to her bank account, and her left kidney – she was, after all, rather attached to it. At least that's what she told herself as she steered the cart around the sunglasses, sun hats, and purses section. One hand on the handle of the cart, she steered around the not-quite-big-enough space, while the other hand cradled a venti, double chocolatey chip crème Frappuccino.

She'd have to factor in some kind of penance-walk into her week for having such a ginormous indulgence. But for now, she sucked the stubborn chocolate chip out of the straw, coughing when it hit the back of her throat, and made her way into the clothing section.

Her Target time was sacred, methodical, and even though she'd been around the aisles countless times before, she still walked each and every one, each and every time. Who knew what shiny new treasures they'd put out since the last time she'd visited? Sure, it was only three days ago, but a lot could change in three days.

She reached out and traced her fingers along the shoulder of a gray sweater hanging at the front of a display. Why did clothes never look quite the same off the rack? You fell in insta-love with something hanging on a faceless mannequin, but when you tried it on in front of those judgy AF dressing room mirrors, it was all kinds of wrong.

Not feeling a clothing-spree vibe from today's trip to Valhalla, she set off for to find snacks, a screeching noise grinding her to a halt. Unhooking the broken clothes hanger caught in the wheel of her cart, she pushed forward.

By the time she got to the cereal aisle, Sabrina had a mismatch of items in her cart. She'd picked up a floppy hat to add to her growing collection, kids sunscreen – because despite her olive skin, she still burned to a crisp, even in the Minnesota winter sun.

She grabbed three pairs of socks, already un-pairing them in her head, because she never wore a matching pair. When she'd picked up a box of tampons in the feminine hygiene aisle, her attention had snagged on a display of adult toys.

The cereal aisle brought out her inner kid, always torn between what she wanted to eat and what she *should* eat. The lure of Cinnamon Toast Crunch was winning out as she scanned the shelves. A soft *pop*, followed by the spilling of cereal onto the linoleum floor made her spin to find the source of the noise.

A little girl, no more than three years old, sat cross-legged with a bag of Lucky Charms on her lap. The box was cast aside, torn open, shards of colored cardboard strewn across the aisle. Pieces of cereal and marshmallows littered her Anna costume and surrounded her like a rainbow of brightly colored sugar. Her plastic crown had slipped off-center and was clinging to her mop of dark ringlets.

The aisle was otherwise empty. There was no sign of the little girl's parents.

"Hi." Sabrina closed the eight-feet gap between them and crouched low. "Does your mommy know you're here?"

The little girl's eyebrows stitched together in a confused frown. She shoveled another handful of cereal into her already chewing mouth before offering a saliva-covered pile of recon-stituting marshmallows to Sabrina.

Giggling, she shook her head, untangling the little girl's crown and putting it right on her head. "No thank you, but we should probably find your parents. I'm pretty sure they're going to be worried about you."

"Jude!" A dark-haired man sprinted toward them from the end of the aisle. He raked his hand through his stylish hair before scraping a palm across his stricken face. "I..." He bent over, hands on his knees before straightening and rubbing his chest. He crouched next to the little girl. "We've talked about you wandering off, baby girl."

The little girl giggled, shoving a handful of cereal at her older brother's face.

"Not funny, Ju-Ju." He straightened her crown.

Her ovaries clenched. Sabrina, unsure of how to extricate herself from the situation, opted for the back-away-quietly-and-hope-no-one-notices approach. It was all going so well until the traitorous toasted oat pieces crunched underfoot.

The man's head jerked up, as though he'd only just realized someone else was there, and he did a double take. So did she. Russell Stewart from her French class, crouching in front of her. He spent his Saturday mornings hanging out with Anna of Arendelle, interesting, still didn't cover her embarrassment at having met him in the men's room, but it eased her wound just a tad.

"Russell?" Whose voice had come out of her mouth? And why did it sound so raspy?

The worry and fear painted over his face as he'd run toward them dissipated, replaced by a mask of calm indifference. But his eyes... they weren't just indifferent, they were cold. As icy as Elsa's freakin' castle atop snow mountain.

Sabrina was heart-on-her sleeve fire. Every emotion that rippled through her, she wore like a badge of honor. She was passionate and outspoken, and as strikingly handsome as Russell Stewart was with his chiseled jaw and pale blue eyes, she had no idea how to handle... ice. She shivered.

Despite being on the hockey team, Russell Stewart kept to himself. He was often missing from parties and group activities, shrouded in an air of mystery. Seeing him interacting with his little sister, the panic, fear, overtly raw emotion that had distorted his otherwise stoic face, squeezed her heart.

"I'll just..." She pointed a thumb over her shoulder, and

turned to leave, hugging the box of Cinnamon Toast Crunch against her chest.

Cereal crunched underfoot, but she didn't turn, she just kept walking, pulse thundering in her ears.

She liked to people-watch. It didn't hurt when the people she watched looked as delicious as sin as Russ did. They'd barely spoken two words to each other in their whole first year in class together, so he couldn't hate her, could he?

"Let's get you cleaned up, princess."

A smattering of Lucky Charms fell to the floor as Jude stood. The sound of a hand sweeping against fabric, for some reason, made Sabrina smile.

"Hey! Uh... I don't know your name, but you forgot your cart."

Her cart, right. She could pretend it wasn't hers so she wouldn't have to look at his unfairly attractive face again. She could pretend she hadn't heard him.

"No, don't. Jude!"

Before she could act, a tiny hand slipped into her palm and tugged her arm. When Sabrina turned, the little girl pointed at her cart and yanked her toward it.

Russell raised an eyebrow and gave a shrug. He stepped toward Jude, arms outstretched. "C'mere, punkin."

Jude looked up at Sabrina, then back to Russell, before dropping Sabrina's hand and flinging herself at Russell's leg. It was the cutest thing she'd ever witnessed, but it seemed Russ had missed the glint of sheer joy and love in the little girl's eyes. *His* eyes were on her cart, or more accurately, on something *in* her cart.

Wonder Woman socks, Tampons, surely he'd seen those before, unless he'd lived a sheltered life... What in her soon-to-be purchases was so exciting it was holding him rapt?

Her stomach coasted off the edge of a cliff and dropped in freefall.

His eyes were pinned to the vibrator box. He tipped his head as though he was trying to either read the box, or figure out where it went and how it worked.

Beads of sweat broke out over every inch of Sabrina's body as Russ's curiosity morphed into something else right in front of her eyes. She didn't know him well enough to know what the look meant, but despite the Ice King radiating chilly fuck-off-and-leave-me-alone vibes, something warm flickered in his gaze.

She cleared her throat. Strike that, something hot. And if she didn't take her cart and leave, she'd need to strip off and jump into one of the freezers in the frozen section to survive.

He jerked his chin at her basket, face deadpan. "Have fun."

Unable to look him in the eye, she grabbed the handle of the cart and fled.

Russell Stewart had seen her buying a vibrator, in Target. She'd have to change schools, leave the state. Maybe she'd move to Canada.

"More, Daddy!"

Sabrina stumbled over her feet, attempting to spin the cart in front of her for support so she didn't crash onto her face.

Daddy? Was it possible that Russ Stewart was the little girl's father? How had she been in class with this man for over a year and not known he had a child? She pulled her top lip between her teeth. It wasn't that unusual – there was plenty she didn't know about people in her class. But a kid?

She cast a furtive glance over her shoulder. Russ's forehead was leaning against Jude's.

"No more cereal, bug. You won't eat your lunch. We need to go find someone to get me a broom so I can sweep up this mess of yours. Then we gotta get you a birthday present, *then* we gotta go see Mimi."

The little girl's face lit up like Time Square at the mention of Mimi.

"Deal?"

The little girl nodded.

Smiling to herself, Sabrina rounded the corner into the next aisle. This side of Russ was nothing short of adorable, but it left her with questions she had no business wondering about.

Was Russ in a relationship? Who was the girl's mother? Didn't Russ room on campus with one of the other hockey players? Who had the little girl when he was at school, her Mom? Mimi?

As she picked up her groceries, the question that kept coming up, was whether or not Russ was going to give another thought to the fact he'd just busted her purchasing a vibrator.

Continue reading Two for Holding now!

Also by Lasairiona McMaster

Two for Interference - Minnesota Snow Pirates book 1

Freezing the Puck - Cedar Rapids Raccoons book 1

Two for Tacos - A Snow Pirates Novella

www.Lasairiona.com

If you're a long-time reader of mine, you'll know this series came from *nowhere*. I'm not even kidding... straight outta left field. One moment I was finishing Jeremy's novella epilogue and working on the outline for Ana and Ky's duet... and the next an indie publisher was asking me to ghostwrite a romance novel for a trial on Amazon's new platform, Kindle Vella.

I considered it, but I didn't want to write under a pen name, and Vella doesn't afford authors the option to co-write. So we were at an impasse. The suggestion was planted in the darkest recesses of my brain and sprouted overnight. It bloomed into a full series in the blink of an eye, and I knew I had to jump on this, fast, before the fickle characters packed up their ideas and went to play in another toybox.

Two weeks after the publisher sent me the first message about the idea, I wrote the words 'Chapter One', just over four weeks later, I typed 'The End'. I wrote like a woman possessed. The words poured out of me onto the page, and I spent a large portion of my time shouting down my inner demons who were screaming at me for having the audacity to try something new.

This book wasn't next on my to-do list, hell, until April 2021, it wasn't on my to-do list at all, but here we are. I really hope you enjoyed it.

I think it's important for me to mention here that Linc's favorite, contemporary Irish author? Oliver Curran? Yeah, he was my dad. My father passed away in November 2019, he was an artist, his favorite scenes to paint were Irish famine scenes, and he was most known for his blue mountains that always looked as though they were blowing in the wind.

At first I used his name as a place holder in my manuscript, but after a while, and some feedback, it felt right to keep his name in there, as a little nod to him, his work, and his encouragement of me to strive to do great things.

What can I even say about Cleo and Linc?

As someone who has struggled with body image issues from the ripe old age of eleven, I have always wanted to write a self-conscious, insecure heroine. Too often I've read stories about curvy heroines who rock their curves, embrace their sexuality, and own it when they meet their Adonis hero who wants to worship them like a goddess. I'm absolutely here for that, please don't get me wrong.

But as a thirty-six-year-old woman who still hasn't found peace with her shape, her size, her*self*, I wanted to write something a little bit different. Something for those women who not only struggle to accept the love of others, but who also struggle to love themselves.

Cleo was that heroine: strong, smart, and beautiful, but unconvinced of herself, other than her book smarts. Meeting someone in a way that her intelligence shone before her prospective partner saw what she looked like, allowed her to ease into things just a little bit. As you saw from how things unwound, however, she still couldn't quite believe it wasn't all just a cruel joke, or that Lincoln wouldn't change his mind.

Cleo's brutal inner monologue and vulnerability reflected

my own. Parts of this book were incredibly hard and draining for me to write. But I coaxed myself through – with regular breaks and margaritas. I wanted to reach the women out there who, like me, don't always like what they see when they look in the mirror. The women who question themselves every day. The women who don't feel like they're enough. Sometimes, if you just try to look at yourself through the eyes of those who love you, instead of through the warped lens of your inner demons, you'll realize just how fucking hard on yourself you're being. Give yourself a goddamn break. You deserve it. You're pretty freakin' amazing. And, yes, I'm talking to you.